# CLAIRE WAS BREATHLESS

The small wooden trap that led out onto the castle parapet squealed in protest as Aimery leaned against it. It opened readily enough to starlight; to a huge, silver disk of a moon—and to music, the same music that played in the hall, with its sounds just as strong and sweet as they had been there. They could have been in the hall; they could have been dancing.

Aimery grinned at her. Claire had the strangest feeling she was seeing a part of him few others had seen: a bright, carefree part of him that he normally hid.

"I thought you would like this," he said. "We can dance here together. You will be safe."

Odd these last words, especially since Aimery did not know if he was saying them more for Claire or for himself. He was only sure he meant them.

He took his vows of chivalry seriously and had worked hard for his knighthood. And while there had been not a few women in his past, they had all wanted him as much as he had wanted them. He would not take advantage of this young girl now.

He wanted to kiss Claire, he suddenly realized; wanted to feel the softness of her pressed against him. He couldn't do that, but he *could* dance with her.

He reached out his hand. She hesitated for a tantalizing instant and then he felt her warm fingers once again. The rest was easy. She followed his lead, swaying to the incessant beat of the timbrel and the flute's magic spell. Moving when he moved, pausing when he paused; dancing with him under the bright night stars.

A perfect moment—but it didn't bring Aimery the contentment he envisioned.

He wanted more . . .

# Maiden of Fire

## Deborah Johns

ZEBRA BOOKS
KENSINGTON PUBLISHING CORP.
http://www.kensingtonbooks.com

ZEBRA BOOKS are published by

Kensington Publishing Corp.
850 Third Avenue
New York, NY 10022

Copyright © 2004 by Deborah Johns Schumaker

All Kensington titles, imprints and distributed lines are available at special quantity discounts for bulk purchases for sales promotion, premiums, fund-raising, educational or institutional use.

Special book excerpts or customized printings can also be created to fit specific needs. For details, write or phone the office of the Kensington Special Sales Manager: Kensington Publishing Corp., 850 Third Avenue, New York, NY 10022. Attn. Special Sales Department. Phone: 1-800-221-2647.

Zebra and the Z logo Reg. U.S. Pat. & TM Off.

First Printing: August 2004
10 9 8 7 6 5 4 3 2 1

Printed in the United States of America

## Author's Note

The Cathars, a group of heretical Christians, flourished throughout the gracious land of Languedoc during the early years of the Thirteenth Century. However, the revolutionary nature of their beliefs threatened the established Church and the feudal political authority of the King of France. In 1209, Lotario dei Conti di Segni, taking the Papal throne as Innocent III to become one of the most ruthless Popes of all time, launched a series of terrible Crusades against the Cathars. These wars lasted until 1244, and eventually spawned the Inquisition. Although their Cause was supported by the leading noble families of the region, who fought valiantly alongside villagers, townfolk, and peasants to retain their freedom, the Cathar rebels were completely crushed by the more powerful Frankish forces of the North.

Or were they?

*Lo lop es mòrt! Lo lop es mòrt!*
(The wolf is dead! The wolf is dead!)

Popular Cathar Ballade about
the fall of the hated
Simon de Montfort
during
the 13<sup>th</sup> Century
Albigensian Crusade

# PROLOGUE

*Montsegur, 1314*

The clouds parted and Peter of Bologna at last saw his objective, so close now that if he stretched far enough and hard enough, he might touch it. But then Montsegur had always been like that—just beyond his reach. Yet, even in this, the darkest night-hour, when all the Good lay fast asleep within its fortress walls, there still seemed purpose and energy to this great city. Peter felt it beckon to him. He felt it urge him onward.

Stark stone walls, granite churches and the castle itself, hovering over all, that was all he could see of it. But it was enough. On this dead night, Peter—a Templar Knight, a warrior monk, a priest and thus a man not overly given to the fanciful—fancied that some devil had spit Montsegur, fully complete and intact, from hell. What did matter was that the city was *there*, the last of its kind. Just as he was.

Montsegur's light had drawn him through horrors that were beyond imagination. Yet he had at last arrived and Peter forgot everything else as he reached out his hand and lifted his eyes to its summit. Forgot the long distance he had walked and his weariness. Forgot the filth that covered him and his own acrid smell. Forgot even the child whom he carried, though she was not one to let herself be easily forgotten.

Montsegur. He was almost there. Almost home.

The city–fortress glittered like a diamond in the sickle cast of brilliant moonlight, but not like a diamond that had been carved and polished by the hand of man. Not like one of those he had seen glistening on the Queen and on Princess Isabeau—that witch!—when he and his poor brother knights had been brought before the throne of Philip the Fair. No, Montsegur did not glimmer like that. It was pure and it was. . . .

"Perfect," he murmured, "and mine."

Or at least it soon would be.

For the fortress had been taken once, and decisively so; but Peter meant to have it back again. He trembled with anticipation, just as he had done so long ago on the battlefields of the Holy Land when he had been young and pure and holy and the earth had been holy with him.

A night bird trilled, a cloud shifted, and Montsegur disappeared into the darkness. The spell was broken and Peter of Bologna, an old man once again, looked outward and realized that his destination was still a long and dangerous hour's climb before him.

"Montsegur has stood since well before Count Raymond's time—that be Count Raymond Roger of Foix," said his peasant guide in a rough Languedoc accent that Peter, Italian by birth, could barely comprehend. "But he is the one most identified with its defense. The evil heathen, the *Frankish* bastards, scur-

ried up this very same path in the dead of night. Then
they. . . ."

Peter shushed the man with a wave of his hand. He
well knew the disaster that had overtaken Montsegur,
and the child did not need to know. At least not yet.

He reached for the small girl and shifted her from
the sumter upon his back into the shelter of his arms.
She was light, almost weightless, but he felt an over-
whelming need to hold her, now that Montsegur had
disappeared once again; to realize that at least she was
already his. He had not intended to wake her but he
had. She stared up at him with her deep eyes; the same
fathomless clear green eyes that had so riveted him the
day he had stumbled, hunted and exhausted, into her
village. More than the touch of her warm hand upon
his cheek, more than the wise words she had whispered
to him, the child's eyes had told him that she was the
one.

His Magdalene.

"You are hurting me," she said now. She had a clear,
solemn voice and Peter thought it remarkable that a
three-year-old child could sound so mature. But then
he could be mistaken about her age; perhaps she could
be a year more. He was hardly an expert on children.
Few enough of them had dared to play within the rigid
boundaries of his monk's life.

"Of course." He nodded and then consciously forced
himself to loosen his grip upon her small form. "Of
course. I would not want to hurt you. Ever."

"Are we there yet?" she asked. "Are we near that
special place?"

Even her slight peevishness delighted Peter; he saw
no flaw in her. He heard the sweet dialect of the
Occitan lace her voice and not the brutal French of

Paris. Peter, a Southerner, had grown in recent years to hate the harsh French of Paris. And with reason.

The child was still so young; there was no one to miss her, no one to search her out. She was well rid of her past and her family and he had taken special care that it could not seek her. How could they possibly value her? He had been right to take her away.

"We are almost there, dear child," he said and then corrected himself. "We are almost there, my dearest Claire. They will be waiting for us."

"I'm frightened," said the child. Now she grasped for the hand she had so recently shrugged away. "I'm hungry and I'm cold. I miss my mother. I want her."

"Look, we are almost at the gates of the fortress," Peter told her in a voice carefully pitched to reassure. "You can no longer see them but that does not mean that they are not still there."

He had doubts of this himself. He glanced stealthily toward the guide who was leading them slowly up the mountain to the summit of its trails. Though just a few steps ahead of them, he could barely make out the man in the gloom cast by the rocky outcrops. The torch the guide held aloft piqued more shadows than it did substance. Peter could only hope and pray that the man knew his way. But then he must; he would have to. The Good had picked their secretive way along these paths for generations. If they had not been skillful at it, they would have perished long before.

Yet they had not disappeared. It would take more than torture and fire to extinguish them from this earth. *He*, Peter, was alive and he had found the Magdalene. True, only a small remnant awaited them at the summit of this dangerous path, but soon there would be more. The warrior monk was certain of this.

"Almost at Montsegur," he repeated as one might

chant a protecting litany. "They are waiting for us there."

Peter lowered the girl to the hard winter's ground and, despite her protests, made her walk along beside him. Instinct told him that she must make this last part of their journey on her own. Though she was young, she must be free to enter Montsegur under the power of her own will. She would face many trials in the future. If he had seen rightly—and he knew he had—Claire would need the strength that stoked each of her decisions, and the courage that backed each step she took along the long, and winding, and bitter way that would lead her upward. Instinct strong as snakebite whispered this to him and Peter always followed his feelings. Instinct alone had led him through the Inquisition fires and on to Montsegur. It had never failed. It never would. He knew this just as surely as he knew that he existed; and just as he knew the child existed and that she was important to the plans that he had made with the others.

Peter caught at the guide and took the muffled torch from him so that he could have one more, brief look at the girl. She stared solemnly back at him. She was lovely. Everything he could possibly have dreamed from within his stinking prison cell and more; those magnificent eyes, that incredible cascade of hex-red hair. She would be a beauty and Peter, a worldly monk indeed, shrewdly realized this might prove advantageous. She would beckon men one day; that much was certain. The old man smiled and eased his fingers once more into the girl's hand. Already she bore the mark of a Wise Woman, and this was, in itself, a powerful attraction. Yet, Peter had no lewd notions about the girl; the very idea would have horrified him. She was too pure.

And he was Perfect.

"There will be a nice, warm bed for you at the end of our journey," he said as he handed the torch back to the guide and they started off once again, "and plenty of food and linen sheets. You will be happy there."

The child caught at the brightness of his promises. "Will there be meat as well? Will there be sweet things? Will my mother come for me?"

"Oh, yes," exclaimed Peter, lying brightly. "You will have everything you need and want and she will join us soon."

The guide stopped suddenly and turned back to them. His face shone with ugly hideousness in the torchlight.

"We must hurry on," he said. "The night is ending and the road curves here against the Roc. The others will be waiting. It is dangerous for them as well."

Peter needed no further urging. He nodded and quickened his step. Beside him the child struggled to keep up.

"They came by night," said the guide. He seemed drawn to his story like a tongue to a decayed tooth. He would tell the tale of Montsegur's misfortune even though this strange man had forbidden it. "They were men under Simon de Montfort's command, paid well by that devil–pope, Innocent III, in Rome. They called him Innocent, but his family name was Segni—they say it is a noble name, one of the most important in the South. He paid them all from his deep purse and they climbed this very path. They thought themselves brave, yet they could only make this climb in the dark. Had they seen its steepness, had they been able to gauge the sharpness of its stones in daylight, they would not have had courage enough to take our city. They liked to swoon like women when, next day, they looked out on what they had trampled in the night. One false step and the lot of them would have tumbled straight to hell. Would to God they had!"

The man's rancor did not disturb Father Peter in the least. He was used to hatred; his heart nourished it.

"They were supposed to be knights," said the peasant. "They were supposed to be good men, the best that Simon de Montfort had to offer, and it is the duty of a knight to protect. Is that not within the vows they make? Yet they fell upon us like jackals. They would have killed us all."

"But they didn't," said Peter softly.

"They killed enough," replied the sullen guide. "They killed the Perfect."

Peter nodded but said nothing. He clutched his secret safely to himself and held tightly to the child.

The man reconsidered and said, "Still, you are right. We must be grateful. Those spawns of Satan did not manage to kill us all."

"They never do," said Peter, looking deeply within the darkness of his own heart. "Never. Never."

"Who were the Perfect?" asked the child. Once again Peter was overcome by the absolute wonder of his fate and of his choice. That he would find this child and that she was so right for the role that destiny would give to her.

He patted her hand reassuringly and felt comforted himself.

"The Perfect were good people who were cruelly persecuted by the authority in Paris." Peter's words were said with the enunciations of memorized rote. "They were Cathar clerics and they perished with most of their people during a black time of persecution many years ago. But you, dear child, will save the remnant that is left. You will be our greatest Magdalene."

Fatigue had prompted him to say more than perhaps

was necessary, but Peter felt his words touch her. Certainly he had hinted at them enough as they made their stealthy way from Foix. Suddenly, the child startled him. She shook her head. She held her ground. Strength radiated from her as she disputed him for the very first time.

"No," she said. "I am not Magdalene, I am Claire. And Claire I shall always remain."

There was no use arguing with her. She would learn, and Peter was both too tired and too triumphant to be worried by mere words. There would be plenty of time to bring her around. He had found her and he had stolen her. Everything would work out in the end. For now he nodded, looked past the child and off into the distance toward Montsegur.

He smiled.

# CHAPTER 1

*Montsegur, 1331*

Aimery, Count of Segni, was there, standing right beside the Grand Inquisitor the day the Wise Woman walked in. Of course, they did not know that Claire of Foix was a witch at the time. They would discover this later.

It was just past sextes—the morning prayer bell—and the bonfires that had welcomed him as the new lord of Montsegur were hardly banked when the woman entered. Aimery could hear the jovial laughter of rollicking peasants as it bounced up from the castle keep and through the Great Hall's walls. The people were exceedingly glad for the day's holiday, and happy enough that the coming of the new lord had caused it. That the Grand Inquisitor had accompanied him and that a trial would soon commence interested them as well. It promised more holidays and more feastings. The burning of such a great heretic as William Belibaste—and there was no doubt in anyone's mind that he would eventu-

ally begin his taste of hellfire here on earth—would
guarantee them three days freedom from the fields.
Already, merchants from as far away as Lyon were pe-
titioning for space at the market the Abbey would hold
for the great occasion.

Aimery paid no attention to the merry making. Nor
did the knights and men at arms who had accompanied him over the Haute Savoie from Italy hold his interest. He stared at the woman coming toward him. He
watched as she wove her way through the finery of his
nobles and of the bishop's court looking very much, he
thought, like a simple shuttle lacing through a golden
loom.

Intriguing.

"Who is this girl?" he whispered to his brother-in-
law, Huguet de Montfort.

The other man was deep in conversation with a
black robed priest, but turned awkwardly when Aimery
spoke to him. " 'Tis the new scribe," he said, "sent
from the convent of St. Magdalene to set down the proceedings of this trial."

"They've sent a female?" inquired Aimery, still staring at her as she approached. He was lord of this place
now, and did not need to hide his interest.

Huguet shrugged his injured shoulder. "Jacques
Fournier, the Inquisitor, is anxious that this tale go onward. No monks being available, he was reduced to requesting assistance from the nuns. Their cloister is
renowned for its learned women but it seems the only
one who could be spared was this novice, and the
Bishop–Inquisitor was forced by necessity to accept
her or do without the scribing."

"He cannot do without," said Aimery. "This trial
must be fair and that fairness well documented. Did
you say this young girl is a novice? She seems much

too lovely to be wedding the Church. Beauty such as hers would seem to call to a more earthly marriage."

"As though you Segnis consider beauty a part of mate taking," said his brother-in-law with a smile.

Aimery smiled back at him. He and Huguet had been close friends since their paging but they shared little in common physically. Where Aimery of Segni was tall and fair, with the sky blue eyes that had been part of his family's fame for generations, his companion was dark haired, small and wiry; too slight for a knight. But then his great and masterful ancestor, Simon de Montfort, had been slight as well.

"Gnome-like" had been whispered behind Huguet de Montfort's back on more than one occasion, and he knew it. Aimery had fought the lad he'd first heard laugh at his friend—he called it his first knightly battle—but even he had to admit that the Count of Montfort was no beauty. Yet, it had not surprised Aimery in the least when his lovely sister, Minerve, whose hand had been sought by a cousin to the King of France, had settled upon this mild and slightly wizened man as husband. Nor did wealth have anything to do with her decision. While it was true that the Counts of Montfort had gained land and position during the Crusade against the Cathars that Aimery's own ancestor, Pope Innocent III, had initiated, they had quickly lost both and within two generations many of the family were again but petty nobles. Rumor murmured that the heretic Cathars had cursed the family and still meant to have revenge against it. But Aimery was not one given to idle superstition. Huguet de Montfort might not possess beauty or wealth but he had other, more important, qualities. Aimery had championed them before the reluctance of his mighty family and had prevailed, though secretly he doubted that Minerve had needed his support. Once she determined on Huguet, she would have him. No one knew this better than her brother Aimery.

"This scribe is a novice," repeated Huguet. "She is betrothed to the Church."

"Betrothed," replied Aimery, Count of Segni, "is not the same as wed."

The woman captivated him; his eyes never left her. She wore the simple white-stuff of an apprentice nun. Her eyes were lowered; her face cocooned in the stiffness of a wimpled veil. She seemed the perfect model of the obedient piety she represented; and yet, there was something not quite perfect about her. One small thing. Aimery's fine eyes, keened from years of warring, narrowed as they regarded it. Yes, one small thing. Not perfect.

Yet, sitting beside him, Jacques Fournier—the Grand Inquisitor—noticed nothing.

The enormous Great Hall was packed with knights and men at arms but they were so busy that they did not heed her, or so thought Claire of Foix. She was nervous, but too well trained to show emotion; she kept her head lowered and made sure her wimple securely veiled her face. Today, she was the only woman in this whole vast chamber, though of course women were brought here. They came when the Inquisitor was in residence. You could feel their fear upon the air; you could smell it. It was not difficult to sense their phantom presence. But Claire could not allow herself the luxury of feelings. She knew that she must be very careful and that she must learn. The enemy's men were boisterous; intent upon their gaming and their drinking. Standing quietly in their midst, Claire was given ample opportunity to study them; to use her power and to know.

Just as Father Peter had taught her.

"As though they would know a true witch," she thought contemptuously, "as though they could even sense one."

Yet, for all their imbecility, Aimery of Segni and his men still claimed William Belibaste within their dungeons. And it was Claire's sworn duty to see him free.

Resolutely, she raised her clear eyes and looked around. The Hall was great in size but much more simply furnished than she had thought it would be. The walls had been freshly whitewashed—in honor of the new lord, she imagined—but they were plain and there were no costly tapestries from Cluny strung upon them, no frescoes envisioning the lewdness of a Babylonian Paris. Instead, the room contained a scattering of wooden trestle tables nestled by low, splintering stools and an occasional carved chair for the Great Knights—and for the Inquisitors.

The court dais and its trestle were barely raised above the others. From the rafters hung the scarlet and cream banners of the Count of Segni, lately appointed liege lord of Montsegur, as well as what she imagined to be the standards of his lesser vassals. But even these waved back and forth with grave discretion upon some unfelt breeze. The chamber was plainer, less bawdy, than what she had expected; than what Father Peter had led her to believe it would be.

The men were another matter. They were everything Peter had warned they would be; even worse, thought Claire. Most—the knights, squires and pages—were easily recognizable for the brightness of their swords and daggers and the swaggering way the knight's golden spurs jingled against the castle's paving stones. Laughter echoed off the white-washed walls. The few Inquisitors were another matter. Their clothes were somber; their faces hawked and intent. They did not joke along with the others. They did not play at gaming. They had come on serious business: life or death, heaven or hell. They had weighty issues on their minds. Claire hated them.

As she turned her attention away from the dais in disgust, a movement from the raucous crowd caught her eye and held it. A man drew her attention with a discreet cough. Claire knew who he was and the knowledge heartened her. Peter had made his way within these fortress walls to stand beside her in spirit, to fortify her; just as he had promised. Claire smiled secretly, heartened. Her Father had not left her to face these mad men all alone and she knew that he never would.

Just then a sunbeam angled through the largest of the windows and touched the covered head of one of the Inquisitors upon the dais. He jerked his head and his sharp glance caught at Claire. His eyes narrowed. Hers quickly lowered.

"Girl," he called. "Come hither. Quicken your pace to me."

He might as well have been calling to one of the dogs that lounged among the hearthside scraps, or so thought Claire of Foix. Yet, she obeyed him and edged closer. A few knights leered but stepped back to make her path clear. No one wished censor from Jacques Fournier. A dog snarled and snapped at her but the firm hand of a squire upon his studded collar held him back. Claire sensed danger in the air but she was used to peril; had lived with it for all of her double life. If danger alone could hurt her, she would have been long dead.

"Eminence," she said and made a deep reverence to the Grand Inquisitor.

"You have been sent to us by the Convent of St. Magdalene?" he inquired.

"Yes, my lord."

"And what is your given name?"

"Claire," she whispered and then more clearly, "Claire of Foix."

There was a gasp and a titter. Peter had chosen well in giving her this family name. It carried resonance in this part of Languedoc. It spoke a history.

"Of Foix?" repeated the Inquisitor. He beckoned her closer. "Then you, above all others, will know why we are here."

Claire nodded.

She studied her enemy. She took two very slow steps forward so that she could do this with disguise. The Inquisitor was tall and finely built; his long, dark robes fashioned of a plain but expensive woven silk samite. Yet his voice was sharp and rough, a peasant's voice that was slightly out of keeping with the fineness of his tunic and with the educated choice of his words. Claire wondered at this. Alone in her room, she would examine this later. And of course she would speak of this anomaly with Father Peter.

"I thought the Counts of Foix long dead," said the Inquisitor, "and the rest of their heritage with them. I thought them all killed in the sieges and in the work of the Great Crusade against the heretical Cathars."

"Not all the Foix were heretical," said Claire with studied humility. She lowered her eyes and let her voice reach out to him from the confines of her wimple. "Many of the family repented. After the crusade against them, they recanted the false ways and came back to the true. They listened to the preaching of Bernard of Clairveaux and your own St. Dominic. They realized their error. My father was among them. He was distant cousin to the last count but his fortunes had shifted and he had lost the rank of noble."

"What is his name? Why have I not heard of him?"

"Because he was the poor, weak member of a wealthy and strong family," Claire replied. "Men such as my father rarely leave a mark. They are not noted."

This answer—true enough—seemed to satisfy the man who questioned her. He nodded to Claire and bade her continue.

"My father's grandfather recanted to St. Dominic de Guzman, who was founder of the priestly order to which you, Eminence, belong. Of his own free will, my grandfather promised that the women of his family would be consecrated for five generations to the Dominican Convent here at Montsegur. We are given to repair the great wrong of our ancestors."

"That is why they sent you to me? Because you are convented nearby?"

"Yes, my lord," lied Claire smoothly. "That is why I have come."

"Not true," snapped Jacques Fournier and Claire felt fear whistle through the room. "You were sent to me because you know Latin, and for no other reason. Now tell me how you, a female, came to be so proficient in that holy language?"

"How do you know Latin?" insisted the Inquisitor.

"I know Greek as well and some Hebrew," replied the girl, who had practiced well her words. "It is a sacred mission of our convent to set out a great tapestry that marks out the history of this place and our small role in it. I was chosen from childhood to learn the sacred languages so I could be useful in this task."

The man stared at her through eyes as sharp as glass

shards. That stare would miss precious little and Claire grew wary.

"Do you know who I am?" said the Inquisitor.

"Yes, my lord. You are Jacques Fournier, Bishop of Pamiers."

"And Bishop of this place as well. At least until a new one is appointed."

Claire nodded to this. She said nothing.

"Do you know why I am here?" continued Jacques Fournier, more amiably now.

"To bless this castle and this land for the new Count of Segni who has come from the south to take it as suzerainty."

Someone chuckled and for the first time Claire became aware of the man beside Fournier, but she could not spare a glance toward him.

"That is true enough and well-spoken." The bishop leaned toward her just a little, as a cat might if it held the intention of sporting with a mouse. "However, I doubt the convent would have let a novice from its confines for such a simple scribing task as the handing over of a castle to the new lord and the blessing of it. Did your Abbess not tell you why you were truly sent?"

"She told me." Claire looked up and directly at him. "I am here because you have managed to capture a heretic Cathar—a renegade, a remnant. His trial will soon commence and you have need of someone to scribe its process and to illustrate it with fine art. That is what my Abbess said. That is my true duty here."

*You must swallow your pride and look an angel. You must humble yourself before him. It is the only way you can help the Perfect.*

She heard Peter's words deep within her mind and she hearkened to them.

"I am here to be of help," she added demurely.

"Then tell the truth," snapped Jacques Fournier. "Then tell me *exactly* how you learned your Latin. Recount for me the aberration of a woman scribe."

Peter had prepared her well for this question. Upon Claire's answer hung their ability to save Belibaste and perhaps the rest as well. Claire remained silent for an instant so she could focus her deep self before she spoke.

"The story of my consecration is no secret. I was orphaned of parents when but a child," she said. "I know nothing of them. Only that they were simple folk, now dead and gone; perished in a sudden village fire. I had no relations able or willing to claim me. We were quite poor. A priest who was himself seeking shelter with the nuns found me wandering upon the hillside. He heard my story and brought me with him when he begged succor at St. Magdalene. His was a fortuitous choice, at least for me. The nuns knew that my ancestor had dowered me to them. They took me in."

"You remember nothing of your family? Of your father and your mother?"

A memory flashed through Claire's mind—Mama, Papa laughing; a simple table, a warm hearth. She saw them clearly, recognized them; though she had not thought of them in years.

"I remember nothing," she said aloud. She fought hard to keep the quaver from her voice.

The unexpected memory of her parents had shattered Claire's focus. She became acutely aware that the murdering men in that room had silenced and that their full attention was focused upon her. She sensed danger here. Her heart scudded but she forced herself to remain quite still.

After a moment the bishop nodded. "Continue," he said.

"I was a particular favorite of the Abbess. I was young and from Foix. She thought it important to personally educate me so as to assure there be no taint of heresy in my upbringing. To make sure that that time was at an end. She assumed—"

"That you had been early raised in the heretical faith?"

Claire forced herself to look directly into the eyes of her Inquisitor. She used her power, though she knew this to be dangerous with a man so obviously astute.

"I was from Foix, a heretical stronghold—just as Montsegur itself had been. My Abbess wished to take no chances that I had been taught anything dangerous or untrue. This is well documented in the convent records, as is the fact that I had no knowledge of any false teachings. I remembered nothing of my past. And this was normal. I was but a few years old when I arrived."

*Again she saw that remembered, smiling woman, and that happy man.*

Although it was early June, a fire had been lit to warm the coldness of the Hall and now a log from it fell from the grate, crackling sparks onto the stone floor. Two dogs snarled and scuffled over a discarded bone, but they were soon hushed.

"But, like the others, the Abbess presumed that I—"

"You, Claire of Foix, have many times this day used the words 'presume' and 'assume' in reference to the thoughts and actions of your Abbess," said Jacques Fournier with deceptive quiet. "Yes, you have used each of these words more than once. I ask you now, Claire of Foix—are you heretic or not?"

"I am not heretic!" Her voice was surprisingly strong and sure. Even she—well trained and Perfect—could not tell from whence this unexpected power came. It took her aback. It frightened her. But as usual she showed nothing.

The bishop leaned closer, his head sticking from his cowl like a turtle's from its shell. He wore the dark purple of a bishop; not the scarlet of a cardinal. Yet Claire could smell ambition upon him and she knew his advancement to be just a matter of time. She knew somehow that Jacques Fournier would go very far in life. He might well end his days as Pope.

"I hear that you are also called Magdalene," he said. Claire's hands iced but still she showed no fear.

"The priest who rescued me called me that and others took up the name," she said and then added an afterthought because Father Peter had told her not to stray far from the truth in the dangerous game they played. "It was a pet name. Mary of Magdala was his favorite saint in the lectionary. My convent is dedicated to her as well. It was quite natural that some would call me by her title."

The Inquisitor nodded but, "I understand that the Magdalene has strong connections to this place," was all he said.

The others grew restless with this long quizzing of a woman. Claire did not turn around but she felt their impatient scuttling behind her. She heard fidgeting and the covert slapping of bone dice. Even the dogs grew restive from boredom and the heat and left their scraps to scratch at fleas.

"Did your Abbess explain why we have sent for you, a woman?" asked Jacques Fournier, the Inquisitor, after a pause. "Did she explain the true importance of this trial and why it cannot be delayed?"

Claire nodded her head once briefly. "The Cathars have become active once again. The heresy proves to be not as dead as the Church once thought. I am to make myself useful to you in your final destruction of it. I am here to be of service to you and to the Truth."

"Well put," said Fournier. He glanced around. "And in what way will you wield this service to me, and to the Truth?"

"I am to use my knowledge of Latin and act as scribe in the trial of a man accused of heresy."

"What is this man's name, girl? Speak it up."

"He is called William Belibaste," replied Claire obediently.

"We were fortunate to have lured such a large fish into our nets," mused Fournier. "There is no doubt of his guilt and, perhaps to his credit, he begs no mercy. Still, a fair trial is vouched him and it must be richly documented that this proceeding was justly held and that he was given ample chance to recant. William Belibaste is a Cathar Perfect, a member of their priesthood. We hope he is the last of them and, with the grace of heaven, we hope he will recant."

All around her, the warriors, bored with the proceedings, chattered and laughed. Claire kept her head low as she edged closer to the Inquisitor's raised and ornate chair.

"He will not recant," she whispered.

"What is that you say, girl?" The Inquisitor sat sharply upwards. "Do you know something of his heresy? Is there something in your own blood, Claire of Foix, that calls to it?"

"All in Montsegur know of the Cathars," said Claire simply. "All here know the history of the war against them. Has Monsignor, himself, forgotten?"

"I urge you to keep a temperate tongue in your

mouth," said the Inquisitor. "Indeed, girl, I have not forgotten the events of that unhappy time and I urge you as well to keep their remembrance fresh within your heart. Let them caution you, as they should caution all in Languedoc."

He turned upon his chair looking first directly at the young nobleman who stood beside him and then glancing about at the others with his sharp eyes.

"These are sad times," said the Inquisitor, "in which we must call upon a woman for scribing. Normally a woman must be kept to her place. Indeed, the Cathars allowed them to be priests and holy people and this formed part of their grave heresy. But this court had no other choice in this matter. Our own learned Brother Edmond has been stricken with a sudden malady, so ill is he that last rites have been ministered, and there is no time to petition north to Paris or south to Rome for a sainted monk to replace him at his task. This trial of William Belibaste cannot wait. It must proceed, and at once. This heretic must be tried at once. Already there is the rumor of a planned uprising to wrest his freedom. We are strong but we must be cautious. This very thing has happened before. Indeed, at Avignonet, the holy Inquisitors were killed whilst they knelt at their prayers—and this but seventy years ago. Such blasphemy shall never be repeated. This girl here, being an expedient, will live within the cloister of her convent as usual but she will emerge to come into the castle and scribe down proceedings of this trial. We want no idle thought that this man's heresy was not completely proven. We will make no martyr of him!"

Sword hilts thumped against trestle tables in acknowledgement of the Inquisitor's rousing words. Yet, the knights assigned to guard the Inquisition had no real or keen interest in its proceedings and but waited to be back at their dicing once again. Or so thought Claire.

"We have not time enough to send for a man. Belibaste must be tried before his people try to free him. You, girl, will be brought each day from your convent and then taken to it again at night. Each day you are to take down the trial's proceedings. We want no hint that this man was sent to the stake wrongly. Everything must be well documented."

Claire nodded.

"Well, then." The Inquisitor motioned to a tonsured Franciscan who immediately sprang forward with parchments awaiting seal and signet. Fournier lowered his head to his task. "Sir Aimery, Count of Segni, will see that an escort accompanies you to the convent."

"Sir Aimery, Count of Segni," said a calm low voice from beside him, "will escort the novice to her convent himself."

Startled, Claire looked up and over the Inquisitor and caught the Count of Segni's interested gaze. She had been so intent upon Jacques Fournier that she had not really noted him before.

But he had noted her.

# CHAPTER 2

It was universally known and clear as sunshine that the prospect of a notorious trial pulled the curious to a village like flies to summer honey. That and the oath taking ceremony of Montsegur's new lord had caused its narrow, cobbled streets to overflow with visitors. Claire and Aimery and the honor guard that accompanied them threaded a careful way through air thick with the smell of roasting meats and sweet ales and the laughter of peasants, glad of the half-holiday. Children chased each other beneath the dark, close overhang of its jumbled buildings, disrupting the pantomimed play of mummers and causing jugglers to lose their concentration and cascade bright, string balls onto the cluttered streets.

Eyes lowered, hands clasped, Claire walked silently. She did not glance at the noble man beside her. Peter had warned her, and she had paid strict attention to his admonitions. She knew what to expect of men like Aimery of Segni. Though calling themselves noble and, indeed, carrying themselves with all the arrogance this status implied, Claire knew that underneath their frippery, their bright tunics and pointy-toed, soft boots, they would be as base and loud as any peasant. Worse even. Had she not witnessed as much in the Great Hall this morning? A man's fate was to be decided there, his very life hung in the balance, yet Count Aimery's knights and men-at-arms had laughed and gamed throughout the solemn proceedings. Had she not heard their whispers and their gossips as she stood before the Grand Inquisitor?

And it was obvious that the new Lord of Montsegur was not better than the subjects he had brought with him. She glanced up now and stared at him from beneath the demur curtain of her lashes. Well, perhaps he did not look the part of a bawdy. He was tall enough for it and manfully built. But his tunic was fashioned of a light, fine wool that strained only slightly along the breadth of his shoulders and he wore not brightness save the jeweled hilt of his sword. Her eyes narrowed and her gaze moved downward. His boots were of soft dark leather. Finest deerskin, she thought. However, they were not painted with bright moons or falling stars. Their toes were not belled and pointed. Nor did horns seem to sprout from his head.

Claire was not fooled by his calmness, nor even by his appearance, though she acknowledged grudgingly that many people might find this blond giant exceedingly handsome. A blind person would have noted the way women looked at him as their party wove its narrow way to the city confines. But Claire knew him for what he was.

They had but a short road from the castle to the convent's stone walls, yet the count had deemed two squires and six pages as necessary escort for the easy distance. They swaggered behind the count's banner, obviously intent upon impressing the more impressionable maids of the village. They were so many that occasionally they bumped against each other on the narrow byways and brushed Claire against the rockhardness of the Count of Segni's arm.

She did not like that. Nor did she like the whole idea of such a grand procession. Two of his banners fluttered beside her in a desultory, summer's breeze. These banners alone could have told the tale of him, she thought; cream and scarlet, his standard depicted a wolf held firmly within the golden talons of an enormous, unfurled eagle.

Fitting, thought Claire with disgust.

She could easily imagine Aimery of Segni as an enormous bird of prey. She could picture the glee with which he would assail the innocent and the helpless; the way he would destroy William Belibaste, if he were able. However, he would not be able. They would stop him. *She* would stop him.

"News traveled far of the feast to be held here at Montsegur." It was the Lord of Segni's second attempt at conversation. Speculation on the weather had gotten him nowhere. "I've seen glovers and silk weavers from beyond the mountains of the Haute Savoie. Indeed, many here come from Como and there are even skilled dyers from Lombardy come to ply their trade. Of course, any celebration is just a gathering-excuse for Southerners who are naturally drawn to dance and jolly-making. I come from the South; from the very lowest tip of Italy, in fact. We are always primed for merry living there. I hear Languedoc is very similar and that it is a land famed for skilled lovers and the legends that they kindle. People are naturally drawn to this type of flame, don't you think?"

" 'Tis hardly a topic upon which I would hold an

opinion," replied Claire primly, "seeing as how I am convent bred."

"And yet, the subject interests you more than the weather," replied the Count of Segni mildly.

Claire glanced up quickly enough to catch the glint of mischief in his eye. And they were such lovely eyes; she couldn't help noticing. Bright blue they were, and clear as the summer sky that stretched above them as far as man could vision. Claire had never glimpsed their like before. So clear, so bright, so very blue— they might have hidden heaven. Dazzled, she smiled into them. And the Count of Segni smiled back.

"Cloistered or not, I am sure you have heard tales of the Troubadour culture," he said smoothly. He placed a guiding hand upon her arm. "It started here—all the ballades and love songs and legends—and this land still bears the kiss of its glory."

Claire said nothing. She walked with her eyes lowered but in reality they took in everything. She had lived at the Magdalene's Convent for twenty years and had often heard tales of Montsegur when it was in its glory under the Cathars. Hers had been a quiet life. She had spent her time cocooned within its cloistered walls, working at her lessons; paying strict attention to what Peter told her. Yet, she had heard of the Troubadour culture. It was always mentioned as part of Languedoc's grand history, a part of what they had lost at the time of Crusade. She knew that under the great Queen Eleanor of Acquitaine—a woman who had been powerful enough to marry first Louis of France and then divorce him to finish her life as Queen to England's Henry II—the troubadours had been encouraged to write their songs of exquisite love, and jongleurs had taken the melodies and sung them throughout all of Christendom. Yet, Claire had never heard any of their love songs before today.

As if on cue, one minstrel's song rang out, stronger and clearer than the others:

> *Blushed was she and lush as sunshine*
> *With breasts that called all men to nip*
> *Honeyed by Love; ripe as late fruit.*
> *So is our Lupa.*
> *Our own she-wolf of Cabaret.*

Claire reddened at the lyrics. The jongleur sang to the accompaniment of a lute and small tambourine. Two brightly dressed women played the instruments and they smiled and winked suggestively as Claire passed by beside the Count of Segni.

Surrounded by his escort, Claire caught one wench winking suggestively at the lord but she could not see his reply. He had turned away. Claire could imagine it though, from the woman's bold, red face and her giggle. Encouraged, she raised her bright skirts just far enough to show a shapely ankle. The others squealed with laughter.

They were having fun; and even to Claire it seemed an innocent enough pastime. The jongleur laughed so hard that his voice faltered; he lost his tune but as they passed, one of Count Aimery's squires threw a few half coins into the dust. The musicians squealed and swooped, tucking their unexpected booty into their bodices and small sumters. Father Peter had always taught her that only the spiritual mattered and yet these jongleurs sang of kisses and the curve of a woman's breast and the heat of a man's breath upon her neck. It was so different from what she had been taught; and yet the people seemed genuinely to be enjoying themselves. A few grabbed wives and sweethearts and danced around the dusty cobbles of the streets. The women laughed. She would discuss this with Father Peter, as she discussed everything with him. Only he had the power to calm her mind once again.

Because walking so close to the Count of Segni was not at all calming. In these confined, closed streets, narrowed near him by the festive jumble of people, she was so near to him that she could smell the tang of the pitch-pine soap he used. She could catch the hint of good leather and the deeper, pure scent of man. His arm continually brushed against hers, and even though she refused to look at him, she was so *aware* of him. And she was much, much nearer than she would have liked.

The count motioned and his entourage wended its slow way once again. But on this bright, clear day, the path before them seemed strewn with pleasant obstacles. The jongleurs moved off; a troop of mummers took their place. Beneath the cathedral's shadow, Claire saw stalls where merchants sold spices and leather gloves and cloth-stuff. A tiny boy earned half-coins by jumping an even smaller dog through a beribboned tambourine hoop. When the dog hopped through, they both danced around in glee. Claire laughed with them, clapping her hands.

"Then this truly is your first fair," said Aimery. He still smiled but Claire looked away from him and curbed her laughter.

A silk merchant from Como, almost hidden behind his wares in an elaborately painted stall, held out a small length of silk ribbon. It was a splendid, fathomless green; the color she imagined the sea to be; and it seemed such a lovely, serene object amidst all the noise and chaos that surrounded them. Instinctively, she reached for it and a slight breeze tickled the silk against her fingers.

"This would be perfect for my lady," said the canny

merchant, emboldened by Claire's gesture to turn in-gratiatingly towards the count. "The color quite matches my lady's eyes."

Claire quickly loosed the ribbon but Aimery reached over and took it into his own strong hands.

"Indeed, yes," he said, holding it up and squinting first at the green silk and then at her, narrowing his eyes in exaggerated concentration. "They seem to be a perfect match."

The merchant was quick into the game. "It could have been colored with my lady's eyes in mind," he said. "The Lombard dye-smith told me it was his master-piece, absolutely the best coloration he had ever achieved. The Lombards are noted for their expensive blues, of course, but their greens are also worthy."

"Too bad my lady Claire would take no interest in such fripperies," said Aimery, handing the silk back to its owner with slow, exaggerated care. "She is much too serious for such pretty nonsense, or else I would be sorely tempted to gift her with this small remembrance."

Claire lowered her eyes, perfectly still. In truth, she had been tempted—for the briefest of instants—by the beautiful light touch of that green silk ribbon. She would have to speak about this to Father Peter as well.

She was eager now to change the subject and take his mind from the embarrassment of her longing for the fine, bright silk. "My lord, do you not think it a great coincidence that a Lord of Segni has come to take possession of the Fortress of Montségur? There have been no Segnis here since the land was placed under interdict by Pope Innocent III, and was he not your ancestor?"

"My great-great uncle, as was the pope who fol-lowed him."

"Montsegur is a great castle," she continued, "worthy to be home to such a noble name as that of Segni."

"Kind words," said Aimery with some amusement, "though I am the first to actually possess these lands. Montsegur was but a pinpoint on the map for my illustrious ancestors."

"But they, especially Pope Innocent, were determined to hold it," said Claire, very slightly slowing her pace, "as was the Count de Montfort."

Aimery shrugged. "They had the crusade and this was a heretic land."

"Don't you think that it is a great coincidence that you are here again and that Simon de Montfort's great grandson is here with you?" Claire quietly insisted.

They rounded a corner and Aimery deftly reached out a hand to right Claire as her pattens slid upon slick cobbles. He did not remove it as they continued on their way.

"There is nothing coincident about my being here with Huguet de Montfort," he replied. "We have been friends and comrades in arms since our paging days; he is married to my sister and the father of her four strong sons. We have come, as our ancestors did before us, to secure this rebel land once again. Rumors of another Cathar uprising have reached Paris. I am vassal to the king. Perhaps he naturally thought of a Segni to secure Languedoc."

"Considering your history?" said Claire.

"Considering *my* history," replied Aimery, "for, like you, I belong to the impoverished faction of a powerful family; not quite out of the nobility but close enough to exclusion to be looked down upon. I was given no castle at birth. Montsegur is my first holding and actually, it is my first home."

He smiled and the smile made him seem unguarded and younger and she realized, suddenly, that he *was* young, perhaps just a bit younger than she was herself. She had received few smiles in her life and she was not at all certain she wanted this one. Her face abruptly fell. She looked away. She kept her eyes resolutely lowered and centered her mind by counting her footfalls as they patterned the soft dust. The noise from the festivities in the Cathedral Square grew dim as they neared the tranquil stone wall that surrounded the convent.

*Learn of him. Learn of him quickly. Ours is a desperate effort. We will need to know all that is possible.*

Claire could almost hear Peter's voice from beside her, from within her. She had a strong urge to look around to see if he was hiding near. But her convent loomed ahead. The long, slow walk to its tranquil environs was almost over; still, perhaps she had learned something during it that would prove useful to the Perfect and to their cause.

"Tell me how you came to Montsegur," she whispered.

"Tell me how you came to be within convent walls."

That was fair enough. She could tell him most—she'd already done that—and then he might tell her more.

"I was born to it," she said, "just as I spoke this morning before Bishop Fournier. My parents were killed—well, they died when I was quite young. The priest found me wandering. He brought me here."

"Indeed, that is what you said before the Inquisitor's court," agreed Aimery, "that this life was chosen for you."

Claire did not like his choice of words. "Perhaps at the beginning; I lived it after that."

"Yet, you still wear novice white and you are old to do so, considering you came so early to be convented. Mayhap you have not fully committed to someone else's plan for your life."

"*Heaven's* plan," she snapped.

"Oh, yes. Heaven's." Aimery sounded dubious. "Yet, you are mightily pretty to be veiled, at least you seem to be from the little of you that one can glimpse from beneath your aprons and wimples. And a pretty girl has many offers in the village—even if that girl is an orphaned child. At least a lad possessed with a nice milking herd would have pledged for you, or a mason with good tools and apprentices. The nuns would never have kept you against your will. Why would one so pretty choose to be shut within a convent? *This* is the conundrum that I mean to master."

Claire scowled, opened her mouth and barely caught her tongue in time. He was baiting her and she knew it. She folded her hands beneath her voluminous aprons just as she had seen Mother Helene often do at St. Magdalene when she wanted to impress someone with her solemnity. It became very important for Claire to let Aimery of Segni know that she was not a woman to be trifled with, for he seemed to think her trifling, indeed.

But the Count of Segni was not to be so easily discouraged from his teasing. "And you have those remarkable cat's eyes."

Again Claire said nothing, though one of the younger pages glanced at her and then dared a giggle at his master's wit.

"And red hair," continued Aimery, "is the mark of a witch."

At last he had the response he wanted. Claire's hand skipped from the safety of her novice aprons to the white wimple that covered all her hair—or almost all of it. She felt the tiny curl of hair upon her forehead.

"I've seen enough to know its color," continued the Count of Segni equably. "I saw that strand from my seat on the dais but I doubt that others noted it. I doubt the Inquisitor remarked it; he would have said something if he had. 'Tis an interesting color, especially for one promised so early to the Cloister and who feels herself to be so *vocationed* to it."

He reached out and touched that one, lone strand of hair upon her wimple, gazing at it with the same, slow attention he had given the merchant's silk.

"My hair was not my choosing. I cannot help it," replied Claire.

"That is true enough," replied Aimery. They had reached the stern, stone walls of St. Magdalene's convent. He hefted his sword twice against its heavy oak doors. The sound reverberated through this silent part of the hilltop. "I have nothing against the color of your hair. Indeed, I think it lovely. Still, I have two cousins dowered to convents in this part of France and so I know the custom is to shave the hair from novices who enter. They claim this as a mark of piety. And yet St. Magdalene's has allowed you to keep your hair beneath its chaste wimple. I wonder why. Indeed, I wonder why."

# CHAPTER 3

"What do you know of William Belibaste?" asked Aimery of Segni of his brother-in-law as they watched a scramble of young squires play at jousting on the list fields.

"That he is a Cathar rebel and thus a nuisance." Huguet de Montfort kept his eyes straight ahead.

Aimery cocked his head and smiled wryly. "The man is up on charges of heresy and sedition. I would call these accusations more than a nuisance—at least if I were he."

"But I am not," replied Huguet equably. "I am your friend and no one would want to see a friend ride in to take possession of his castle with the Grand Inquisitor and all his mischief slung in right beside him."

"Especially if that Inquisitor is Jacques Fournier."

"A man sworn to his duty, and bound to his word."

The friends were a good pairing, though not even his own mother would have dared to call Huguet de Montfort a beauty. Dark where the Segnis were fair, he had the sharp nose and thick, unruly hair that had run through his family for generations. Now he watched silently beside the Count of Segni as a mounted squire galloped enthusiastically toward the quatrain, his lance point aimed straight at its painted heart. The mannequin spun wildly from its blow. The young boys cheered and stamped their feet.

"The Cathars were heretics, as well," said Huguet, still staring at the group of squires and smiling. "Though I am not too clear as to their particular infraction. Something to do with the old Manichean theories—the body is evil, spirit is good; that dichotomy."

"Seems innocent enough."

"But pernicious. It has been a leading heresy since time began and one that has been quickly and ruthlessly quelled, wherever it has risen up."

"But why? From what I hear the Cathars were peaceable enough, at least they were in the beginning."

"Oh, very. Movements flourished here in the South of France and, of course, across the Haute Savoie in Northern Italy but these rugged lands are considered its chief home. The Cathars believed in a deeply spiritual life; at least, one that they considered to be so. They prized simplicity, purity, beauty and harmony; they cradled the Troubadour civilization and all the refinements that mark it. There are those who say they nurtured our own chivalric codes as well. Anything to do with spirit was perfect; anything carnal was to be avoided at all costs. Unfortunately, this sets good and evil always at war and a man is continually battling with these elements within—and with no guarantee that good will prevail.

He paused as another young squire launched himself into the fray, barely managing to keep his seat as his powerful destrier strained forward. The others around him squealed in delight.

Huguet smiled as he continued. "The Cathar Credentes had very advanced ideas for their time, and for ours. They believed, for instance, in a female priesthood. They formed part of what were called the Perfect, right alongside the men."

"They were Christian, were they not?" said Aimery.

Huguet nodded.

Aimery continued, "Then there is more to this than religion. I cannot imagine Rome would have taken on such a massive mission as crusade, if the foe were not also considered a strong political adversary."

"It was crusade launched by our ancestors," replied Huguet quietly, "to be precise, your great-great-uncle Lotario of Segni as Pope Innocent III and my great-great-grandfather Simon de Montfort as general of the invading armies. Others figured prominently in the undertaking—Bernard of Clairveaux, Arnold Amaury, Bishop Fulk of Marseilles and eventually St. Dominic and the Inquisitors. Nonetheless our two families were the cornerstones for whatever happened in this land."

"You mean for the slaughter at Montsegur."

"And at Montsegur, Albi, Toulouse, and of course Foix. The Counts of Foix were perhaps the staunchest opponents but it was a useless defense—one region against all the rest of Europe and the Church. It took some years but in the end, the Cathars were most ruthlessly sought out and destroyed."

"Did they not see what was happening to them?"

"Towards the end they fought back, at Toulouse and Foix, and here at Montsegur."

"Then perhaps it is fitting that they have brought William Belibaste here for trial. I imagine he is part of some revival of this movement, part of their priesthood; the Perfect, did you say?"

Huguet nodded. "The Perfect."

"Well, he must be tried," said Aimery, both Count of Segni and a good warrior. "And he must recant or he is doomed."

The two men looked on as another young boy tried his luck upon the list field. He thundered down the track, his lance aimed high towards the quatrain. The steel cracked high, giving life to the motionless wooden figure. Its stretched out arms turned upon the riding squire, knocking him squarely to the ground.

"He will learn for the next time to watch his aim," said Aimery, laughing along with the others, though he never enjoyed seeing a warrior bested, even at list field practice. Never.

"It is interesting that you say the Cathars had a female priesthood," he said. "Interesting because we also have such an anomaly in our own female scribe."

"Ah, the pretty novice," said Huguet as they turned back to the stern face of Montsegur's castle. "I see you've taken a notion to her—escorted her to the convent personally, and took a leisurely time of it, I might add. Not like you; you are usually so keen to your affairs. I can't imagine you sparing a whole turn of the hourglass to exploring the charms of some simple convent girl."

"You find it odd that I should escort our young scribe back to her convent?" replied Aimery. "You find it teasing?"

"In you I do," said Huguet. "Perhaps it might fall to one of your squires to escort her, but it was never your duty. Not even the Abbess Helene would have expected as much from you, had she been scribing and not this young girl. The task was never yours and it surprises me that you would take it to yourself. . . ."

"Especially as I am near-betrothed," Aimery finished for him.

"Yes, that." Huguet hesitated. "And certainly no one would want to compromise your alliance with the mighty House of Valois and be cousin-by-marriage to the King of France. Still, there is something more important than that. You and I have been friends since childhood and I know you as an honorable man. The novice is comely, at least she appears so from the little one can glimpse of her beneath her veils and aprons. I cannot imagine—it is not possible that you would choose to toy with a woman who is professed."

"She is not yet professed."

They had reached the castle's heavy, timbered door and for an instant Aimery turned from it to look out over the land that was now his. He claimed an enormous fortress; the castle dominated the little village huddling round its fist and then reached out to loom over the rugged land round it—and to point across the Haute Savoie towards Italy and home. Aimery had traveled a long path from Italy and sometimes—especially on days like this when he missed the sheer, hard brightness of it—he wondered if he would ever see his birth-land again.

This is my castle, he thought, but it is not my home.

"And you are the most honorable man I know," continued his brother-in-law. "It never entered my mind that you would wish to compromise the virtue of any woman, much less this promised scribe. Aside from the sacredness of her position is the fact that you are near-betrothed to Isabeau of Valois, cousin to the King of France, just as your sister was near-betrothed to another of the king's cousins—when she nearly toppled relations between Paris and Rome by choosing me instead."

"And *fighting* for you," added Aimery. Both men smiled at this memory of the beautiful, headstrong

Minerve and her determination to have the landless and almost penniless count of Montfort. They, too, had traveled a far path these last years.

"Speaking of which," continued Huguet. "My lovely wife has arrived and brought the complete brood of our children with her. The eldest, Rupert, is in page-service to the duke of Burgundy and most anxious to see his uncle of Segni. You are a hero to him, you know; and to half the other young pages in Europe. You have made a mighty name for yourself as crusader in the east."

Aimery felt a frisson of unease scurry through him at the thought of his sister and her young children at Montsegur during William Belibaste's trial. But he smiled at Huguet and said, "Tell Minerve I will be with her directly. I have but one small matter to attend to first."

And before he could be questioned, the Count of Segni strode down the massive stone stairs of Montsegur Castle and back toward the village fair.

# CHAPTER 4

"So he noticed your hair," said Peter.

Claire nodded.

"It is interesting that he should remark upon it. He seems a most observant man; I doubt even the Inquisitor would have grasped the significance of that one small curl. However, we knew Sir Aimery to be most astute. Have I not warned you of your hair?"

As usual, there was only the mildest of reproaches in Peter's voice as he spoke to Claire; more like a father to her than a priest, and the only family she had left. Short and stout with a tonsured head, a wizened nut-like face and wrinkled habit, he looked the man Claire knew him to be: a kind and gentle and true person who was devoted to their peaceful cause.

They walked side by side through the cloister of the Magdalene's convent, as the evening's twilight settled round about them. Claire placed her hand in the crook of the priest's arm, nestling it against the rough cloth of his habit. An ancient nun stopped her painfully slow and arthritic ramble to smile down at them from a high window. She thought of her own early days in the convent and remembered how important these moments spent with a truly holy man could be. The old woman sighed contentedly. Peter of Bologna was a truly holy man; everyone within this flourishing convent knew that. He had lived among them for many years and had become their confessor. He had risked his own life to bring their dear Claire here. And he had remained devoted to her.

"How dear," thought the nun. "How wonderful, after so long a time, that they are still together."

Fortunately, she was much too far away to hear their conversation.

"Still, perhaps his attentions will prove providential," Peter whispered to Claire. His face closed in around this thought with the eagerness of a squirrel making off with a new nut. He patted Claire's hand.

She nodded and then opened her mouth to tell him that not only had Sir Aimery noted her hair, he had also touched it. She could still feel the tingling, unwanted warmth of his fingers against her forehead. She had gone immediately to the washing jug, dipped her hands into its cooling waters and tried to scrub his touch away. She had not succeeded. Nor did she now succeed in telling their priest of him. She held him secret, but Peter did not seem to notice anything amiss.

"Aimery of Segni is a warrior," he said as he quickened his pace. The beat of his wooden clogs against the stone floor stabbed against the evening's peace. "And warriors are all the same. They crave bloodshed and battle. They want, want, want; there is no peace from their wanting. They cannot even comprehend the happiness that we find in our simple life, and that is the real reason that they hunt the Cathar Perfect so mercilessly. They don't understand us; how could they? They are so very different from the Good."

He sighed over the perfidy of those who lurked just beyond the quiet confines of their convent.

"But you were once a warrior," chided Claire quietly, stroking his arm. "You were a Knight Templar and there were Templar Knights battling beside the kings of Europe in all the great Crusades."

"Indeed, there were—until the kings turned against us."

Claire knew Peter's terrible tale, had heard it many times before. Yet she longed to hear it once again. She had spent an hour with Aimery of Segni and then the rest of the afternoon disturbed by the remembrance of it. She longed to crowd him from her mind with the familiar; she wanted again to hear something she had heard often and could understand. It would take her mind from the fact that, for the first time, she held a secret that she dared not share with her beloved Father. For the first time, she had been touched by a man; he had run his hand along her hair. And she, Claire, was Perfect. She had been consecrated to the Cathars when she was still but a child, in a secret part of this convent. How Peter had chuckled over this. Who would think to look for the Perfect within the ranks of a convent consecrated by St. Dominic himself? The Dominicans were widely known to have instituted the Inquisition; it was fitting that the Perfect should have the small revenge of hiding within their mantle's sheltering folds.

But Peter did not oblige her. He would talk of nothing save Aimery of Segni.

"Did he say more?" he asked her. "Did he say more about your hair?"

Claire hesitated. "He called it witch-colored."

Peter paused and thoughtfully nodded. After standing quite still for a moment, he resumed a slow pace through the cloister. Water splashed into a fountain they could not see. Above them the moon had risen with slow majesty to crown the shagged beauty of Languedoc. It hung full and thick and whitely mottled; a picture of impishness in the night sky.

"Aimery of Segni is possessed of a sharp eye and possibly an even sharper mind," said Peter. He leaned attentively closer, as though he and the young nun were in deep prayer. "And always has been, despite his dissolute ways."

"Then you know of him?"

"Everyone knows of the Segnis. They are quite famous. They have been so for generations."

"But *I* know nothing of him. The only thing I know of mercenary knights is that they sometimes call themselves Inquisitors. And that they killed my family."

"That is all you need to know and you will do well to remember this. Always," said Peter as he patted Claire upon the hand. "And it would do the proud Sir Aimery good to hear your words of humbling. Not know of the Segnis? Why, they ceased thinking of themselves as mere earthly knights at least a century ago, when Lotario Segni took on the Papal mantle."

Again the priest paused, so deep within his own thoughts that he seemed to forget the girl beside him. "From the moment of his accession to the Papacy, there was no peace for our people—no, not anywhere within Christendom. As Innocent III, he routed us and imprisoned us and had us burned at the stake. He was determined that this land should be subject only to his authority. Just as the king of France and another Pope—Clement V—would not rest until they had hounded my brother Knights Templar into their graves and carried off our fortune. It was the same here. The Perfect and the Credentes who looked to them had constructed a safe haven here and all were welcomed to it. While they were treated little better than dogs in the rest of Christendom, in Languedoc women were allowed to become Perfect. They ministered the Sacrament. The Credentes—as we called ourselves—and the Cathars, as they called us, lived simple saintly lives. Troubadours sang of their graces. Many say there was something about that peace and harmony that personally offended Lotario of Segni. He wanted it stamped out. That is what they say—but it is not the true reason that he mounted his crusade against fellow Christians."

Claire felt something sweep past her, felt something brush against the cheek that Aimery of Segni had touched. Startled, she glanced up in time to catch two night-birds sweep into the muted expanse of dark sky.

"They said it was about the faith, they said the true faith needed defending. But of course this wasn't the real reason for the barbarity; just as it was not with the Templars. As always, the real stakes were land and power—and money, of course. It always gets back to the money. They killed the Templars because they believed they hid a treasure and discovered that what monies were had were not enough. Then, still greedy, they turned to the Cathars. This was a rich land and many who followed the Faith were noble and quite wealthy."

Peter again paused, as though considering, and then

fixed his bright eyes upon Claire. For an instant she saw the moon's light reflected in them as he moved close. " 'Tis rumored that the Credentes smuggled their treasure down this hill and hid it, once it was certain that Simon de Montfort's troops would have the upper hand. We knew this land intimately. They did not. The Cathar treasure was meant to be hidden and to stay hidden. Few even know for certain of its existence. But I believe that Jacques Fournier knows of it." He paused. "As do I."

The moon smiled down at them. And once again Peter, a very old man, seemed to forget that Claire was there. He stood at the very edge of the clerestory and gazed fiercely into the night. They had reached the end and Claire turned back, but Peter reached out a clawed hand and held her fast.

"The Segnis and the Montforts of this world have always gotten what they wanted from it," said the priest. His words hissed out into the gathering gloom. "This time they will not. The next Troubadour's tale sung of them will end differently. They have tried and tried, and then tried once again, but they have never managed to take everything that belonged to us. They have never managed to kill us all. Now we are back, though still hidden. And now we will have vengeance. We will take back what is rightfully ours."

"So we will meet with the others soon; with Ruch Anger and Guy de Loc and Mother Helene," whispered the girl beside him, "and we will all free William Belibaste before it is too late."

The priest turned back from his own secret vision to smile at her. "Ah, yes, Helene and the others; everyone working together and so hard to free our last Perfect," said Peter. "And, indeed, Belibaste will also be freed in the end."

Claire lay beneath her linen bedding and gloried in the silver light that flooded through the small window of her sleeping cell, making the room almost—but not quite—as bright as daytime. She loved June, when the moon's light angled in and flowed across the small bed where she had slept since childhood.

Peter had decided that they should soon meet with the others.

"It is dangerous for us to be together, especially for you, my little one," he had whispered. "Belibaste's fate will doubtless depend upon our plans."

Claire had nodded. She believed him, as she always had.

Still, there was much in her new situation that frightened her and she had hurried to the haven of her small cell, which contained the few simple things she called her own: her simple bed and cross and prie dieu; the familiarity of her homespun linens. The smell of fresh lavender pervaded all of Languedoc in summer and was especially strong here because she had gathered sheaves of it into an umber colored earthenware pitcher and placed it on the splintery small stool beside her bed.

Everything as it should be. Her own place. Her home.

It must have been only an instant before she saw it, though it seemed longer. Much longer. But it was there. An intrusion, laid out quite boldly upon the moonlight covering her small bed. Without thinking, she touched it.

It was the green ribbon she had seen at the afternoon's fair. It still felt soft and slickly perfect in her outstretched hand.

Instinctively, she knew how it had gotten here, who had brought it here and carefully placed it. And instinctively she wondered just what this knowledge meant.

# CHAPTER 5

"You are called William Belibaste?" the Inquisitor mildly inquired.

The man before him nodded. If there was still rebellion left within him, it was obvious that he had decided not to waste its energy on these early questions. There would be worse than this to come and he knew it. He would doubtless need all his strength then.

"Then please give your name loudly in your own voice so that it can be written by my scribe."

Jacques Fournier nodded curtly toward Claire who sat perched on a stool behind him, almost hidden by quilled pens and inks and parchment and linen papers. She had wanted it this way; she had wanted to be hidden. There was no desire on her part to see more of William Belibaste than she had already seen. She had looked up once, very briefly, when he entered and had seen how his great shape was bent over and how he shuffled. She had heard the clanking of his chains. She had smelled his fear.

"I am William Belibaste," the man said. His voice

whistled out to them, sounding as though it brushed against dry, dead leaves.

"Have you the ability to read and to write your name?"

"I have ability neither to read nor to write. I am a simple man. A peasant."

"You can affix your mark. You know that much, at least?" Jacques Fournier's voice was not unkind.

"I can leave my mark," said Belibaste, "when it is called for. You should have no doubt of that."

Laughter gurgled up from somewhere deep within the crowded Hall.

"Good," replied Jacques Fournier. "We ask but that, and of course that you tell the truth. Will you agree to these simple requests?"

Belibaste chuckled.

Fournier ignored him as he bent over his parchments. He placed a pair of steel and leaded-glass spectacles to his eyes.

"Please inform this court where you were born and when." Fournier did not look up as he pronounced these words.

"I was born within the Corbieres region of France; of that much I am certain. Of the rest—exact time and place of my birth—I am not certain. As I say, we were poor folk and we had no priest to scribe our comings and goings."

For a moment there was only the sound of Claire's quill as she scratched it with diligence across the parchment.

"Continue," said Fournier. "Surely you must know more of your own childhood—your parents' names, the existence of young brothers and sisters. Tell this Court all of that; we must know it all."

"I remember nothing," repeated Belibaste. "I am peasant born. I have no roots. I have no family."

Fournier leaned forward in his chair. He rested his arms upon the polished trestle table before him and tented his hands at his face. He stared quietly at Belibaste for a long while.

"Then tell us of the murder," he said, "the one that you committed and for which you were justly tried and condemned. Since you seem to have no other history, we will commence with that which is known."

If Belibaste were surprised at this question, he did not show it. Claire glanced up quickly, caught his eyes, and then turned again diligently to her task.

"It happened during a brawl. My only justification—though 'tis a paltry one—is that I was very young. I was also very drunk on new ale. But I killed a man and certainly there is no reasoning that fact away. There is no excuse. He was a shepherd, just as I was. We had both come into the village with our sheep. I can no longer remember which of us picked the quarrel or even what it was about. It mattered little then; it matters much more now that I am older. I can do nothing for it now. A man's life—I have spent my own life since trying to repent. It was my repentance that brought me here."

"You did not come willingly," reproved Fournier, "so let us not make pretence that you did."

He turned to the other Inquisitors. There were three of them; younger versions of himself, dressed in dark colors and with serious eyes.

"This man," said Fournier to his colleagues, "is not here on trial for that murder. It is in the distant past. He is charged now with instigation to heresy."

The bishop turned back to the accused and continued. "Yet, even then, you fled before the constables of France. You did not let your need for repentance prevent you from fleeing the lawful authorities."

William looked down pointedly at his gnarled hands, at his homespun clothing, at his bare feet. "There is no justice for such as me in France," he said simply. "There was not then; there is not now. I fled from the king's constables and I took my brother with me. He was already hunted by the Inquisition and had been for years. Though a simple man, he held to beliefs that were not considered orthodox. He was a Cathar." Belibaste paused for a moment and then repeated. "He was a Cathar. He believed a free man should be able to think for himself, but the Inquisition did not believe with him, and so we were forced to run together."

Belibaste paused and Claire felt her soul drawn to his, linked with his, until she reached his memory. She felt the night and the cold and his terror. Her stomach knotted with his hunger. She felt his remorse and his shame.

"I will continue on now to the point of my history that will interest you," said Belibaste. "Our flight led us to Philip d'Alayrac, who was also a hunted man."

A trill of interest scurried through the room at the mention of this name. The Inquisitors looked up from their parchments, their eyes narrowing. Soldiers who had been playing at dice stopped their rattling. Even the dogs quieted upon the cold hearth.

"Continue," said Fournier as the others held their breath.

William Belibaste did just that. "D'Alayrac belonged to the revival," he said, his voice strong, his eyes no longer looking downward. "He belonged to the revival of the Cathar Perfect."

Aimery watched Claire as she set down the dreary

proceedings. He watched as her long fingers dipped a quill into ink and then scratched it across parchment. He watched her brow furrow; he noticed that she rarely glanced at Belibaste. There was a mystery about her; something he could not readily explain. He thought it might have something to do with the warm wisp of red hair he had glimpsed. It had seemed so saucy and bold against the pristine whiteness of her wimple. It had emboldened him to purchase the green ribbon she had so fleetingly and guiltily admired and to gift her with it. Even now, he wondered why he had done this, why he had acted so impulsively. He was not, by nature, precipitous; and, after all, she was near-betrothed to the Church.

The Hall, though large, was hot and stuffy. Aimery, a warrior used to his horse and to the open skies, could hardly bear the closeness of it. However, this trial was part and parcel of the sinecure of Montsegur. He thought ruefully that he had finally gotten the impressive fortress he had worked for. Now he must rule it.

But it was tedious work and his mind wandered from the drone of it. Besides presiding at this trial, he had spent his morning hiring a bailiff and attending to his other business. Who would ever have thought his duties as lord of Montsegur would be so tedious, or so dull? Yet that is exactly what Aimery had found them to be. Well dressed men from as far away as Corbieres and Albi had shown up at the castle keep with references and recommendations, each firmly believing that he was the perfect one to fill the lucrative post of running Montsegur castle for its young seigneur. Used to generalling warriors, Aimery quickly grew impatient with their posturing. He had felt the dire need of a wife who could manage this nonsense.

And the hiring of a bailiff had been by far the easiest

of his morning's tasks. There had been a squabble to settle between two glovers who had both paid tithes to have a stall directly beneath the Cathedral eaves, in the event that William Belibaste was found guilty of heresy and sentenced to death.

"There will be many a visitor to come on that day," said one arrogant, silk-clad man to his new lord, "and I want prime place for my goods."

It took a conscious effort for Aimery not to let disgust show on his face. After all he was new here—a foreigner, an Italian—and he must learn to rule this place.

"There is no guarantee that William Belibaste will burn," he had said to the glover. "He is only being tried now and his trial will be a fair one. You, man, will take your place among the others on the far side, within the Cathedral. The man from Paris may take place in the choicer section under the eaves."

The glover had opened his mouth in protest and then thought best of it. The new lord's face brooked no opposition. Instead, the merchant lowered himself into a deep reverence and then turned and walked smartly from the room. He looked up only once at Aimery. There was hatred in his eyes.

"You have made an enemy of that glover this morning," Huguet now said from beside him. Around them Belibaste's testimony droned on. "He is listed upon the Church registry as one of the richest men in this place, used to being deferred to. He did not take well, your giving his choice spot to an outsider."

"Especially as I am an outsider myself," replied Aimery with an exaggerated Italian accent. Both friends laughed.

"I am annoyed with all this talk of witchcraft and burning," he said. He pitched his voice so that the knights and monks that surrounded him could hear it. "Belibaste has been convicted of nothing as yet."

"He is a known heretic," replied Huguet mildly. "And he has vowed not to repent."

"Yet he might," snapped Aimery. "He can always change his mind. He does not have to be part of his own destruction."

He was surprised by his own vehemence. This man's fate should not matter to him at all; at most his trial should prove a bad omen, nothing more. And yet, something in Belibaste's plight urged his compassion; it disgusted Aimery that his first major duty at Montsegur was to preside over such a distasteful business.

"He should be able to think as he pleases," he said. "The Cathars have been suppressed for a hundred years. Certainly this man and his few followers can cause us no real harm."

"The king is afraid of revolt," replied Huguet.

"You are speaking of a peasant revolt?" A slow, dubious smile etched its way across Aimery's handsome face. "Those never work."

Huguet's clear eyes grew earnest. "Indeed, they do work. In Italy the Cathars, who were thought to be so piously against bloodshed, rose up against the Inquisition and slaughtered its adherents. Not even the anathema, with its threat of eternal damnation, could bring them to heel. The Cathars rose up here in France as well. On the Feast of the Ascension, adherents of this cult—peasants—rose up against two judges of the Inquisition. The rebels came from this very town of Montsegur. One witness came forth afterwards saying that he had viewed them upon the road, but had mistaken them for laborers headed homeward after a good day's work. There was only one thing wrong with them—these workmen carried battle axes."

"There will be no revolt here while I serve as lord of Montsegur," said Aimery. "William Belibaste will have a fair trial; one hopes he will be acquitted. Nonetheless, I will brook no illegal means in the acquisition of his freedom and anyone who tries to incite rebellion will face the consequences of his actions. I have set my word upon this."

A rustle brought their attention back to the proceedings in the Great Hall. The Inquisitors pushed back their ornate chairs and rose and surreptitiously stretched their aching backs. The prisoner shuffled from the room guarded by two surly men at arms.

Aimery watched for a moment as Claire gathered her few supplies into a leather sumter. He saw her close her parcel tight with good, flax twine. And then, without a parting word to Huguet, he walked quickly across the room to join her.

A lone priest had reached there before him. He was a short, round fellow, Aimery noted, dressed in the nondescript homespun of the Order of St. Francis. The two of them—the old priest and the young nun—seemed to be in deep conversation. When he caught sight of the new lord of Montsegur, the priest made a deferential path for him. Keeping his head bowed, he gave a slow, deep reverence before disappearing into the crowd.

# CHAPTER 6

If Aimery had expected the young scribe to be reticent and not mention his present to her, if he had expected her to blush or to falter, he changed his mind before they were barely ten feet without his castle walls. He learned that Claire of Foix was not the type to blush or falter.

"I've brought it with me," she said to him. "You must take it back."

She pitched her voice low so that it could not be easily heard by Aimery's honor guard, but it still remained forceful. She did not whisper.

So surprised was he, that Aimery walked silently beside her for a moment, gathering his thoughts. He had been at Montsegur a full week now and the festivities of his arrival were gradually fading. Only a few brightly painted merchants' stalls still clung within the Cathedral's shadow. The young child and his dog had disappeared, as had the mummers and the traveling troubadours. June was filled with feast days and celebrations; everyone would be off in search of new places with new coins to fill their purse.

Not that Aimery noticed their absence as he walked beside the Maid of Foix.

"It was a present," he said at last. "Something you had admired and that I wanted to gift you with. I thought it went well with your hair."

He realized his mistake when the words were already out.

Claire turned clear eyes upon him and she did not blush. She displayed none of the coquettishness or false restraint he had come to expect when women said things to him they did not truly mean.

"You make too much of my waywardness," she said. "I have been spoiled by the nuns who raised me, that is all. They stretch certain rules for my benefit; they give me certain privileges. Besides, shaving one's head is not really part of the convent canon; it is more of a custom. I came to St. Magdalene when I was but a child. There are women there—women who have had no children of their own—who look upon me as their child. I have been indulged, and perhaps shamefully so."

"Then I imagine you will shave your hair tomorrow just to spite me," said Aimery as they started on the open path that led to Claire's convent, "because you know it gives me so much pleasure just knowing that it is there, and that I am one of the few to have seen it. At least I imagine I am. This almost makes it a secret that we share."

If he had planned to ruffle her, he did not succeed. Claire shrugged her shoulders. "It is a paltry secret, indeed, when it is one that is shared with a convent full of women," she said. "I cannot imagine why my hair should interest you at all. I want you to take that ribbon back."

Aimery stared into the cloudless sky. He had to sternly suppress an urge to whistle into the wind. He had no idea what he wanted from this woman; no idea, really, why he had hurried to the Como silk merchant to purchase the accursed ribbon that was now causing all this discussion, but he knew he had no intention of taking it back. He was truly enjoying himself for the first time since he had come to Montsegur. Still, he thought it best to veer her mind toward something else. She just might force the ribbon on him if he pressed her about it.

"Do you think William Belibaste guilty of heresy?" he asked. This topic was answered prayer and Aimery knew it. Everyone in Montsegur held an easy opinion about William Belibaste and his trial for heresy. Aimery thought he saw Claire shiver at his question. He thought he saw her move just a little apart from him on the path.

"I have not been called by the bishop to give opinion to what I hear," she said. "I have been called to scribe these court proceedings, not pronounce upon them."

"Yet you must have some interest in them," Aimery insisted. He was grateful she no longer spoke about the ribbon, demanding that he take it back. He pressed his point. "You are from Foix originally and, from what I hear, Foix was a hotbed of Catharism in the last century."

"*Hotbed* is a word not generally associated with the Credentes," said Claire. "It is too rankly passionate for them. They were pacific and simple people. They did not believe in giving in to the baser emotions—at least from what I've always heard."

She waved a dismissive hand. She seemed to want to put an end to this discussion. Aimery did not.

"Then you've heard more of them than I have," he

said as they paused an instant beneath a giant oak tree's leafy shade. "I know nothing of their beliefs and it might help me to understand these proceedings—to understand why this heresy is taken so to heart by the Inquisition—if you would let me know just a little of what you have heard of it."

And then, for some reason, he added, "It might aid me in helping Belibaste."

Claire hesitated. Her eyes did not leave Aimery's and he thought he saw indecision flit through them. They started up the path again, their steps beating tattoos into the packed earth.

"There is precious little that you can do to help him, even should you want to do so," Claire said at last. "Not even noblemen have been able to stand for their people against the Inquisition. God in heaven knows, throughout this last century, enough of them battled against it here in Languedoc."

But she had hesitated, and now Aimery pressed his advantage. "Then will you explain this history to me? Not the battles and the burnings—I can get this from any number of sources. It seems that all in Montsegur, from my brother-in-law to the lowest sheep guard, has some theory on what happened here and who was wrong to whom. I need to know what relevance the past has to *now*, to why the Cathars have once again sprung up and why William Belibaste let himself be captured."

"He did not let himself be captured," snapped Claire. "No man would."

"Then tell me why he didn't. I need to know what the Cathar's believed if I am to rule this land well."

She seemed to consider this.

"Everyone knows the story here," she said. The leafy limb of an oak tree brushed against her white wimple.

"As I say, we are told it at our mother's breast. And there are many mothers—peasants, mostly—who frighten their children into submission with the threat of Innocent III and his grand war. It has gone down in our memory as the Albigensian Crusade. On the other hand, the Cathars are remembered sympathetically. They were peace loving and generous; believing only that this world of flesh is evil and yearning for a world of absolute spirit, which was good."

She warmed to her subject; Aimery noticed that she moved a little closer to him on the narrow path. "This belief permeated all of Languedoc, reaching from its mighty castles into its peasants' huts. It mothered the richly refined culture for which this region was noted— and envied. However, this credence also put its adherents into direct conflict with the Authority at Rome as well as the King in Paris. That is the key."

Aimery nodded.

"Innocent III was the first to call for a Crusade against the belief," she continued. "He allied himself with the King of France who had long wished to subdue the independence of his vassals here. The allied armies, led by Simon de Montfort, swept through Languedoc, pillaging the land and laying waste its population. *Burning* them as heretics, until now only a few of them remain—or at least I hear that there are few of them—and these are hidden away; fearful that at any moment the Inquisition might sweep down on them again."

Aimery nodded. Claire had spoken of many things, but he had learned nothing new from what she'd said. And her omissions were curious: she had said nothing about the rumor that the Cathars were witches and sorcerers—the same charges that had been used, with great effect, against the Knights Templar only a few years before. Professed or not, she was still a member of a religious order. Surely she would have heard these accusations. Without realizing it, Claire had pleaded the Cathar cause passionately without once giving a reason for her passion. Aimery's shrewd eyes narrowed at this. It was another mystery, one of many.

The day was bright; the air just heavy enough to be languorous. Aimery put aside his duties, the pesky tasks of choosing a bailiff and assigning merchant stalls at a makeshift market. He was enjoying himself. Claire's earnest conversation engrossed him. He found her frank talk enthralling. The only passion his own near-betrothed ever exhibited generally concerned a novel way of knotting her hair. Isabeau of Valois had no patience with anything that did not directly concern her person. On more than one occasion, Aimery had found himself grateful that an active life had precluded his spending much time with her in the past, and that continued activity would doubtless keep a safe distance between them once they were wed.

This was married life and he accepted it: the Segni lands and money in exchange for the power that accompanied the Valois surname. Love, passion, even the earnestness of a good conversation, could be found elsewhere. Was he not finding them now with this sweet maid and her serious talk? All in all, this was a satisfactory way to spend the sand-span of an hourglass. These simple moments were the only fine time he'd had since coming to Montsegur.

Later, Aimery came to believe this very satisfaction was why he did not at first see the effigy. Or perhaps it was because it was so small, barely larger than his hand. Still, it was hard to imagine why he overlooked the menace. They were almost at the convent's wicket gate when they saw it hanging there.

He noticed it first and moved slightly, as though to block it from Claire's view. He reached out a hand to stop her, but it was too late. He heard her gasp. At least he snatched the thing away before she could touch it. Such a small object, and yet so horrifying; a small nun–doll, with a face carved from stinking pig-fat soap, and its tunic and veiling a coarse mockery of the white linen that the novices at St. Magdalene's wore. A simple thing, a feigning of innocence; its tale told in the burnt charring of the tunic and the unmistakable lock of red hair pinned carefully to its wimple.

# CHAPTER 7

Claire lay on her bed, her body curled tightly onto itself, her eyes staring into the darkness. It had been a stupid ploy, setting the doll where she would surely see it; placing it there to frighten her. She knew all this. And yet she had been frightened by it. She sensed the threat that had been sewn within it, even though she had not really seen the effigy at all. Aimery had been too quick for her. He had stepped ahead and taken it into his capable hands before she could really glimpse it. Still, the threat had been there. Aimery had acted too quickly for her to be frightened—then.

But she was frightened now.

Who would have stitched together such a menace? Who would have wanted to do so?

This is what Aimery asked her. She asked herself the same questions now.

There were no answers.

Of course, the obvious one was that someone had found out they meant to save William Belibaste. Their

little band had been found out. Their plot to free him—
still barely conceived and not truly outlined—had been
discovered. The Inquisitors knew about them.

Claire, schooled in this convent, was not at all naïve
about the power of the Church. She knew its intricate
workings. Since childhood, she had learned that the
Inquisition was the hand of the Frankish North, and
that at any time it might reach out to crush her. She
knew all this. She only wondered how.

How had they found out?

Claire tossed upon the bed, tangled in its soft linen
sheets, as her mind furrowed around this question.
They had been so careful; they had tried so hard to
cover themselves. And they were so few. Herself; of
course Father Peter; Mother Helene, who hid her secret
Cathar leanings behind the sanctity of her role as
Abbess—there were just a few others. They had not
wanted many now. The numbers would come later—
after they had established themselves once again and
after William Belibaste was freed.

There was another deeper worry, hidden just behind
this one. In that instant when Aimery had stepped out,
when his hand had reached for the effigy, she had
stepped behind him. She had instinctively sought shelter with him from what lay ahead. And Aimery of
Segni was her sworn enemy. He was Protector of the
Inquisition that sought to find them out. No matter his
banter, no matter his attempts at light conversation, if
he knew who she was he would have her burned. She
knew all this; she had been *taught* to know it. Yet, she
trusted him. When afraid, she had instinctively sought
his shelter. Even now, much later, she still clutched the
silk ribbon he had given her as a warder and a talisman
against the darkness. She looked down, with some

wonder, on its bright softness as it lay webbed between
her fingers.

This would never do. She must meet with the others.
If they could just gather—she and Father Peter and the
Abbess Helene and the few others of their little band—
Claire knew she would pull strength from them. She
knew she would again feel the calm, sure knowing she
had always determined in the past.

The Northern Franks were murderers and assassins.
The Cathars held to the true, good ways. And one day
they would retake the land that had been so cruelly
snatched from them. Claire held to this thought as the
morning sky tinted lavender outside her window. It was
the old thought, but this time it did not bring the old
comfort.


Jacques Fournier glanced up at the voice of his protector. He was settled in his own expansive chamber,
puzzled by a visit so late in the afternoon, but he was
too much the consummate diplomat to let emotion
show upon his face. Besides, he had news of his own to
share.

"Good day to you, Count." He nodded once, almost
curtly, and then motioned Aimery of Segni to a handsome carved chair. "I carried this down with me from
Paris. They say it was originally destined for the Papal
residence at Avignon, or at least that is what I was told
by the dealer. However, he was from Lombardy and
could just as easily have been telling me what he
thought I wanted to hear in order to raise the price
upon me. He may have imagined bishops always to be
looking for objects that might identify them with a
higher rank."

"Did he say why the pope didn't want it for Avignon?" asked Aimery.

"Too tame," replied the bishop with a shrug. "Not enough carvings of dryads and cavorting nymphs, I imagine. You know how things are at Avignon."

"Different from Rome."

"But that is the schism. It is a disaster, this having two popes, and I cannot see the ending of it in my life-time, nor even in yours. However, I imagine that is not the problem that has brought you here."

Again Fournier motioned Aimery to be seated.

The chair was dust free and perfectly positioned, as was everything else in Jacques Fournier's immaculate and orderly chamber. No dust danced upon the late af-ternoon sunlight in the bishop's apartments; no stray ash lingered in his carefully cleaned grate. The room bespoke an orderly and precise mind, one from which clarity could not easily be hidden—something Aimery had long realized of the bishop.

"I've come to speak of the novice," said Aimery, set-tling his long legs out before him, "the one who acts as scribe."

Fournier gave no indication that he was startled by this remark, if indeed he had been. He merely raised a thin eyebrow and waited.

The Count of Segni continued. "I want to remove her from the convent. I want her in my castle."

"That is impossible," said Fournier mildly. "She has not yet professed. It is impossible to remove her from St. Magdalene's. She has always lived at St. Magda-lene's. She told us this herself and from what I gather, the nuns have grown quite fond of her. She is both at-tractive and unprotected; removing her would cause scandal and scandal is the last thing we need if we are to pursue this delicate trial."

"I want her in my castle," repeated Aimery quietly. "I mean to have her here."

Fournier blinked and something glittered deep within his eyes. He studied the Count of Segni.

"I believe she is in danger," continued Aimery.

"You mean that little incident with the doll—the one you told me of?" asked the bishop with a dismissive wave of the hand. "It was nothing, a child's prank."

"I don't think so," said Aimery. "The doll, as you call it, wore a dress singed with fire. It sported a lock of Claire's own hair. Those are the marks of heresy. The girl saw and recognized them. She was frightened. I was there. I saw her fear."

"But Claire of Foix is novice in a most Christian convent. Except for her work as scribe, she knows nothing of the Cathars. How could she?"

Aimery opened his mouth to tell Fournier about his conversation with Claire, to let the bishop know just how much she knew of the forbidden ways, but then thought better of it. Fournier was the Inquisitor, after all. Instead he said, "There are rumors that Belibaste's fellow religionists will rise to rescue him. It would not be the first time and for all their talk of peaceableness, their uprisings can be singularly bloody. I would have her safe."

"Impossible," repeated the bishop. "Already, some remark upon the attention you show her—a woman professed to a chaste life. It is better that she remains where she is. I see no danger for her."

"As lord of this place, it is my right to insist. I want the Maid of Foix removed from St. Magdalene's convent and brought within the walls of Montsegur Castle."

They stared at each other for a very long moment. Neither man looked away.

"I received a letter from your lady mother, yesterday," said the bishop at last.

Aimery shook his head. "You've not responded to what I told you."

"I am responding," replied the bishop, "if you will but listen. Your lady mother sends both you and your sister greetings from Rome. She says that she is returning again to the South, although the journey fatigues her. She said that she had not been well. She vaguely mentioned some illness. You know how your mother is—she could be already at heaven's throne and only think her illness a mild indisposition. She would be arguing with St. Peter, demanding that she be sent back to attend to some business."

Aimery smiled at this image of the tiny but energetic Countess of Segni.

"I know her well and I can read the fatigue in her letter," continued Jacques Fournier. He leaned slightly forward in his chair, "and in the fact that she mentioned a wife for you—and more than once. She inquired most energetically about Isabeau of Valois."

"It is in the natural course that a woman my mother's age would want grandchildren," replied Aimery shortly.

"As I recall, your sister Minerve has already gifted her with a pride of these. She has four children has she not, and all sons."

"My mother wants an heir to the Segni name. My sister has sired Montforts."

"Your mother wishes to see you settled," said the bishop. "She wants you happy. In any event, the question of grandchildren was not mentioned in her letter. The question of your lands was."

Two finely chiseled creases now framed Aimery's tightened lips. "My lands are not my mother's concern."

But they were, and he knew it. Under the circumstances.

"They are when she is forced to run them." Fournier's lips had grown thin as well. "And she is forced to run them because you are so little in Italy yourself. The lands in the Campagna are your responsibility and you are shirking it and them to come to France to gain titles and lands that you neither need nor want. Your mother has grown too old to be the support for your over weaning ambition."

"But my father would have wanted me here," retorted Aimery. He didn't know where those words had come from and he tried to soften their meaning. "My mother is not forced to watch those lands. I employ a very capable bailiff to oversee them for me."

"You have gone through five bailiffs in the last two years," replied Fournier mildly. "I learned this from others, not from your mother. Countess Iolande is much too young to have told me this, and too wary. I was one of your minor guardians and she well knows my feelings on this subject. You've so much land that you have no idea what to do with it. You cannot govern what you own. You cannot properly attend it. Yet, still you would have more."

"Montsegur is not just any land. This is not just any castle," Aimery shot back.

"But is Montsegur *your* castle?"

Aimery sprang up so quickly that he toppled the bishop's ornate, Avignon-bought chair to the stone floor. "Are you implying, Eminence, that I am greedy enough to take something that does not rightfully belong to me? Why, the King of France himself—"

"Hardly greedy," interrupted Fournier mildly. "Perhaps *driven* might be the better term."

"Driven towards what?" Aimery's quick storm of

anger disappeared as quickly as it had arisen. He reached down; slowly righted his chair; placed himself in it. By the time he finished doing so, he was master of himself once again. "Toward acquiring lands? Toward striving to do what my family expects of me?"

"Your family?" said the bishop quietly, "or your father?"

Once was enough. He would not let this wily bishop goad him or deflect him from his objective. Aimery had already allowed his anger to show. He was determined not to do it again. He would command the situation, just as he, a commander in arms, was used to doing.

"I have no idea what you mean by this reference to my father," he began and then continued on quickly, neatly hoeing down any words the bishop might be holding in abeyance. "I know only that I am master of Montsegur now and as such I will continue the illustrious work that my ancestors began. I will hold this place for the house of Segni and unite this land under the aegis of the Kings of France. I will brook no insurrection—neither a temporal nor a religious one. And while I wish to show you no disrespect, Eminence, it might be well for you to remember that you are under my protection. I am not under yours. It is commonly rumored that William Belibaste's friends will try to rescue him and that they will incite others to join them. We will not have a flower filled path to travel until he is burned for heresy and incitation, if indeed that is his ultimate fate. I, for one, am against the whole of this business, including your part in it, yet I will do what I must to hold this land for the king. But I will not place an innocent girl's life in danger. One could feel the malevolence on that effigy they made of her; one could feel the hatred motivating it. She is the weakest of all who are involved in this business. We have put her in danger's way and I will at least move her now to Montsegur where she can be safe."

"She is not the only one. There will be others in danger as well." Fournier looked shrewdly over at his protector. He would let the matter of Umberto dei Conti di Segni, Aimery's father, rest until a more propitious time. "You hold one of the greatest warrior titles in Christendom but, as with most things in this wretched world, it is coveted and challenged on many sides. As both your bishop and confessor, I urge you to secure it by marrying—suitably—and producing an heir as quickly as possible. If you will not think of yourself and your own responsibilities, I urge you to consider Huguet and your sister. Above all consider your sister. She is with child and the danger here is great."

"I have offered to send her away. Indeed, I urged her not to come at all."

"But she will not leave her husband—and you will need Huguet."

This last was telling and they both knew it. Aimery had been in possession of Montsegur exactly one week and already there were rumors of insurrection. From opposite sides of the trestle table, the two men, bishop and warrior, stared at each other from similarly colored, intelligent eyes. They could have played at chess.

"If you think it unwise that Claire be moved to the castle," said Aimery slowly, "then perhaps we should dispense with her services entirely. Perhaps it is not right to have a novice scribing."

Jacques Fournier cocked a wary eye. He had not missed Aimery's use of the girl's Christian name. "You have been for it from the very beginning. When Brother Clements was struck low and we could locate no replacement for him, 'twas you who said it would show impartiality on the Court's part to let a woman do the noting."

"A woman," said Aimery slowly, "not a nun."

"And what is the difference?" The bishop lifted his gaze from the Count of Segni and raised it to heaven. "They both call unwanted attention to themselves. I am sure that it is already known in Rome that a woman is noting these proceedings. That kind of scandalous news always travels fast."

"Exactly the problem," said Aimery. "No matter what she does, Claire of Foix will call attention to herself—at least, if she continues to dress as she does." He allowed these words to echo on the silence before he continued. " 'Tis something witching in all that white. My men have mentioned it."

"Claire of Foix is the only Latinist available to me!" cried Jacques Fournier. "I have appealed for help, but in the meantime there is no one else to do the scribing and this inquisition must go on. It is imperative that the case against William Belibaste be brought to its immediate summation. You know the dangers in it. You know what happened before; you know of the revolt and the bloodshed. What else would you have me to do but continue?"

"Have the Maid of Foix dress as a normal woman," replied the Count of Segni. "Modestly but inconspicuously. You would be doing nothing wrong in this. There is no need for her to dress as a nun when she is not as yet one. She has not taken final vows and so she is not yet professed. You would be breaking no law of the Church should you chose to forbid her the habit—at least for a time."

Though he still shook his head no, Aimery could tell

that his friend, the bishop, was considering the logic in his words. His face screwed up tight as a walnut around the idea.

"And I would remove the veil from her hair," said the Count of Segni quietly, as though this last were but an afterthought and not the main motivation behind his conversation. "The wimple she wears marks her as a cleric. Instead, let the people think she is one of their own. *Show* them that she is one of their own. In that way there will be less discussion when the verdict comes down. If *she* is there, if *she* is taking the scribing, and if she is one of them, they will not say that the decision was foreordained."

"They will not say that," replied Jacques Fournier sharply, "not of my court. 'Tis fairly run. All have an impartial chance before its judgment seat. No one goes to the fire unless he refuses to recant."

"Or unless he is Perfect," said Aimery softly.

"Or unless he is Perfect," agreed the Inquisitor without hesitation.

"Then show this," said the Count of Segni, rising from his chair. "Let the maiden continue to take the notes. But let her take them looking as she truly is—a maiden."

"I will think on it," said the bishop turning again to the endless stack of parchments on his desk.

" 'Tis all I ask," said Aimery.

It was enough.

There was no going against the lord of the fortress, even when one was under his special protection. Jacques Fournier had been intelligent enough to realize this, just as Aimery had known he would be. The bishop was far too astute to totally trust the Count of

Segni's reasons for wanting the Maid of Foix in his castle.

"You are attracted to her," said the prelate as he blotted the ink dry on his permission. "For some reason you want her. But you must remember your station, Aimery. And you must remember hers."

Aimery had forgotten none of this, but he would have Claire. He was determined upon it. He would have her and that very day—though not in the way the bishop thought. He did not "want" Claire of Foix. He merely had to have her. That was all. Aimery had not forgotten his station; he had not forgotten his duty to Montsegur or to his family. Still, he enjoyed Claire; he enjoyed hearing her speak, watching her at her scribing, enjoyed their walks to the convent, enjoyed buying her ribbons and speculating about the exact color of her hair, the feel of it and the way it smelled. He enjoyed all of this; looked forward to their time together. There was very little else pleasurable in his life, nor had there been for longer than he cared to remember.

Aimery was determined to hold fast to this small bit of joy called Claire, at least as long as he could.

# CHAPTER 8

"I cannot possibly leave my convent," Claire said to him. They were in the small antechamber just off the main Hall. It was early evening and they were alone. She had tried to hurry away after the day's session with William Belibaste. They were still involved with the preliminary testimony, the dry data of Belibaste's life. His birth, his family, his early occupation were still to be sifted with the thoroughness Jacques Fournier demanded in his court. He wanted no aspersions cast upon the ultimate verdict. They had not yet reached testimony for witchcraft and heresy, but this would surely come.

"No one is asking you to leave it permanently," said the Count of Segni to the Maid of Foix, "only for a short time. We have heard that there is a plot aloft to free William Belibaste. We would have you safe from it within this fortress. You must understand that I—we—may have put you in danger by demanding that you scribe for us. The effigy upon the wicket—well, it was disturbing."

"Superstition," said Claire quickly as she looked away. She suspected more about that effigy than she was willing to share, especially with Aimery of Segni who was her enemy. "How can a doll harm me?"

"Of course I don't believe that a doll can harm you," said Aimery, "but I most certainly believe that the man who put it there can, and that he will."

She turned away. "There is no need for my protection. I am from Montsegur. No one would hurt me. I have lived in this town and in its convent all my life."

"Not quite all your life," replied the Count of Segni casually, "only since the age of three. You told me this yourself. I have also had word from Foix. I know all about you."

"All about me?" That he had sought information in Foix neither surprised nor frightened Claire. She expected caution from him. She would be cautious in his place.

Aimery crossed to the small leaded window, his gaze seemingly intent on the setting sun. Claire was glad for his back so that she could study him. She had never had this opportunity before. A quick look here, a glance there; this was all that had been permitted her. Now that he was turned from her, she could study him. He was much taller than she; this much was evident even from a distance; taller, broader, and somehow stronger. Different. She saw the way his samite tunic held tight against the width of his shoulders and loosened just enough at his narrow waist. She saw the way sunlight glowed through his bright hair. She could smell maleness on him. Claire had thought little enough about this in the past, but she had never been around anything so very male before. Aimery was different from her; Claire knew this, and she felt this knowledge as it physically tingled through her body.

She said, "You sent spies to Foix?"

She kept her voice cold and made sure there was a stern set to her wimpled head. In case he turned back. In case he might secretly study her, just as she secretly studied him.

"Not spies," he said. "You must admit it curious that a woman from such a humbled existence as your own—and I mean no impertinence by this—should be so vastly educated."

She faced him squarely. "I've told you the nuns at St. Magdalene's . . ."

"The nuns are not capable of teaching you all that you have learned. They, too, are amazed at your capabilities. The Abbess Helene said that they guided you in rudimentary Latin, but that soon you had quite surpassed them all. It seems you are capable of the most astonishing feats of knowledge. The Abbess quite beamed with pride in you—and not in your Latin alone. She told me that you excelled in letterings, and mathematics, as well. She said you were a knowledgeable alchemist."

Claire pushed aside her fear at the use of this word, so closely linked with the Knights Templar. She continued to stare at him.

"You had no right to spy upon me," she whispered. "You had no right to question."

"I have all rights," he answered mildly. "I am liege lord here at Montsegur and I must know exactly what my duties to this place and its people will entail."

These were the same words he had used to the bishop, but Claire of Foix was not the bishop. She did not accept what he said with grace.

"I am a novice, professed to the Church," she said and her deep eyes glittered. "I will not be told what to do. I will not be removed from my home."

"You have already been removed," said Aimery

slowly and deliberately. He no longer even pretended to look from the high, arrow-slit window. He gazed right at Claire. "Your few things have been brought to a chamber on the noble floor. You will like it. 'Tis near that of my sister, Minerve, who is just a few seasons older than you are. I have the feeling that you will get on well with Minerve. She, too, knows her own mind. And she has a gaggle of sons—four to be exact with another due before summer's ending. Do you like children?"

The question was so unexpected that Claire bobbed a quick yes without thinking.

"Good," continued the Count of Segni. "Minerve's children are well-behaved and boisterous both, if that combination can be imagined, and she is as enamored of them as she is of their father. I have the feeling that you and my sister will become friends."

"I doubt that," said Claire. "Not if she is related to you; not if she shares your arrogant inability to consider the wishes of anyone but yourself. I doubt that I shall have anything at all in common with your sister."

Aimery smiled. "That may well be. Minerve does know her own mind. You will have opportunity enough to decide this. You will meet my sister. You will come to know her well. Follow me now, I will escort you to your new home."


*Not my home. Never my home.*

It was a pleasant enough chamber. One quick look had assured Claire that it was better by far—at least in worldly ways—than the small cell she had left behind her. It was still small but the splintered furniture had been replaced by polished wood; the rough linen sheets by softly embroidered ones; the small, cramped cot by a bed so luxuriously grand that she could stretch cross-wise upon it and still barely touch its edges. And there was a large, east facing window. At night, the moon could still kiss her. She could bathe in its silvery light.

More importantly, she shared this space with no one. One quick perusal assured her of this. Most castle chambers, even those on the noble floor, were communal concerns, and Claire had assumed Aimery of Segni had placed her with other maidens under his charge. He had not. This was excellent. Claire was grateful for the solitude. She needed it, if William Belibaste were to be set free.

She paced the chamber now, her feet beating furiously against its thyme-strewn floors, as her mind raced through the implications of this move. She knew she must get word to Father Peter and the others. Mother Helene would have told them; they would by now know this disastrous turn of event. And it was Helene she wished most to speak with; for once, more than Peter, she was drawn to Helene.

No matter what, she must still get to them. They must form firm plans. In the past they had been content to live from day to day; to see what fate would turn up that might prove useful to them in their quest. They were against Aimery of Segni now and Claire knew well enough that he would not slip. He would give them nothing inadvertently. They must plan. They must snatch.

And no one knew how long the trial would last. The evidence against William Belibaste appeared limitless, especially as he seemed unrepentant and showed no inclination to recant. He had never been one to disguise or to dissimilate. A forthright man left a clear trail behind him and the Inquisition had been scenting at

Belibaste's for years. That meant this trial could end tomorrow if the Inquisitor so decreed it. The bishop had evidence aplenty and to spare. No one knew *what* Jacques Fournier would do; only that he had the power and authority to do anything he chose.

Peter had understood this as well. He had slipped a parchment into her sumter saying that they would gather this night at the convent. She knew the place. The meeting, like all their meetings, would be quick and furtive. Dangerous. But she must be there.

"Of all the days to move me away," she muttered and she felt a stab of fear. Aimery of Segni was not stupid; he was not a man with whom to trifle, but Claire doubted he had guessed her secret—yet. He did not suspect her. How could he? That was not the reason he had forced her here. They, especially Peter, had been excruciatingly careful. Yet she was being watched and she knew it.

She glanced around her chamber once again. Though small, it claimed excellent appointments and it was filled with light from a plethora of beeswax candles that twinkled in pewter cups. She walked to its freeing window. By castle standards, it was large and looked down over the Roc and towards the Haute Savoie and Italy, hidden in the twilight. It was as though a breeze from off the mountainside had passed through it and left the summer scents she had grown to love during her years here—growing grass and earth crops and the soft mingling odor of a thousand wild flowers. She breathed it all for a moment, and then she turned back to the bed.

Claire tried not to think of it, not to even look at it, as she paced her way from one end of her new home to the other. Yet it was irresistible. It fascinated her. She would catch a glimpse of white; she would smell the

scent of flowers. And the room was so small—the bed
so large. Its white linen puddled onto the gray stone
floor. If she was not careful, she brushed against it as
she walked past.

And she wanted to brush against it. This much was
certain. She wanted to run her hand along the finely
wrought needlework that covered it. She wanted to push
her nose deep inside its freshness; she could smell lavender hidden within it, even from afar. Sometimes, in her
deepest dreams, she touched fineness such as this, but
she had never experienced its like in wide-awake life.
Life at St. Magdalene's was frugal, hardworking, and
plain; a life lived for what the Cathar Good could do
when they were able to come from hiding once again.
A life lived for future glory.

This was now. This beautiful bed was before her and
she was attracted to this beauty; just as she was guiltily
drawn to the green ribbon the Count of Segni had
gifted to her. She wore it at her neck, hidden behind the
high collar of her tunic. Her hand went to it now. She
grazed its softness. She was finding more and more to
love about a world and a life that she had always known
as carnal and confusing, as worthless and unfulfilling.
She was puzzled by her own rapid change.

"And it is Aimery of Segni who is changing me."

The sound of her own voice startled Claire into
stopping in mid-step. It had grown late during her pacing. She heard the bells sound compline, the time of
late-night prayer. Quickly she crossed to the window
and looked out. Night had fallen but there was a fat
moon and in its light one lone sentry guarded the parapet. Claire concentrated upon him for a moment; joining the force of her mind with his just as she had been
taught to do by Peter. She saw the man at arms reach a

hand to his mouth to stifle a yawn and she nodded. Her gaze left him and roamed through the castle keep until it came upon the wicket gate. No one watched it; she was certain of this. The sentry stopped his pacing and slunk down upon the stone walkway. He would sleep for a good long time. Claire sensed danger all around her but it did not come from this man. She was as safe, this night, as she would ever be. She could reach the others but she would have to hurry.

First, she would have to change her clothes. There would be questions asked of a nun out and about at this time of the night. She had planned to argue strenuously with Aimery of Segni about his insistence that she wear normal clothing, but she was grateful now for what he had provided for her. She rustled through a chest and snatched forth a dark tunic. She changed quickly but left her hair loose. There was no time to gather it. She must quit this place quickly and join the others—or else she would be caught.

And she could not be caught. It would mean her life.

Aimery of Segni could not sleep. He tossed and turned upon his narrow bed long after the sounds of gaming and festivity from the Great Hall had ceased. His long legs tangled in the linen sheets; his blond hair tousled about his face. *Perhaps it is the heat,* he thought, *or the moon.*

*Yes, 'tis the moon,* he decided. Its light illumined his spare chamber. It crackled on the air about him with the energy of day.

"They say the moon may turn men mad."

Aimery smiled at his own whimsy and threw the sheeting aside. He was not yet mad—at least not quite—and could take this situation well in hand. The drapering at the window could be drawn and the room darkened. The night was warm, hot even. Closing the linen might stifle the air a bit, but it would also keep the moon at bay, and for some reason he wanted that light stifled. It kept him awake and he did not like its disturbance. Tomorrow promised to be a day very much like today had been—filled with decisions and responsibilities and people who needed their lord to settle some difference or to clear a way for some enterprise. This was his life; this was his duty and it behooved him to be ready tomorrow when he was presented with it once again.

His hand had just touched the draping, ready to close out both the light and the air, when he saw Claire. He knew her instantly, although he had never actually *seen* her before this moment. Except for that one wisp of devil-colored hair, he had found her always well hidden within the folds of her novice garb. She was not hidden from him tonight.

As Aimery watched, Claire tiptoed cautiously out onto the carefully swirled gravel of the castle keep. She glanced about. He thought she seemed taller, more confident, without the restrictions of her shapeless nun's clothing. As she walked, the moonlight touched her body beneath its flimsy linen tunic, and Aimery saw the clear outline of her long legs; the firm high rise of her breasts. He stared at her, letting his gaze caress the cascade of her freed hair, which tumbled down her back like liquid fire, thick and luminous. He watched, transfixed, as she slipped first through the espaliered pear trees and then through the small wicket gate that led out into the countryside. It shrieked in protest as she pulled it open. He felt her catch her breath. He wondered that she did not feel the heat of his gaze upon her and turn to confront him. She did not. Instead she slipped through the wicket and disappeared into the night.

Leaving him wondering.

Where was she going? The question did not trouble him. He knew he would find out.


They were a strange, tired group; grown smaller in number rather than larger since William Belibaste's arrest. They huddled together in one of the convent's dim, underground storage rooms. Claire tried not to tense as she heard rats scurry through the thick, damp, underground walls. The Mother Superior, Abbess Helene, had provided this space. She, too, was one of the Credentes, though now she rarely came to its meetings. She was here tonight, though, and six others with her: a notary, two peasants, a monk who had risked his life to slink away from his monastery under cover of the night. In the past there had been three others. These men—for now they were all men save for Claire and Helene—had vowed their undying allegiance and help when first they learned of Belibaste's arrest. They had promised to do all they could to free him. Then they had promptly disappeared. Who could blame them? The Cathars were hunted; their secretive world a far cry from the glory times of the last century when the Credentes had ruled all of Languedoc and had commanded Congresses and Councils throughout the land. Now they were barely a ragged presence. The threat of witch fire had been a mighty inducement to recant.

Peter had always soothed and encouraged them, called them his remnant. He fanned the embers of their loyalty, and their thirst for revenge.

"The others will be back and plenty more with them. Once we have organized the rebellion, they will all join us. They will rush to cast Rome and Paris from off the back of Languedoc!" His brown eyes flashed as he flung his arms out as if to embrace this great land of Cathars and Troubadours. "Soon—very soon—we will take this great land again."

That was to be the glorious future. For now his small group hunkered together and listened to the incredulity in their leader's voice.

"He told you what?" exclaimed Peter.

Claire had told them everything once, but now she repeated it all again. "He brought me to the castle. I was told to remove my convent habit and to dress in the clothing of an ordinary maiden. He had tunics and slippers for me—simple things, nothing too fine. It was as though he wanted to deny me what I have, to take it from me."

Peter stroked the back of her young hand with his gnarled and shriveled one.

"He cannot deny you Perfection, my child," crooned the priest. "He has not the power to do it. You are one of us, just as you have always been."

The others murmured their agreement.

"The bishop says I must hold my hair loose," continued Claire. "He sent word to me that I am to dress and act as a respectable maiden, not as a nun, until this trial of Belibaste is finished. He said that I would attract less attention if I dressed like the others, if I acted like them."

Peter crooned encouragement but he knew perfectly well that the idea to unbind Claire's hair and to put her in normal clothing had not originated with the bishop. He stared at the bright red-gold of her tresses, then at her deep green eyes and the clear, fine lines of her face. For the first time he felt the faint scuttling of fear. It seemed to scurry through the others as well.

"They have never asked for anything like this before," said Roger Aude, the notary and the most educated of their group. "The Inquisition has never insisted that women leave their habits. In the beginning of the persecution they insisted that we recant our beliefs but the *form* of what we did remained the same. Dominic de Guzman merely mantled our structures with his beliefs. The Cathars always had their own convents. We were never forced to change our customary dress."

"And so you think this means the Count of Segni suspects something, or that his bishop does?" asked Helene, the Abbess of St. Magdalene. "I doubt it means anything of the kind."

She leaned across the splintered table to stare at Claire. They had known each other for years now, since the child's coming to Montsegur. Claire, the orphan, had often fantasized a perfect family with Peter as father and Helene as mother and herself as the beloved and safe child. But she had grown up and away from this dream. She had accepted the fact that she would one day be Perfect and that there could be no small, cozy family for her. She would have her duty instead.

Helene, a tall, splintery woman, had rarely touched Claire. Now she reached across and took her hand.

" 'Tis only clothing, after all," Helene said. "And clothing does not matter. It does not make a person Good. It does not make them a Credente. Nothing material can do that. Goodness comes from the soul and from the heart. You have only to keep your spirit pure, my child. The rest, all of it, is only something thrown over that. You must always remember that."

It was close and damp and musty in their small room. The heat made their foreheads glisten. Claire's new clothing clung to her body.

"It is hot here," remarked Guy the shepherd, "nature's way of preparing us for the stake fires."

It was a crude joke and the others tittered at it, but Claire knew by tomorrow their ranks would have thinned even further. She wondered when the first traitor would appear.

"It is impossible to really know why these foreigners have come," admonished Helene. "They may only want the castle. Belibaste's capture might only have been incidental to them. They might want everything from us, but then again they may want nothing."

"Generally, history has taught they will take everything from us," hissed Roger Genet, "and then when they have finished with that—why, they will take more."

Peter had been oddly silent, but they all turned naturally to him now. He was their leader, the fierce heart of their little band. When he spoke, his voice was so low that it was almost hidden by its faint crackling. They strained toward him.

"They suspect that we are near. They suspect that Belibaste has friends about him," whispered Peter. "Soon they will learn this for a certainty, but we will be saved by Claire. She will utilize all the wisdom ways she has been taught. And then she will learn more."

He stared at the girl, fixing her with the full, deep force of his soul. For once he did not smile at her; he did not reassure.

"You must use all of your powers with this child of Satan, this Aimery of Segni. His purpose is to crush our brotherhood, to devastate the Good. He is more dangerous by half than the Inquisitor and he will see us all dead. He will destroy all that we have worked for and us with it, if we do not destroy him first. He must be brought down. He must be killed."

"Why?" Helene shook her head. Her tone sharpened. "Why do you say this, Peter? The Count of Segni has not harmed us. Indeed, both he and Jacques Fournier have repeatedly called for fair trial. If our purpose is the peaceful one of freeing William Belibaste, then why must we violently kill Aimery of Segni to do it?"

"I tell you they are one in the same thing," snapped Father Peter. "Either he is destroyed or we will be. Have you forgotten the lessons of our history? Have you no recollection what happened here at Montsegur? Hundreds of our people were burned right here at the Roc for their beliefs. Women and children, sent to the stake; their ashes scattered to the winds, without even the solace of Christian burial. Is it not plain what his ancestors did to us? Have you forgotten our past?"

"Have you forgotten your purpose?" urged Helene gently. "Have you forgotten the reason that we are Good?"

Peter was adamant. "Would you wish Belibaste dead then? He is our last male Perfect. What will happen to us without him?"

"Of course I would not wish Belibaste dead," whispered Helene, "and I will do all in my power to see him peaceably escaped. But he is not the only man-Perfect that we have. You are. You served as a Templar priest until you joined us, but still you remain a priest. And priests are Perfect; you know that as well as I. You are empowered to give the sacramentum, the sacred passage. In many ways, you are more a true Perfect than Belibaste ever was."

"Because I did not marry," said Peter quietly, "and Belibaste did."

His words pelted the silence.

"The wife is coming," said Helene, at last. "He has requested her and the Inquisition has granted Belibaste the solace of his wife. Even now she crosses the mountains of the Haute Savoie on her journey here. Bishop Fournier has begged hospitality for her within the convent walls. And when she comes . . ."

With her stunning news, the Abbess, not Peter, now commanded their attention.

Together, they leaned toward her.

# CHAPTER 9

They finished their plans just before cockcrow and then scattered like dead leaves to the wind. Claire hurried through the awakening convent with Peter beside her. He lagged behind sometimes, old now, and she would stop to let him catch up. Yet, she was anxious to be away. She sensed danger everywhere within this convent that had always been her home. She found herself longing for the haven of the chamber she had yet to sleep in, her chamber within the fortress of Montsegur.

"I know all of this is troubling to you," said Peter, catching up. "But it has happened. They will give your place here to Belibaste's wife. You have been moved from amongst us and we must make the best of it. We must use it to further our own ends. Nothing happens that we cannot use. I have always told you that, and it is true."

Claire was so tired. Already the eastern sky glowed violet with dawn and early morning candles flickered from the castle's arrow slits. She must be back before she was missed, and there was a full day's work stretching before her, but it seemed that Peter wanted, or needed, to talk.

"I know all of this is troubling to you," he whispered, breathless beside her. "But it has happened. We must make the best of this situation and use it to our own ends. Nothing occurs that will not further the ends of the Good. We can use everything."

"Use?"

Something disturbed Claire in his use of this word. She had never thought of them *using* anything. She didn't think of the Good in that way and yet this was Father Peter who placed a detaining hand upon her arm. This was Father Peter and she must listen to what he said. "What is it that we must use?"

"We must use you," he whispered, "because Aimery of Segni wants you."

"Wants me?" Claire's words were an incredulous echo. And yet, deep within, she knew what Peter would say even before he said it.

"He wants you as his plaything, as his toy," continued the Templar serenely. "He cannot see you as the woman you are—part of the Good. You are dedicated to things he could not possibly understand. His type is like that. They follow in the barbaric footsteps of the French King. They are not *connoisseurs* like the peoples of Languedoc are, like we are. The Frankish people will see something and determine to possess it. It is their way. They must steal and plunder. They must seek to own—at least until something else catches at their fancy. But Aimery of Segni is wrong in this. He will never have you. He cannot. You are dedicated to the Good and you will be our Perfect. But this doesn't mean we cannot use his arrogant presumptions against him."

Claire stopped short. "What of Mother Helene's

plan to free Belibaste, it seems peaceable enough and it will surely function? If we work through his wife . . ."

"Helene's plan will fail. She does not know the perfidy of the enemy that confronts her, and I do. Believe me, my Claire, I do."

All around them birds twittered the morning into wakefulness.

"And you must believe me in this, my own child, more than you have believed me about anything else in the past," the old Templar continued. "You must *use* power against Aimery of Segni to save William Belibaste, to save us all."

The old man sighed, then reached within the folds of his priestly robes. Claire felt the roughness of a flax bag in her hand. She smelled the acrid odor of herbs.

"What is this?" she asked.

Peter patted her hand, soothed her. "Something that will help you, as it once helped me in a moment of great need. You must only concentrate upon him, just as I have always taught you. This should be easy enough. He obviously wants you to contemplate him. And it is your duty to do so—for the Good and for yourself. You have but to remember what the Northerners, the Franks, did to your parents. How they destroyed them for their beliefs. How they left you orphan. Now it is your turn to control them."

Again Claire felt a prickle of deep memory and the fear that always came with it.

*First "use" and now "control." Is this what I choose? Is this what I want?*

But the herbs were in her hand now; she could not give them back.

"Your parents died working to restore the Cathars to their former glory," said Peter. "They died so you could become Perfect, and a part of the Good."

Claire shook her head very slowly, as though brushing at dark concerned cobwebs. "I won't hurt anyone. I won't shed blood."

"There will be no bloodshed!" exclaimed the priest as he pressed the flax bundle more firmly into her hands. "Or at least precious little of it, if we are able to free Belibaste before the Inquisition has its way with him. These herbs will—help you. They will allow you to more easily direct Aimery of Segni's thoughts in the way that we would have them go. That is all—lead them. You already claim the power to do this within yourself; these herbs are but a small help."

Claire's mind had gone back again in time. She was running through the cold; she was running toward the flames. They grabbed at her, they wanted her—and then she saw the face.

*Maman!*

"Remember this," insisted Peter, oblivious to Claire's quick memory. His voice had again taken on the reassuring accents of the man who, once long ago, had saved her; had carried her upon his back through bitter cold and brought her to Montsegur. Once again, he was the kindly, dear man to whom Claire owed her life.

"But you must use your own powers as well," he whispered. "These herbs are nothing without you. You must enter into Aimery of Segni's mind, just as we have always practiced. Concentrate. You must learn what he keeps hidden in his soul."

Claire nodded.

# CHAPTER 10

"You will state your name for this court."

"I am Arnold Sicre." And then louder, as though the small, wan man sitting before the Grand Inquisitor had suddenly grown surer of himself. "I am Arnold Sicre."

It was a peasant's name. They all knew that.

"You are responsible for bringing William Belibaste back to Languedoc?"

"I am responsible for bringing a sorcerer and a traitor to the judgment seat!" the man called out amidst general hurrahing and the thumping of steel tankards against wooden trestles. It was yet early but the Count of Segni's knights and men-at-arms were already drunk on witch-baiting.

Aimery frowned, waved a hand, and they silenced.

"Sorcery has not been proven," said Jacques Fournier mildly, "much less treachery. You will keep a civil tongue in your head."

The man slunk back, nodding.

If there were a traitor here, Aimery thought, it would be Arnold Sicre. He looked created to play this part in life. Short, and with his face pocked with the remnants of some plague, he had the slight build that an impoverished childhood conferred and that could be rectified by no amount of subsequent good living. Though there was no doubt this traitor would live most sumptuously in the future. It was whispered that the bishop had promised him a fortune in bright gold florins for his aid in bringing the last Cathar Perfect to trial. Jacques Fournier had hunted Belibaste for years; he was most grateful for his capture. It might well raise him from his Bishopric all the way to the Papal throne.

They all knew that, above all Arnold Sicre, who now smiled winningly at his benefactor as he continued, "Indeed, I have always stood on the side of Rome and Paris. It is my . . ." His voice droned on, ingratiatingly.

Aimery's attention wavered. It was a dismally hot, close day, unseasonably so for June, but from his place close by the bishop's side, he had full view of the Court's young scribe. This diverted him. She sat primly silent behind her quills and parchments; she did not look up. Still, Aimery was certain that she studied him, and with the same secret intensity with which he studied her. He knew it, but he wondered why. Claire of Foix was a conundrum to him, a challenge. And he had lost few of these. She looked docile, industrious and obedient but Aimery had the strongest feeling that this was not her true self and that she kept this true self very strictly hidden. He was anxious to hear what his sister, Minerve, would say of her. Minerve was quite intuitive about people and their ways.

"I found William Belibaste exactly where you, Bishop—where I had been told he would be," continued Arnold Sicre. "There was a secret band of Cathars hidden in the Sabartès, in the liege lands of the Kings of Spain. Belibaste ministered to them. He was their Perfect."

"A Perfect is a form of priest?"

"So it seems," replied Sicre hastily. "I really had no connection to their beliefs before I searched them out, and I have since forgotten all of their God-forsaken creeds."

"You stumbled upon these Credentes?" Fournier urged quietly.

"They were where you said they would be," said Sicre and then, once again, he hastily corrected his slip. "They were where I had been told they would be, in a little village called Ax-les-Thermes."

For a moment there was only the sound of Claire's quill etching words into the parchment. It did not falter.

"You may continue," said the bishop.

"Once found, they were easily convinced of my sincerity," said the little man. "The Cathars were ready to believe in anyone. They had lived under persecution for a hundred years, hiding themselves away and becoming frightened as rabbits. They were eager to believe in anyone who offered them hope. I, quite naturally, fanned this gullibility by claiming to understand them. And I had excellent credentials: I brought an impeccable badge of honor with me. The Inquisition had put my mother, Sybil Bayle, to the torch. Belibaste and his band knew that. My brother, Pons, had been a known believer and a member of the inner circle of the Perfect. When I stumbled into their midst, the heretics at Ax-les-Thermes took it as a providential sign that I had been sent to them. They did not question my sudden appearance. They did not question me."

"And they asked nothing of your father?"

Sicre shrugged. The movement was nothing more than a brief, sharp lifting of his shoulders, but it had the lingering effect of a sigh. "They were credulous," he said. "I tell you, they *wanted* to believe in me. Besides, I do not think they knew my father had turned against the Faith. The refugees at Ax-les-Thermes did not seem to know that my father had solemnly recanted his Cathar beliefs and then helped organize the raid against the Credentes at Montaillou. They heard only of the martyrdom; they cared nothing of the rest." Again he shrugged. "It must have been difficult for my father, having a Perfect as wife. He may have wanted warm flesh instead of cold perfection come a winter's night."

The soldiers sniggered. Even some of the priests stifled a smile.

Sicre seemed gratified by the attention. His gaze darted all around the vast chamber, though Aimery noticed that he did not once glance towards William Belibaste, sitting chained and silent on his stool before the Inquisition Seat.

"You knew about their customs sufficiently so you were able to feint yourself as one of them?" continued Jacques Fournier.

"I knew enough," responded Sicre, adding quickly, "though I am no heretic myself."

"It was thus you were able to confound them; even William Belibaste?"

Sicre shook his head. "Belibaste knew even less of the creed than I did. Have you forgotten that he was an escaped murderer? He went on to take a wife even though, as Perfect, sexual relations were strictly forbidden to him. Do you not recall that he fathered a child?"

"I recall everything," said Fournier.

"Of course you do," replied Sicre hastily. "Of course."

"Continue, please."

Sicre fixed his gaze upon Bishop Fournier, after obviously deciding that this was the safest place for it to rest. He avoided looking toward the prisoner, though Belibaste's gaze never wavered from his face.

"The Credentes welcomed me with open arms," said Arnold Sicre. "They thought I would be an easy convert. They accepted me."

*"Belibaste* accepted you?" insisted the Inquisitor.

Sicre hesitated. "No, not at first," he said slowly, "and then only with skepticism. It was as though he knew . . ."

*That I would traitor him.*

"As though there were something wrong with me," continued Sicre. "And of course there was. I understood only a little of the Cathar deep beliefs and practices. I knew only what you—what I had been told before my mission. I made many mistakes. But the others around him believed in me, and they were quick to become my friends. Apprentice work was found for me in the neighboring village of Saint Mateu, and it left me free to attend all the secret sessions and the meetings in Belibaste's small house. Within a very few months I had been accepted into the secret Cathar community. I remained there quietly for years and worked hard. I grew to be close friends with the Perfect. Many even considered me to be his natural successor.

"And yet all the time . . ."

Sicre fidgeted upon his stool. "All the time, I had my mission and it was the most important thing to me. I had no doubt as to my true loyalty. I let years drift by and then I began dropping hints to the others about how much I missed the family I had left behind in Languedoc. I told the Cathars of my wealthy widowed aunt and a beautiful sister. I talked often of how much I loved them: I emphasized how rich they were. I sighed over the fact that they had been abandoned without the spiritual succor I had found in Catalonia. Quite frankly, it was exceedingly easy to convince the Cathars that my words were sincere."

Jacques Fournier cleared his throat. "In the end, Belibaste himself convinced you to return to Languedoc to fetch your kin people?"

"He *urged* me to fetch them. He said a nubile bride would always be a welcomed addition to our community, especially if that bride were richly dowered."

"By then he trusted you?" asked the Inquisitor dryly.

"Completely." Sicre grinned, then slithered up a little straighter in his seat. "I set out for Languedoc and was gone from Ax-les-Thermes for many months. When I returned it was with news that my aunt was too frail with illness to travel and that my sister had decided to remain and help her. Oh, yes—I added that my aunt's illness was mortal. She was old and could not survive. This was a most important point. She, a woman both rich and dying, needed the consolation of a Perfect."

"Therefore she needed Belibaste." The silent room pressed in upon Fournier's words.

"He was the only Perfect remaining, at least the only one we knew of," continued Sicre. "I urged him to cross the mountains to her and said she would pay handsomely for his service. I spoke often and at length about the considerable dowry she had settled upon my sister. The Cathars wanted money; indeed, they needed it. When I returned from my visit to Languedoc, I had brought plenty of gold with me. I made that Christmas memorable for their poor band and this was all to the good, because for many of them it was to be their last."

Something caught Aimery's attention and pulled it

toward Claire. He could not tell if it had been a movement or a sigh, but it passed away in the instant that he
fully turned to her. Claire's head was lowered as she
diligently worked her pen.

"And so he came?" asked the Inquisitor.

Sicre nodded. "He came, though by now there were
some who had grown skeptical of me and warned him
against the journey. His wife, in particular, always
loathed me. I never could win her over. She reminded
him that, once before, he had barely escaped Languedoc
with his life. She cautioned care. And Belibaste wanted
to be careful, you could tell that. You could tell that something warned him off. It was just that his own character
proved to be his undoing. A dying woman needed consolation and he was the last Perfect; that this woman
was wealthy and that her death could help the impoverished Credentes was yet another inducement for him."

"So he was not coerced to leave Catalonia?"

"Not coerced," said Sicre softly. "I tricked him."

That was when Claire looked up and met Aimery's
eye. For just the briefest of instants, her hatred seared
him and all the room that surrounded him and then,
once again, she stifled the power of emotion behind the
placid mask of her face.


Sicre grew tired and the tribunal was dismissed.
Belibaste was led away as the Great Hall slowly emp-
tied. Aimery had every intention of striding up to
Claire and escorting her away, just as he always did. He
looked forward to this; it made the unbearable heat and
confusion worthwhile. But Claire disappeared into the
crowd and he was arrested by the chaos and the noise;
engulfed by them. He looked around but could not find
her.

"Damnation," he whispered.

"And was that directed at me, my lord?"

Aimery turned to face his sister, Minerve, his mouth already answering the ready smile upon her face.

"Not at all," he said to his twin. "If anything, seeing you brings heaven's face a little nearer."

Minerve laughed aloud at this. "I think you've spent too much time in this Troubadour land, though plainly proximity has done nothing to improve your horrible brand of chivalric verse."

"I guess I'll never be the model knight of Languedoc," Aimery said ruefully, taking his sister's arm and weaving her through the mass to the Great Hall's main door. "I've no ear for poetic turn."

"Nor need of one," replied Minerve. "It is refreshing to be away from the turns of poetic artifice, especially after I've spent so much time in Paris."

Unexpectedly, Aimery's stomach knotted at this mention of the French capital, but he knew what was expected of him.

"How was Paris?" he asked, and then after only the barest hesitation. "And how was Isabeau of Valois?"

"Your betrothed?"

They were in the castle's corridors now and the crowd had thinned about them, though the air was still oppressive and hot. Aimery longed for an iced piece of linen to run across his brow, to cool it. And he worried about his sister. Minerve was enormously and exuberantly pregnant; one of the few women he knew who would have dared cross half of France when she was so near to birthing.

"But I must be at Montsegur," she had written to him. "After all these sons, Huguet has a right to see a daughter birthed at last. Since he cannot be with me, then I shall surely be with him."

As though any of them had hope of a girl child. Wishful thinking, Aimery had thought and Huguet, the father, had agreed with him. Minerve de Montfort had become legend throughout Christendom for her ability to produce large, strapping sons.

"How are the boys?" he asked her and was rewarded with minute detail about the intricacies of their lives. Aimery, the eldest—his godson and namesake—was even now, at barely six and in his early paging days, already showing evidence of exceeding skill with the small sword. Edoard and Guy showed a keen eye and great marksmanship, respectively, and Minerve swore that little Simon's first word had been tournament.

"He spoke it clearly as daylight, and when he was barely two months. Don't laugh so, Aimery. One day he will hold the record lists at Paris and you will see that it was true. Simon will be my greatest knight of all. I have this feeling already."

"And Isabeau," Aimery asked again. "Did you see my betrothed in Paris as well?"

"Your betrothed," repeated Minerve. She wasn't smiling. She laid a hand upon her brother's arm and led him to the slight air and sunlight of an arrow slit. The din died out about them. The others had gone for a quick nap or an even quicker meal before the trial for Belibaste continued once again. They were alone, but the heat still pressed in all about them.

"You've seen her then," he said. "How is she?"

They were so much alike, and not just because they shared the same bright sun-colored hair, the same deeply blue eyes. He could tell by the slight puckering that marked his sister's forehead that she didn't want to talk about Isabeau, and at the same time he realized he didn't want to hear about the Valois heiress, nothing at all. Things have come to a bad turn, he thought ruefully, when a man dares not inquire about the woman he is slated to marry, when he actually dreads asking about her. But then, he realized, he'd always had this slight misgiving about Isabeau, the heiress of Valois. It was fortunate one didn't have to love, or even approve of a person to marry them; although that was one point upon which he and Minerve did differ.

"We—you and I—have spent little time together since I came to Montsegur," said Minerve. "I think Isabeau might be the reason for our reticence—my not wanting to talk, your not wanting to hear. Of course I saw her at the Palace of the Louvre. It is not so very large after all, and she is your betrothed."

"My near betrothed," corrected Aimery. "We have not as yet finalized the arrangements. There are still financial plans, considerations of lands and holdings that are dowered to her by the Valois. The lawyers and Lombard bankers are still active."

"Your near betrothed," dutifully repeated Minerve. "In truth, I often saw her. The Louvre is not so large a palace that one can easily hide oneself within its isolated crannies. And Isabeau is not one to secrete herself."

"Or her actions?"

"She seems well."

"*Seems* well?" It wasn't like Minerve to conceal her meaning behind words. It wasn't like him to press her there either, but he did. "You said you saw each other often."

"We saw each other," said Minerve. "We did not often speak. We had different interests, different friends, and we pursued them."

They had neared the great slab of stairway that circled upward to one of the castle's defensive donjons. Aimery laid a piece of chance-linen upon the granite step and helped his sister sit. She struggled down, fanning her hand, opening her mouth to speak.

"I don't want to hear about the weather," said Aimery, cutting her off. "I want to hear what you don't want to tell me about Isabeau."

They stared at each other. Minerve, lifted her eyebrows, shrugged, did not look away.

"I have nothing to add to what you already know," she said. "Isabeau is . . . what she is. You did not choose her for her virtue."

Aimery hunkered down on the stone beside her, not quite knowing why he pressed her on this, not quite knowing what truth he pursued.

"Tell me what it is that you don't want to tell."

Minerve hesitated, perched on the edge of the uncomfortable step. "I will speak plainly," she said, at last. Though it was evident to Aimery that this would take some effort on his sister's part. She was not given to Court gossip. "The Valois, Isabeau's family, came to power quite unexpectedly. No one thought her uncle would ever rise to the throne as Philip VI. You know they call him *le roi trouve*, the found king. He was put into place to stop an emergency. Before, Isabeau was a mere distant cousin to a king of France; now, with Philip's accession, she is this particular King's niece." Minerve paused and looked squarely at her brother. "She is a very silly woman to be that close to power."

Aimery waved her words aside. "Isabeau is not young and frivolous. She has already been married once and left widowed. Her uncle, the King, is pious; some say even obsessively so. The sole object of his life is to prove the beatific vision; he wants to know if the saints see God immediately once they reach heaven. At one point, he even threatened to excommunicate the pope when he disagreed with him about this!

This is Isabeau's family; this is where she comes from."

"Do you think I would spread wives' tales?" asked his sister quietly.

Aimery shook his head, and for some reason he—a warrior born—dreaded what was coming next.

"You asked and I will tell you what I witnessed. I will tell only what I saw," continued Minerve, her face still grave. "Isabeau's friends are not the best. Guy de Guinne, Raoul de Perceval, Eustache d'Alembert. You have spent time at Court. You have heard of them."

Minerve brushed a midge away with a smooth movement of her hand. "These were the friends Isabeau chose when she came to Court and they have remained her friends in the years since. Close friends. There was talk—and this was gossip—when her husband died. Talk that she had helped him on the way with poison because he opposed the life she led openly at Court; he opposed the company she kept."

Aimery had heard the gossip. He had chosen to ignore it. Isabeau was young and very wealthy; she could easily be the object of envy. He could not ignore what his sister was saying to him now.

"She lives openly with Eustache d'Alembert, right beneath the nose of his young wife and right in the shadow of your proposed betrothal. Everyone knows that she is his mistress, and has been for quite a long while. In fact, it was he who decided upon the fete."

"Which fete?"

"The one meant to celebrate your betrothal."

"The lady Isabeau and I are not yet fully betrothed," he said mechanically.

Minerve ignored him, shifting her bulk a little on the uncomfortable stair, anxious to be finished with this equally uncomfortable tale. "It was a scandal. Giving a fete for a widowed woman about to remarry is considered scandalous enough in Paris. And as for Isabeau, living openly with this other man . . ." She let her voice trail and her brow grew more troubled. "I wish there were someone else to tell you this. God knows I didn't want to do it. But at least, if you insist on marrying her, you should know what to expect."

" 'Tis gossip."

"I was there at court. I know what happened. Do you doubt my word?"

"Tell me of the fete."

" 'Twas late at night, in the Grand Hall of the Louvre. Isabeau was there, Eustache was there."

"And you?"

"I was there at its ending."

"To spy upon Isabeau?"

Minerve did not flinch or look away. Their eyes met, glinting shards of hard blue, one against the other. "I was there to protect your interests. I know you well. Isabeau is not what you would want in wife."

"Tell me of the fete," Aimery repeated.

"It was supposed to be a Bacchanalia," she said, "mirrored on the orgies of ancient Greece, and naturally much wine flowed. Bacchus is the ancient god of wine, after all. The women came dressed as nymphs and dryads; the men as satyrs. But Guy de Guinne and six of the others decided that mere costuming was not enough. Why dress the part when one could place resin upon his naked body and glue goats hair to it? Naturally the men were masked but everyone knew who they were. And just as naturally it was decided that no torches could be allowed. Resin is intensely flammable; the flash of fire could have annihilated those covered in it."

The number of midges had grown. They buzzed about the arrow slit; darkly outlined against the sunlight. It had grown uncomfortably warm, and Aimery longed for a breath of fresh air.

"What happened then?" he asked his sister.

"Disaster," she answered. "Despite the admonition against torches and firelight, Eustache d'Alembert burst into the room with his flambeau. A spark touched Sir Guy and soon the other nymphs were engulfed in flames as well. Only two were saved—one by jumping into a vat of water and another protected himself from the sparks by jumping beneath the skirts of Sybille Thierry. Otherwise they would have died the same horrible death as the others." She paused, and tears glistened in her clear eyes. "It was horrible. Even those who had not attended such a disastrous party could hear the screams of the dying. They echoed for days— for an eternity—through the palace corridors. The king was livid with rage, at the outrageousness of the feste and at its consequences. He ordered Isabeau from Court for her part in it. She has been banished to Picardy, under the guardianship of the Sire de Coucy. Of course Eustache d'Alembert went with her. She has no intention of giving him up, Aimery. The king has not been able to make her; you will not be able to do so. Their relationship was always a great scandal, but now it has evolved and evolved until it is nothing less than a tragedy."

His feet crashed through the underbrush, as though they knew he wished to put a great distance between himself and what his sister had told him.

*Nothing less than a tragedy.*

And yet, how could Minerve understand his determination to marry Isabeau of Valois? His sister had looked at him expectantly, anticipating that he would rise up with indignation and repudiate Isabeau, not want to take her on as wife, not need her.

And yet he did need her. This betrothal had been his father's dying wish for him, a way to for him to show his illustrious family that he, too, was worthy and that he was powerful enough to ally his son with the greatest family in France.

Aimery remembered his father. He had seen him cowed beneath all the subtle, telling insults that a wealthy, powerful family could heap upon one of its own who had not advanced as they had, who had disappointed. The used tunics and faded silks, the poor placement at table, the invitations to great events that did not seem to make it to their impoverished, stone house; Aimery remembered them all. And though the slights made no difference to him, he had cringed for his father and he had determined to make it up to him.

"And you will," Aldo dei Conti di Segni had repeatedly said to his son. His eyes had been bleached by despair and his breath stank of stale wine, but Aimery did not notice. He had been too riveted to the future and to those things he might do to make his father's life better; to make it shining once again, and full of promise and new.

After the honor of his knighthood, marriage to Isabeau of Valois had seemed the next logical step on his chosen path. Even before the ascension of her uncle to the throne as Philip VI, she had been closely related to power and prestige; the surname Valois was one of the most prominent in France. However, their father had died and Minerve, with the backing of their mother, had turned down Isabeau's dissolute brother for Huguet de Montfort. That had not deterred Aimery. He would claim Isabeau of Valois—and all she stood for. She would be his.

And she was—or almost.

His feet struck furiously against the packed, summer earth, the jingle of his golden spurs muffled by the lush buzz of insects and the twittering of birds. He had no idea where he was going. He only knew he was furious with Minerve; that he had to get away from what she had told him and, worse, what her words implied.

It was easy enough for her to talk; easy enough for her to have abandoned duty to family and married the poor count, Huguet de Montfort. That he had gone on well enough—indeed, that he became a splendid warrior knight and hero—had been just a stroke of luck. It could have gone much differently. It had gone very differently for their father. What Minerve had said shouldn't really bother him. It *didn't* really bother him, he assured himself as his spurs beat furiously against the ground. He had always known about Isabeau—not everything, perhaps, but enough—and he had always accepted her as she was, just as she must accept him.

Aimery had a sure access to power and to vindication for his father in this near-betrothal to Isabeau of Valois and—by St. Louis!—he had no intention of letting his sister's prejudices deter him. She was set against Isabeau, and always had been. His sister had never esteemed the Valois. Besides, he was a warrior knight, hired by kings and feudal barons throughout Europe to defend their interests. He would rarely find the time or means to be fixed in France with his wife. Once he settled a legitimate heir upon her—and he would see that the Segni heir was legitimate, he would definitely see to this—his wife could do as she pleased. Many, many noble marriages were like this; based on family, based on land. His would be as well.

So involved was Aimery with his thoughts, and with his anger that at first he didn't even hear the splashing

water. It was too soft, too musical, to penetrate the
blackness of his thoughts. The tramp of his angry footsteps blocked it out. Then he stopped for a moment,
puzzled by where he found himself, lost on his own
land; and he heard the unmistakable splash of a waterfall. He could have sworn it was this; he recognized the
sound. And it sounded—nice. It soothed him, and he
moved toward its tumbling music.

The earth grew soft and spongy under his kid boots
as he came upon the grotto. The line of trees came
close but did not quite reach the pool, so the midday
sunlight was not blocked from it. It was cool here
though, and peaceful; as though it had been hidden
from the bustle that was the town and castle of
Montsegur. Bees buzzed overhead and birds twittered;
small water crocuses shot bright spots of color amid
the grass. The waterfall splattered carefully from a
rocky overhang into a clear, deep pool. Fish jumped
about in it; Aimery saw their fleeting, silver flash.

He didn't see Claire though—at least not at first. It
was obvious, though, from the way she stood, motionless and quiet and on the far side of the pool from him,
that she had seen him and was trying now to hide in
stillness. He wouldn't let her.

"Claire," he said.

She stood knee deep in the pool; the loose, white
linen tunic she wore billowing about her in the water.
She had freed her hair and it fell in one thick magnificent wave of fire; down, down her back almost to the
water itself. Isabeau had red hair, he suddenly remembered, but it was nothing like this. Claire's glistened in
the sunlight; the full answer to the one strand he had
first glimpsed the day she boldly strode up to the
Inquisitor's throne, to take her place as scribe. She kept
her hands at her sides, did not cross them over the

flimsy stuff of her clothing, and he respected her for
that. He knew she must want to cover herself; any
woman who had a body as lush and wild as hers would
automatically reach to cover herself. It would be instinct; intuition would tell her what her body could do
to a man. What it was doing to him.

She did not cover herself; she did not look away; she
did not move. He could barely see her breasts move up
and down in rhythm with her breathing.

"Claire," he repeated, and then, "Were you swimming?"

She found her voice then, "I don't know how. I . . ."

"Then I will teach you."

She would have opposed him; she opened her mouth
and he could see the protest in her eyes. But Aimery
was already in the pond; striding through its waters
fully clothed, coming toward her.

"I won't hurt you," he added.

She often came here, especially when the day had
been as hot and as crowded with people as today had
been. She would escape to this secret place; had been
doing so for years, since she had discovered it as a
child. And no one knew; not Mother Helene, not Father
Peter. That's what made it special. She came here in the
summer, on hot, sticky days when the air around her
was as thick and sweet as honey; and in the midst of
winter when the tiny waterfall froze in crystal wonder
and the wind beat silver shards against her face. Her
life was so regimented, so *full*—even in the convent—
that she longed for some quiet refuge she could call her
own.

God had heard her prayers. He had answered her
with this place.

She had always been alone here—until now.

Aimery of Segni, ruler of this place, came nearer to

her through the water. The still pond parted around him, it rippled against his breeched legs. The sky above him was cloudless, the exact warm blue of his eyes, letting the full force of the sun glow down to halo his golden hair.

And he was smiling at her. And she had always longed to swim.

"First you must learn to float," he said, so near her now that for an instant his leg brushed against hers in the water. He moved it aside, putting his hand at her waist and at her shoulders, tilting her slowly backwards. She felt herself tense at his touch, felt goose bumps all along her spine.

"Trust me," he said.

*Shouldn't . . . can't . . . won't.*

She shut off her mind, listened to her body. She wanted to swim, had always wanted to learn to do it. It was her choice.

One hand beneath her shoulders, the other beneath the small of her back, she felt the water like cool silk against her body, all at once. Claire sensed the pool breathing around her body as she became part of its rhythm, heard the quiet buzz of activity all around her and the splash of a darting fish; floating on the water's surface, feeling her body as it melted into it—and oh, so aware of Aimery's touch.

Yet, not unpleasantly aware. His was not what she expected of a man's touch, not at all. His hands upon her, his fingers splayed along her spine felt as gentle and caressing as the water, as light as spirit. So light, in fact, that she felt no difference when he eased them away and she lay tucked upon the water, eyes closed; and for the first time in her life, feeling safe and secure.

# CHAPTER 11

It couldn't last. It shouldn't last. Claire realized this as she ran through the forest back to the granite castle commanded by Aimery of Segni; his fortress, not hers, and she would be wise to remember this. Whatever had possessed her, to let him touch her like that, to let him see her body through her thin shift? For, of course he had seen her, all of her. How could he have helped himself, with the sun streaming through the trees to highlight her body and the water making her clothing cling? But she had wanted to do it, loved doing it; floating on the water, learning to swim.

When Aimery said to her, "We'll meet again tomorrow, I'll teach you more," she had nodded and then quickly hidden behind bushes to towel herself with her tunic and skirt and slip them on again.

Now, she wasn't so sure.

He was gone by the time she'd dressed; an apparition that disappeared as quickly and silently as he'd come, and Claire was grateful for it. It left her time to think, as she walked the overgrown path to the castle;

to try to make some sense of the roil of emotions she felt.

*Shouldn't . . . can't . . . won't.*

This time the words had Father Peter's voice to them, and they had been repeated enough during the many years she had spent under his care. She had loved the purity of them; loved that following them was making her Perfect.

But lately other words had replaced them.

*Learn of him. Use your power.*

Certainly she could learn more of the Count of Segni alone with him at the pond than she ever could learn of him surrounded by the heat and chaos of the Inquisition chamber; even living in his castle, she avoided him, rarely saw him. The lessons were a way that she could obey Peter, and help the Cathar cause of freeing William Belibaste.

Yet, this wasn't the reason she had nodded yes to Aimery's offer for tomorrow, and she was woman enough to realize this. He offered to teach her something *she* had always wanted to learn; helping her to do something *she* wanted to do. It was a strange feeling, frightening even; the first time she'd ever chosen to do something without discussing it with Father Peter first, and she knew she would not discuss this with him, no matter that he had encouraged her to learn all she could of their new overlord. She knew, instinctively, that Peter would not like this new development. The other Cathars, even Mother Helene, might not mind—but Claire knew that Peter would.

Thoughts of the swimming lesson floated through her mind for the rest of the afternoon. She tried pushing them away at first by working at her scribings; she

wanted the proceedings of Belibaste's trial meticulously preserved so that once he was freed, the world
would know the injustice of the case against him.
Claire set about her task diligently enough but the buzz
of a midge would distract her, or the song of a bird. She
would find her hand stayed and her mind distracted,
and she would be back at the pond once again with
Aimery's hands holding her steady, and the coolness of
the water all around.

*I wonder what he thinks of me.*

This would never do! She must take hold of herself
and of her thoughts. If she could not control her mind,
then she must control her actions. Peter had told her
this over and over again. Claire's quill clattered to the
floor as she jumped from her low stool, and away from
the memory of Aimery's touch. Claire, trained in the
Power, knew she must work through her agitation. She
could not let it master her. She had the strangest sensation that if she did, it might overwhelm her; and that
within it, well hidden, was something that she did not
want to see.

In her chamber once again, she busied herself in
taking her own few things out of their flaxen sumters
and placing them atop the tunics Aimery of Segni had
sent up for her. He had given her nothing ostentatious,
nothing she could not wear if she were an ordinary
maiden and not Perfect, but they agitated Claire all the
same. Each tunic had its own particular color—a soft
yellow and a blue and a green that matched the color of
the silk ribbon that she carried tucked within the pocket
of her apron. There was nothing white, and white was
what she was used to. She put the new tunics over her
old ones and then pulled everything out and put her old
clothing on top. She grabbed a straw broom and furiously swept out her chamber and swept out the thyme

and rosemary that had been laid upon the floor. She needed more; she must replace it. It would be good for her to be out of this chamber and into the fresh air of the kitchen gardens. Surely the thought of Aimery of Segni would not follow her there.

Stealthily, feeling like a thief, Claire crossed to her door and listened. No sound echoed through the corridors; not even the laughter and clatter of cooks and serving maids as they made ready for the evening's meal. Montsegur Castle seemed lost in a spell of slumber on this hot and hazy late afternoon.

Montsegur's fortress had been without a liege lord for many years and its kitchen gardens were most probably long overrun and neglected. Still, they might have what she wanted and needed, sweet thyme, dusty roses and late lavender. These would bring freshness to her chamber, and something more as well. Thyme for sweetness, rose for peace, and lavender for healing; they might work their magic upon her. Claire suspected it might take a bit of their wisdom to undo the spell that Aimery of Segni had worked upon her at the pool.

*I wonder what he thinks of me.*

The garden was worse than she had anticipated; weeds choked what had once been tidy, orderly rows, massing them into a tangled jumble. Yet Claire glimpsed brightness here and there: the roses she needed, a hint of an herb's sweetness, the flash of a geranium that peeked forth triumphantly, after having fought a hard battle to live.

This determination toward life was something Claire understood, and she would nourish it, she would midwife it. She struggled against the weeds and the undergrowth until she heard the call to vesper prayers tinkle out from the small steeple at St. Magdalene's. Claire looked up, startled that so much time had passed, and then quickly picked up the flaxen basket she had loaded with picked flowers and herbs. She had found more than she expected, and she hummed a light tune as she hurried back to Montsegur. Her mood had vastly improved; she was tired and covered in grime, but she had sweated away the effects of her lesson in swimming and she felt calm and at peace. She felt like herself again.

Claire opened its great doors and again paused to listen but there was nothing, only the distant rumbling of voices coming from the Great Hall. She had not been missed. Holding tightly to her basket, she lifted her skirts and fled up the winding stone stairway and through deserted corridors, determined that no one would see her, that Aimery would not see her. Perhaps if he did not see her, he might forget about her—and then, maybe, she could forget about him.

By the time she reached the entrance, her heart was pounding. "At least I'm here now, and I can be by myself," she murmured as she shut the heavy door behind her.

"Excuse me, are you Claire of Foix?"

A bright female voice rang out from deep within the shadowed chamber. Startled, Claire whirled at the sound and sent the whole of her flower basket tumbling onto the floor.

At least, that's what she remembered.

She was aware of a shape lumbering toward her, advancing in a strange, slow-fast movement, as though someone was trying to stride through honey.

"It's my fault. I will gather them again."

"No, 'tis mine. Let me do the gathering."

She heard two voices speaking at once, and recognized one of them as hers. The rest, fortunately, was a blessed blur, brought on by stars dancing in front of her eyes when she reached over to gather her flowers and bumped her head against the hardest surface it had ever felt.

"Oh!"

It took a moment for Claire's vision to clear and for her to grasp the fact that she sat, tumbled on the floor, in front of another woman, grimacing and rubbing at her own head.

"Claire of Foix?" repeated this strange apparition. The woman struggled straighter, and as she did Claire saw that she was enormously pregnant; and that her eyes were clear and blue as heaven's sky and that her hair seemed filled with its sunshine. It was almost unnecessary when the woman said, "I am Minerve de Montfort, sister to the Count of Segni."

This could be Aimery before me, thought Claire, she looks so like her brother.

And the other woman was laughing; howling actually, lying back amidst the strewn flowers and herbs with one hand clutching her head and the other held fast to her stomach. She was practically doubled in two with mirth. But the jiggled, pregnant stomach frightened Claire and made her find her tongue.

"You must stop!" cried Claire, alarmed. "Stop laughing so hard. You might hurt yourself, something terrible could happen."

"Nothing terrible can happen to me with birthing," said the otherwise delicate Lady Minerve. "This is not my first son, after all; he will be the fifth!"

Still, looking at Claire's alarmed face, she made an effort to contain her laughter, hiccoughing once or twice and righting herself among the flowers. For an instant, the two women stared at each other.

"You are lovely," said Claire finally, "and you look

just like your brother. Of course you must know that; people must have been saying it to you for years."

"Not *exactly* like him," said Minerve, pointing to her very large stomach, "but enough so that the world would know we are in close relationship. I take your words as a compliment. Quite frankly, I find my brother beautiful; indeed, if it were not for my husband, he might be the most beautiful man upon this world. You must forgive my manners. Aimery said you would not mind my waiting for you here and I was frightened to miss you again. I've been trying to meet you since I first arrived. I think it marvelous they have found a woman to do the scribing."

Claire heaved herself up and gave Minerve a hand but the other woman over balanced, caught at Claire, and the two tumbled down once again. This time, caught by the contagion of Minerve's merriment, even Claire laughed until fat, great tears rolled down both their cheeks.

"By St. Louis!" exclaimed the Countess de Montfort, wiping her eyes. "I've not laughed this hard in all the time I've been at Montsegur. This tumbling and falling has done me nothing but good! I know it was wrong of me to come to your chamber and even more wrong to startle you as I have but it is worth every breech in behavior—that is, it will be worth the breech if you will only forgive my intrusion. This laughing has been a boon to me, just as I am sure it has been to my son!"

This time when Claire struggled up, she managed to hoist the hugely expectant Minerve. The two women stood panting and looking at each other for a moment, and then Claire, too, burst into laughter.

"But you are so *very* pregnant," she exclaimed.

"Enormously so," agreed the Countess de Montfort.

Again her lovely face wrinkled into a grin. "Especially when one considers that the child will not be born for another two months."

"But you look . . ."

"Ready to foal two?" Minerve shook her head and followed Claire back to the small chairs that sat near the leaded window in her chamber. Two fat beeswax candles already sputtered in their pewter holders but it was summer, darkness came late, and the sky outside the window still glowed pink. Claire gave Minerve a down cushion from the bed and the other woman pushed it into the back of her chair and settled down comfortably. "I feel well and am so huge that, if only one child lies hidden within all this encumbrance, I fear we will find him already big as Hercules when he finally emerges."

Again they smiled. Two maids bustled in, placed torches in the wall sconces and made deep reverences to the young Countess de Montfort before bustling out again to bring straw brooms to clean up the flowery mess. Claire blushed. Minerve seemed so approachable that it was easy to forget who she was and her high rank, especially because Minerve seemed so ready to forget it.

"You must truly forgive me," began Minerve earnestly once the door had closed behind them. "I know 'twas rude of me to venture into your room without having your permission. It is just that I was determined to meet you. Since my arrival from Paris, I have been only rarely to the Hall to see the trial of William Belibaste. And, like you, I take my meals by myself. But you are so learned and my brother admires you greatly, as does my husband. They both think your working in Latin extraordinary."

"For a woman," said Claire.

"For anyone." Minerve settled more deeply against her cushion. "They made you seem interesting, even extraordinarily so. Aimery told me you were lovely as well."

"I am flattered and thank him for the compliment, but he has exaggerated his assessment for my benefit."

"Oh, no," Minerve assured her. "My brother never exaggerates. He always says only what he finds true. He said you might enjoy sitting with me some days in the Lady's Gallery over the Great Hall. I have no friends here; he said you have none either. I thought we might befriend each other and work our tapestries together. I am hopeless with my needle and have been working on the same square of flax-linen for ten years."

For the second time that day, Claire opened her mouth to say no to a Segni, and instead found herself agreeing with what Minerve suggested.

"I have no skill at tapestry, but I could work on my scribings. They need leafing done and colors added. I could do that with you. In fact, that might be nice. I get . . ."

"Lonely," Minerve finished for her and the two women looked at each other silently in the candlelight. "I do as well, but this situation might work well for both of us—that is, if you don't mind children."

"I don't imagine I will," she said slowly. "I've never really been around them."

"Then mine are hardly a fair introduction. They are so rambunctious they seem twice their number. But they will do; they have to." With a sigh Minerve heaved to her feet. "So I will see you tomorrow, when you have finished with your work—that is, if you don't mind. Oh, and my brother also asked me to convey his own compliments as well and to ask you to a feast in the Great

Hall on the morrow. The Count of Foix will be there and Aimery thought it might be well that you attend."

Minerve narrowed her eyes and for an instant they glowed with the same shrewd intelligence as those of her brother.

"I know my brother likes you, Claire of Foix," she said. "I think I do as well, and I hope we will become friends."

*You are a Segni and married to a descendent of Simon de Montfort,* thought Claire. *We can never be friends.*

Aloud she said nothing.

# CHAPTER 12

Claire knew she could not possibly attend any festivity in the Great Hall. She was promised to her convent and, more than that, to the Good. She was to be their next Perfect, and being Perfect was still the most important thing to her. It was her life. The trouble was, life seemed less certain than it had just a bare two days before. She shouldn't spend time with Aimery of Segni, yet she wanted to swim; she shouldn't go to the feast for the Count of Foix, and yet she wanted to meet him. She realized that suddenly. She wanted to meet him; maybe he would know something of her parents, something Father Peter did not know because he had been only a pilgrim through Foix when they were killed, and did not know them.

She longed for Peter, for his counsel, his certain knowledge of what she should do next. Peter was within the convent, but more than distance seemed to separate them now. She, Claire, had floated in the arms of the Count of Segni; she had spoken of friendship with a hated Montfort. Yet, she remained Perfect, and she was determined to act this way.

"I cannot do it."

She made her reverence to Lord Aimery as they made their way from the next day's court session. He had not had to follow her; she had come directly to him.

He looked at her now with grave amusement. "Why, if it's not the Maiden of Foix. I trust you slept well last night. Swimming may prove to be deliciously tiring."

"I slept well, thank you," she said. "But the lady Minerve said you ordered my presence at a banquet tonight for the Count of Foix. I beg leave, sir, but it is impossible for me to attend such a thing. You must know that."

He reached over and deftly took her by the arm, leading her away from the throng. "I cannot believe my sister *ordered* you to do anything. She is not the type to take orders from me, much less pass them on to you. I *asked* that you attend the festivities that will surround the Count of Foix when he comes to Montsegur to present his annate tithes. I thought you might want to attend, as you are from Foix yourself. The Abbot from St. Denis will be here; I have even invited the Abbess of your convent."

"Mother Helene?" questioned Claire, instantly alert. "And will she come?"

"She's not sent word, yet I expect her. 'Twill be a harmless enough gathering. The Count of Foix has surprised us all by arriving in person to present his tithes. This should be an added inducement as you are originally from Foix. No order was issued. You misunderstood my sister."

"The Lady Minerve was kind to me," said Claire, stopping to look him directly in the eye. "She did not order me. I beg your pardon for having used that word. I employed it only because I thought she carried out your wishes."

"Wish is a word I can accept," agreed Aimery. "I *wish* you to come to the banquet this evening. In fact, I wish it very much. I think you will enjoy yourself with Minerve as companion."

Actually, Claire thought this as well, but she struggled against the web of his words and the charm of his sister. "I can't go to banquets. You know very well that I am professed to the Church."

Even to her ears the excuse sounded worn and tired, repetitive even. Certainly the idea of the convent and her devotion to it could be challenged by her trip to the pond.

Aimery realized it as well and pounced upon the advantage. "Should you happen to be the only religious present," he said, "I have already clarified your position, both as it is seen by me and by the world. You are not as yet professed; you have not taken final vows. The novitiate is, by definition, a time to explore. And if yours is a true vocation, you have nothing to fear from a night's festivities."

"Mine is a true vocation," snapped Claire, the secret Cathar Perfect. "One that needs no concurrence or support from you, Aimery of Segni."

"We will see," he said.

Lovely, he thought as he watched her walk away. And so different from what he had expected. His teasing of her had started as innocent play to ward off boredom; even the gifting of that small green ribbon had been a way to pique the shell of her composure, to make her think of him when he wasn't there. He couldn't believe such a lovely creature could actually have chosen the convent of her own accord, and he was determined to dig to the mystery of her. The change had come—when? When he'd seen the menace of her singed effigy at the wicket? When he'd brought her to his castle to live?

No, it had been the pond. Of course it had been with the sun hung like a halo above them and the water rippling out through her witch-red hair. He had glimpsed so much of her that day; more than she probably imagined because her eyes had been closed. She had not wanted to see. Still, he had seen her—and more, had felt her. The light, almost weightless brush of her body against his fingers; the innocent way she had trusted him to lead her safely through the water, and had not panicked when he had removed his hands. There was a deep, silent core to Claire; she seemed to know exactly what she was doing and why. And suddenly he envied her for it.

*So different from Isabeau.*
*I wonder what she thinks of me.*


That afternoon's work was dry as tinder. Bishop Fournier droned through a thorough questioning of Arnold Sicre as to the intricacies of his trickery of William Belibaste. Claire diligently took down the traitor's words, rarely looking up from her task; afraid to see whose eyes she might encounter. And she made plans. Peter could save her from this danger, just as he had saved her so many other times in the past. She had but to get word to him and he would make arrangements for their meeting. Peter would tell her exactly what she should do. And they were so close—had always been so close—that somehow, her father Peter would just know that she needed him. And he would be there.

As, indeed, he was when the breathless Maid of Foix pushed open the door that led to the concealed place where the Cathars met. Claire knelt beside him and quickly poured out her tale to her friend.

"But, of course, you must attend the feast for the Count of Foix," said Peter when she had finished. "There can be no question of your not going. This is a marvelous opportunity—indeed, it is an astonishing one. The others will agree with this; even Helene would see the advantage of it."

"He has asked the Abbess as well," said Claire.

"Interesting," said Peter, looking away, "though our dear Helene has been quite busy lately. I doubt she will go. You will be enough to further our cause. You are obviously the next favorite?"

"Favorite?" echoed Claire.

"My lord of Segni seems to have taken a strong interest in you," Peter said.

*He called me his friend. He offered to protect me.*

Claire did not share this thought with Peter. She could only stare at him. The priest hurried on. "Already his care for you is the talk of Montsegur. He has taken the most indiscreet step of removing you from the convent into his fortress walls. A move like that cannot help but fan an afternoon's gossip, especially in so small a place as Montsegur. Indeed, by now all Languedoc is curious as to his intentions. There is speculation that he will attempt more; that he will want you as his mistress. Hush, hush child. 'Twould not be the first time that the lord of a castle has taken his pick from a convent's virgins."

"Aimery is not like that," said Claire. She had not

meant to call him by his Christian name. "He would not want to compromise his new position as lord of Montsegur."

"Not that Aimery of Segni will *have* you," said Peter, patting her hand. "Of course, that would never happen. You would prevent it. Still, he must *think* that he might. All know that men are much more ardent for the chase than for the capture. You have but to keep his interest, to use him; and this will do much toward our freeing William Belibaste."

"The others would not agree to such a thing," replied Claire. "Roger and Guy and Estoril will not agree. The Abbess Helene will not agree."

"It doesn't matter what Helene agrees with, at least not any more. And the others need not know; that is, they need not know if you do not tell them." Peter wheedled his small stool closer to Claire, but she stood and slowly began to pace the small room; away from him, her mind a jumble of strange, new notions.

*Friends, Aimery had said. Yet, was that what she truly wanted?*

She thought of Aimery: his sunlit hair and open manner; the width of his shoulders in their crisp, samite tunic; the silk ribbon he had given to her and that she still carried. She thought of him in the waters of the pool.

"But even if they did know," came Peter's voice from behind her, "it would not matter. You are Perfect; everything you do furthers the good of the Cathar cause. Are you not still dedicated to it? Have you not always been so?" He paused. "Was it not your choice?"

*My choice. My choice?*

Claire shook these thoughts away; spoke of others.

"It is wrong," she said. "It is wrong to use another person to further one's own ends."

Peter stared at her in astonishment, but his face again quickly assumed its customary kindly glow.

"You are wrong in thinking that the others will not agree with me," he insisted. "They will. You will see."

"Mother Helene?" Claire shook her head. "She will never agree with your motives, Father. She would never have me adorned and made worldly. It goes against everything that we believe."

"That does not matter," said Peter sharply. "What matters is that we prevail. Helene is just as devoted to our cause as I. Why, if she were not . . ."

"If she were not?" repeated Claire.

"But she *is*," replied Peter. "The Count of Segni has taken obvious interest in you. 'Tis your duty now to blow upon the kindling of this interest until a fire builds that will serve the Good. What does it matter that you wear frivolous finery for one night—or that you let him kiss you?"

"Kiss me? He's shown no interest in me that way."

"Yet he may. He wants it and if this is what he wants you must give this small victory as well. Would you want William Belibaste's death upon your conscience merely because you held too tightly and too selfishly to a scruple? You are our instrument. You must go to Aimery of Segni because he beckons you and he has both the information we need and the power. You will go to the festival planned for his taking the castle and you will dress the part he has called you to play. A lowered bodice, a freeing of your hair—what harm is there in that? You still have the herbs I gave you, do you not? They will protect you."

Confusion made Claire angry. "I will not do this. Why should I put upon finery to attend this banquet? Why should you even suggest that Aimery of Segni might want to kiss me? The Cathars have no need of ornamentation. We are valued for ourselves and for our spiritual nature. We do not use our bodies to seduce."

"In these wicked times," replied Peter, just as angry, "the Cathar Good had best look to keeping their pure souls within their wicked bodies! You sit daily at the Court and take down its transcriptions. Do you not realize that Aimery of Segni and all his kind would gladly burn the lot of us for heresy?

"This is no time to hold fast to fine notions that were formulated in a gentler age. The Cathars once ruled these hills and numbered bishops and powerful nobles among their adherents. The call to worship would bring a thousand men! But that time is finished. It is gone forever unless we force it back." Peter hobbled away, his back to her, staring at the dank, gray walls of their secret cell. "My brother Templars were just like you, naïve and trusting. I could never convince my Grand Master, Jacques de Molay, that Philip of France would turn against him. 'He is my friend. I am godfather to his only daughter.'" Peter's mimic of an old man's voice was harsh and rasping. "I tried to warn him, then I tried to defend him. But how can you defend a man from a danger that he refuses to accept as real? Well, Jacques was burned for his stupidity; burned before the King and his henchman Pope. My friend died cursing Philip and his family down through thirteen generations. The curse held, but Molay died nonetheless."

Peter's voice now grew wispy with remembrance. "Believe me, Claire, as I tell you this upon the soul of my dearest friend, that if the Cathars are to survive, if ever again there is to be a resurrection of our pure movement, then we must learn what we can about these men and use their weakness against them. After all, it is *their* weakness, not ours. Which is more important to you—that you go around wimpled or that

William Belibaste is saved? This is your only choice. Think clearly and then answer me. Is not his life worth a small change in your ways?'

Claire nodded. She remembered the pool—and she knew that she had already changed.

Peter reached up and touched her hair, just as Aimery had touched it before him. He loosed it gently from its iron pins and left it to fall in a thick tumble along her back.

"Then you must listen to my reason," he said softly. "And you must do exactly as I have said. Entice Aimery of Segni. Learn what he knows and share this knowledge with us. Help us in the way we most need your help."

Again Claire nodded. But secretly she was already composing a message to Mother Helene. She would leave it in the Abbess's chamber before she left this night.

# CHAPTER 13

The parchment lay as smooth as a shadow upon the pristine stillness of Claire's white bed. She dropped her sumter of pens and hurried eagerly to read it.

*My dearest child,*
  *I pray you, meet me tonight at the Roc just after the last late-night compline bell has sounded. I have much that I must tell you. I know who placed the effigy and why. I have learned of the treasure.*

The message was unsigned. It needed no signature. Claire had grown up with Helene and she recognized her Mother's firm, smooth hand. Claire's heart thumped as she read the note. She cared little about the myth of treasure but the effigy at the wicket frightened her whether she admitted it or not. It had disturbed Aimery as well but in the end the burnt doll had accomplished its purpose, she realized. She was in Montsegur Castle. That had been the whole plan.
*How had Helene come to realize this as well?*

She felt apprehension tingle through her body. She must get to her Mother and quickly—but how? If she set off now, she would be missed. The Count of Segni had determined she must attend his feast for the Lord of Foix; and Peter had echoed this insistence. If she disappeared now she would be missed. No, better to do what her Mother suggested; they would meet tonight at the Roc as she had planned.

"And I am making too much of this," Claire said aloud. The actual sound of her own voice served to quiet her fears. "If it were urgent, Helene would have asked me to come immediately, this very instant. There must be a reason she would have me wait until after the nighttime prayer bell."

Still . . .

So deeply was she tangled within the skein of her own thoughts that she barely heard the Countess de Montfort as she bustled in. Still resplendently pregnant, Minerve wore a shielding flax apron over the costly silk of her tunic, and a simple matron's wimple tamed the fair overflow of her hair—though not too successfully. Bright wisps of it framed her smiling face.

A small parade of servants followed her. They struggled under the weight of a brass bathing tub, splashing pails of steaming water, a wooden screen, clothing chests and sumters and a plethora of other objects that Claire could not even begin to identify.

"I am *so* sorry, you must forgive me for being late," bustled the Countess de Montfort. "My eldest, Rupert, was determined that he should be allowed to squire for his Uncle Aimery at the coming lists and he absolutely cannot do that. He is much too young; he has barely begun his paging days. Then after that, Edoard, my second born, decided he should be allowed to go falconing but, of course . . ." Minerve stopped with a laugh. "You have absolutely no interest in the intricacies of my role as brood mother. You want to dress for your first feast. And I have come to help."

Claire made her a brief, welcoming reverence. "Help with what?"

"Why, with preparing you," said Minerve as she motioned the servants here and there. "How else could you be ready for this night's banquet? You have no clothes."

"But I have those from Sir Aimery," insisted Claire.

"Aimery knows nothing of women's dress," scoffed Minerve. "That's why he charged me to help you."

"I can put on anything. I don't care what I wear."

Minerve's eyes widened incredulously. "Not care what you wear? Why, every woman cares what she puts on. Half the fun of any event is planning what one will wear to it. I am already planning what clothes I should have made once my new son is born. It's what gets me through."

She looked about and received fervent, concurring nods from at least two of her female servants.

"Still, you *have* been convented," she said, "and that may serve as your excuse. We will see you are well bathed first, and then will come the rest."

While they spoke, the servants had set up the bathing tub, filled it with steaming water and draped its back with linen sheeting. They placed the wooden screen around it.

"You may leave us," said Minerve, "but make sure you return in the sands-span of an hourglass, no later. We will have much to do."

The sands-span of an hourglass for bathing, thought Claire. Impossible! Once the door had closed she tiptoed to the steaming tub.

"There are rose petals in it!'

"And elixir of rose as well!" whispered Minerve as she handed Claire a chunk of fragrant soap. "It is all part of the womanly spell you will weave tonight. I know the modesty of convent ways, so I will sit without this screen and let you bathe yourself. You will have much more privacy here than ever you would have at the village bathhouse! We can talk while you are busy at your task. I love to talk—as you will certainly come to understand."

This would doubtless take some getting used to. At the convent, bathing was quick and perfunctory, carried out in water so cold that it raised gooseflesh on Claire's arms even in August. The goose-fat soap they used cleaned well enough, but sometimes left her smelling worse than when she had begun. She put a hand tentatively into this water. It warmed her; it smelled like heaven. She eased herself in.

"Settled?" called out Minerve from outside the wooded screen.

Claire sighed, "Yes."

"I have the absolute feeling that we will end as friends," said the Countess de Montfort. "God knows, I have no other friends in this forsaken place."

"Nor do I," Claire surprised herself by saying.

Both women laughed tentatively from behind their separating screen.

"But you must overlook my bossing ways," continued Minerve. "My brother calls me quite despotic, as though he should be the one to say it."

Again she laughed, though this time Claire didn't. She lay back in the water, breathed deeply, and listened.

"Aimery is commanding because he is a warrior," continued Minerve, "and because he is so driven."

"Driven?" replied Claire. She stopped splashing in the water; kept herself quite still. "Who would dare to put the whip to a count of Segni?"

"Our father," replied Minerve simply. "He, too, was a count of Segni—Aldo was his name—but not the first son, and not even heir to a castle when he married my mother. They desperately loved each other, at least at the beginning, but both their families opposed the match. My mother was a Trenceval of Languedoc, thus the bearer of a very ancient name, and her relations would not have her married to someone they considered an upstart. It did not matter to the Trenceval that two of his ancestors had followed each other as Pope. This did not influence them and, indeed, they were rumored to be in sympathy with the old Cathar religion and so there was no love lost between them and happenings in Paris or Rome. In the end, though, my parents were allowed to marry. My father had great dreams, but little of what is necessary to realize them. They possessed no castle and little of the money needed to maintain my father in his knighthood. In those days, my brother, my parents and I lived in a simple farm house. There were times that my mother was forced to work at basketry and herbing in order to keep our few lands together whilst my father was away seeking adventure and wealth in the Eastern crusades. He never obtained either position or wealth, and so in the end he transferred his ambition to Aimery and to me. *We* would make his mark in life."

Minerve paused, as though she were back in those wanting times and in that small farmhouse; when she spoke again, steel whipped through her voice.

"Aimery was set on pleasing our father. He was ever this way, from the time he was a little child. Yet, can you imagine the difficulty in pleasing a man who was satisfied with nothing? At all cost, our father would have my brother do what he had never been able to do himself. Aimery must conquer; he must possess lands and castles, not just in Italy but in Languedoc as well. Aimery dei Conti di Segni must be the greatest count of them all! The pressure was enormous, but my brother welded himself to it. He let my father's wishes overrun his life. Indeed, our mother said he even over-came the plague because our father would have been disappointed in him had he not bested death."

"Aimery had plague?"

"And almost died of it," said his sister. "We were quite young; but eight and Aimery had just started paging."

"You didn't catch it? Usually that contagion spreads like witch fire, and everyone is burned by it."

"Fortunately for my sake, they had sent me into the country and I was still there. It was a grueling moment and yet . . ."

"Aimery survived."

"A miracle," agreed his sister. "It very rarely hap-pened that someone survived that curse. Especially when it was said he brought the sickness when he re-turned home from the court of Amedeo of Savoy. My mother attributed his salvation to a novena she made to St. Dorothea. She told everyone that this was the rea-son her child—her only son—was saved."

"Perhaps it was the prayer within the novena, and not the novena itself."

"If so, then it worked its blessing only for children. The same grace did not save my father."

There was silence for a moment. Claire did not want to hear these things about Aimery of Segni. She did not want to hear of his childhood; of its bleak poverty and what he had had to overcome. It made him too *real* to her.

"And I will not have him real," she whispered.

"But he *is* real," said Minerve from behind the wooden screen. "You must take him as such. After his death, it was as though Aimery clothed himself in our father's blighted ambitions. Whatever had been thwarted must be made right. My brother must win castle after castle and he must conquer Montsegur merely because it was in Languedoc and the people here had looked down upon our father. In truth he hates this land, hates the responsibility of this fortress. He should leave it all and go back to Italy where he is happy. God knows, he has won lands aplenty there! And he intends to go on and go on and even to marry, and then nothing will be worth the price he will pay." Minerve stopped abruptly, letting her voice trail off.

"But we must honor the memory of our parents, we must do what they would want and revenge them," said Claire softly.

"Are your own parents living?"

"I was three when they died," Claire whispered. "I can barely remember them. But I have heard what happened. They were burned."

Minerve's voice was filled with compassion. "Was there a fire in your village?"

"No," said Claire thoughtfully, not sure why she felt like confiding; not sure what she planned to say until she said it. "They were poor people, found guilty of a crime and they were executed for it. At least this is what I have always been told. Only, lately . . ."

"Lately?"

"In my mind I see it differently, though sometimes I don't think I can be actually *seeing* it at all. I was so young, only three; how could I possibly remember? Yet I catch glimpses of the fire and it was all around them—but they were not staked to it, and there were no witnesses. There are always witnesses at an execution, even the Inquisition insists upon that. And yet I know my parents were alone and they were surprised by what happened to them. I can feel their shock even more than their fear. You'd think that if they had been tried they would have been at least *expecting* their fate." Claire shook her head. The water surrounding her had suddenly grown cold. She did not like these memories; had always pushed them away. "I was so young. I could be remembering wrongly. I could have made everything up in my mind. I wasn't actually there—how could I have been?"

She gathered the linen sheets around her and abruptly stepped from the tub.

"Ready?" cried Minerve as Claire emerged from behind the wooden screen. Her troubled eyes did not quite match the forced brightness of her voice. "Now where are the servants? We will need them all. I have chosen something wonderful for you. Something bright and flamboyant and wonderful; something I am sure you will like. Now, don't shake your head against me, Missy. Put yourself in my hands for just this one night."

# CHAPTER 14

Aimery had expected to see a change in Claire, had even anticipated it. After all, he was a warrior and as such he possessed an eye used to seeking out the pivotal in situations, an intuition that could visualize change before it appeared. Instinctively he knew there was more to her than the masquerade of rough flax and shapeless burlap that she hid behind. He'd found that out in the pool when she had floated in his arms. The veiling and loose tunics and aprons did much to disguise the loveliness of her tall, slender figure, just as they had been meant to do.

Nothing disguised her now. She took his breath away, coming toward him slowly, slowly; making her Claire of Foix was truly lovely—wondrously lovely. The promise of that one red-gold ringlet had developed into an almost amazing cascade of richness, thicker even than it had appeared in the water and fuller. Held back only by a thin gold wire, it framed her face and tumbled free down a shimmering bronze tunic to rest almost at the gentle small curve of her back. There was nothing lavish about her; she wore no costly jewels but she took his breath away as she came slowly onward and not even Minerve's gentle gloating smile could embarrass him from staring at her. From reacting to her. Aimery felt his body stiffen; felt it yearn for Claire, even though she was a novice and he knew it, and full well realized the responsibility he bore for her, no matter how strenuously he might argue to Bishop Fournier that she was not, as yet, professed. Perhaps the rumors in this wild place were true that the House of Segni had perpetrated nothing but suffering upon the people of Languedoc. He, Aimery of Segni, would redress that wrong, at least with this Maid of Foix. He knew that he could—and that he would.

Aimery bowed first to his sister and then to Claire as he gave her his hand and led her to the dais. He had accepted this fete as a duty of his suzerainty, the honor a liege lord must show to a leading vassal when he presented himself at Court, and so he had taken great pains to impress his new subjects. The Great Hall had been thoroughly cleaned of all the accumulated detritus that a great many men and too many dogs could so easily leave. The walls had been newly whitewashed and the tables with their silver and pewter ornaments shone with waxing. Enormous banners in the Segni colors of scarlet and cream flew overhead from the rafters along with the shining pennants of every vassal lord that served beneath their pennant. As he looked upward, seeing them flutter, he could not help thinking: *I have done this. I have achieved what I set out to achieve, what I was supposed to achieve.*

He had organized this night with all the stoic attention to duty that marked everything he did at Montsegur. He had not expected to enjoy his own banquet;

he never had in the past. Claire's touch upon his hand changed that. Suddenly the Great Hall exploded in gaiety, as musicians thundered rousing music on the timbrel and on the lute. A juggler tossed his bright balls into the air with what the Count of Segni saw as truly dazzling skill. He wanted to call Claire's attention to it; to see if she saw how truly masterful the small, bedraggled man actually was. Aimery tapped his foot. He smiled down at the woman beside him and realized that he was suddenly, and inexplicably, having fun.

He felt as young as the youngest of his pages—and just as devious—as he held Claire's small, soft hand and smiled his brightest smile at the noble and well-connected Gertrude, Countess of Triconet, whom rank had placed beside him at the long trestle table. He didn't want her there, he wanted Claire; and now that he was lord of this castle he could bring whomever he chose into precedence with him. And he chose the Maid of Foix. This was his table, this was his castle and today was the day on which he received its first annate tithes. Still smiling, he motioned to his steward and had the Countess's place changed, just a little. Placed only two seats from him, and beside the Count de Montfort, the Countess of Triconet was still grandly situated. She remained on the dais. She should be happy enough. True, she did not *look* very happy, her face had gone quite pale beneath the red dust on her cheeks and her eyes flashed spite at Claire. Aimery did not care.

The woman made a polite reverence to the Count of Segni and blinked quickly at Claire, eyeing her in much the same manner as a vulture might gaze upon his prey. Barely was the curtsey finished before she moved deftly to take her place further along the table, her gold jewelry tinkling and leaving a heavy roiling of spiced perfume in her wake. Claire felt her cool gaze again as she took her place beside a wondrously solicitous Huguet de Montfort.

"The Lady Gertrude will have her revenge for this," the Count of Segni whispered into the ear of Claire of Foix. He loved being this close to her; he loved her smell.

"Please don't make a spectacle of me," she whispered. "I should have been happy to be seated at a more appropriate place considering my ranking. I am neither nobly nor richly born."

"I am lord of this castle," said Aimery mildly. "I decide who will sit where."

Still, Claire's point was well taken. He had wanted Claire beside him; he had not meant to offend the Lady Gertrude. He smiled down the table at her and made mental notation that he must take special pains to flatter her out of her biliousness. This would be another of his duties as lord of Montsegur.

But he wouldn't think about that now. He was too content, too happy.

Aimery motioned and an army of servants marched into the room with silver trays heaped with food. There were cheeses and frosted oranges and green water lettuces to begin, followed by plaice that had been caught that very morning in his own lakes and partridges and boar shot on his lands. He watched, surreptitiously, as Claire picked her way through the food he had placed before her; watched the delicate way her throat worked as she sipped at the amber wines that had been brought from his estates in Italy across the Haute Savoie.

"Try this," said Aimery, holding out a frosted sweetmeat. Claire hesitated but then reached across and, steadying his hand with her own warm one, took what he offered her. He was delighted when she asked for more.

Aimery laughed out loud, a startling sound. "I have high admiration for a woman who enjoys her food!"

Again he reveled in the brush of her lips against his sticky fingers.

"But only one more," he playfully admonished, "or else you will end by looking like the man who created them."

He motioned towards a doorway where an enormous man, dressed in bleached homespun and dripping sweat, threateningly waved a huge wooden spoon at a very small, very slight boy who was clothed exactly like him.

"My cook," said Aimery with a flourish, "brought straight from Paris by my enterprising sister. He is husband to her dressmaker. Perhaps you have met Madame Monique? Not yet? Then you will. My sister will most assuredly see to that. This cook has worked in the king's kitchens and is so fully aware of his importance that even I, as lord of this castle, am loathe to go against him. I will need a wife to do that."

*Why had he said that? And why to Claire?*

She was taken with her own thoughts. "Your cook was in service to the King of France?" she said astonished. "Why should he leave . . ."

"Paris to come to come to Languedoc?" Aimery finished for her. "Indeed, my cook is Parisian and would heartily agree with your questioning. Like all true natives of that city, he curses the gods who forced him to live anywhere else. Alas, he sealed his own fate with his actions. His work in the Louvre gave him access to the king's wine cellars where, it is rumored, he began to spend more and more of his time. His fondness for the contents of that vault was the only weakness in an otherwise sterling career—but it was a mighty failing. The king dismissed him. His choice was to work for me or to take his chances with the Bohemian princes— and, well, Bohemia is Bohemia. That is why you find him here."

Claire laughed outright. Aimery was delighted. So was Minerve de Montfort, who looked over at Claire with a wink and a smile.

They laughed on as the new musicians bowed out with a flourish from behind a tapestry, and the lively sounds of the timbrel and flute gave place to Rogre de Tencacel and his mandolin. Tencacel, one of the most famous troubadours in Languedoc, sang lustily and well of a slightly naughty incident that had recently happened at the English court. His sung tale was met with wild cries and cheering and the thumping of metal against wooden trestles. The noble Countess de Trenceval wiped away tears of mirth and dabbed at her long nose with a piece of fine lace that Huguet, ever solicitous, held out for her.

"Your people have the best of all worlds," whispered Minerve as she leaned across her brother toward Claire. "Languedoc is a land and a culture created from the spark of romance—or at least it was until these un-fortunate persecutions of the Cathars ruined much of what grew here. I am orthodox in my own beliefs, as is my brother, but neither of us sees the use in burning a man's body as an inducement for him to change his mind. Aimery would free William Belibaste right this moment if he could, and he may yet find a way to do just this."

Claire stared straight ahead. It was a temptation to confide in her, to ask for help. She liked Minerve and was beginning to trust Aimery, but could they really help with William Belibaste? No, of course they would not. They were not Cathar; his freedom and his life had no meaning for them. Besides, Peter had always warned her from Gallic good intentions. There was no hope for her from Minerve de Montfort or from Aimery of Segni. She would do well to remember this.

A kettle drum rolled as brightly liveried servants strutted out with the *pièce de résistance*: a spice cake replica of the pennons of Montsegur and of Foix that were so skillfully assembled that they seemed to actually undulate in a spun sugar breeze.

Claire concentrated on the intricacies of the cake—she had never seen anything like it before—and oohed and aahed with the rest of the assemblage. She would forget anything else.

She was smiling, she was laughing, but she was not with them and Aimery knew it. He watched the slight traces of a frown etch their way across Claire's smooth forehead. Something was troubling her, something deep; but he doubted that anyone else saw the signs of it. Both Minerve and Huguet were chattering on, smiling and waving, tapping their feet upon the flooring in anticipation of the dancing that was to come. Aimery caught Claire as she cast a stealthy, quick glance at the new Count of Foix.

I should introduce them, thought Aimery; that was my stated purpose in having her here. Foix was her childhood's home; she was born there and will be interested in becoming formally acquainted with its count.

Yet, he knew that somehow this wasn't the moment. The time would present itself and he would be ready, but for right now he had a plan. He would return the smile to Claire of Foix. He was determined upon it.

The Count of Segni rose from his seat and clapped

his long hands together smartly as all around him noble revelers squealed in anticipation.

"We will start placement for the dance!"

Claire had never danced before. Naturally there had been dancing in the village, on feast days and marketings and when the lists were held at Montsegur, but she had always viewed the merriment from the great height of convent walls. To see people dancing together, to see them move back and forth and touch each other, had intrigued but not enthralled her. Dancing was not for her and she had not missed it.

Or so she thought.

Tonight was different. Aimery would make it different.

Perhaps it was the feel of silk against her body, or the scent of roses from her bathing water that still clung with the force of memory to her nose. Perhaps it was the fact that she had had wine tonight—she, who rarely drank anything at all save water. Now as she watched servants clear the room and heard the lute and mandolin players trying out notes upon their instruments, she felt—alone, isolated. As though she, too, might want to take part in the coming fun. She saw women sway in their seats, throw their heads back.

*What would dancing be like?*

She longed to find out.

Still, this longing quickly passed; it flitted through her mind and was gone. The bell for compline would soon sound, and Mother Helene would be waiting for her at the Roc. She must get away—which was why she so readily agreed to the Count of Segni's next suggestion.

"You must be tired," he said. "I can see it on you, but first let me take you somewhere, let me show you something." He shook his head as her wariness deepened. "Don't ask me of it. Just follow me. I will not keep you long, and then you'll be free."

And she needed to be free. There was still time in the hourglass before compline. If she did what the Count of Segni wanted, she could quite soon be free. Otherwise, who knew how long he might detain her? She was here because he wanted her here, she wore the clothing he had provided, she lived in the castle he now held as fortress. And she had not chosen any of these things; they had not come to her by right.

*Know your enemy. Use him.* Peter's counsel.

Aimery controlled some of her actions, but not all of them. How could he? He knew nothing of the Good and her devotion to the Cathars. Wherever he led her, whatever he chose to show her would be quickly done with. She would let him think he governed her and still she would manage to do what she must do, what she had vowed to do.

Still, she wondered as he threaded her through the dancing couples and out into the dark passageways of his great castle.

"Where are we going? Where are you taking me?"

"Hush. I'll show you the way."

For the first time his honor guard did not trail them; they were completely alone.

She followed him, hand in his hand—the same hand that had held her safely in the water, warm flesh against her flesh. Behind them the music played on, but the deserted hallways muted its clarity. Claire still heard the echo of the timbrel but the sound of the flute was quickly lost. Claire strained to hear it; she missed the sound. She thought of Helene and how she would soon meet her, even as she stepped beside Aimery as they moved through Montsegur's stone corridors and up the narrow steps that led into its fortified donjon.

"Up here," said Aimery as they reached the end of their steep journey. Claire was breathless. The small, wooden trap that led out onto the castle parapet squealed in protest as Aimery leaned against it. It opened readily enough to starlight; to a huge, silver disk of moon— and to music, the same music that played in the hall, with its sounds just as strong and sweet as they had been there. They could have been in the hall; they could have been dancing. Claire stepped through the portal, into the night's light.

Aimery grinned at her. Claire was surprised how carefree and light this grin made him appear, and she had the strangest feeling that she was seeing a part of him that few others had seen; a bright, carefree part of him that he normally hid.

"I thought you would like this," he said. "I happened upon this magic my first day at Montsegur. We are directly over the Great Hall at Montsegur and an oddity in the castle's masonry slivers its sounds perfectly here. I discovered that I could hear whispered conversations, if I chose. I imagined music would be especially clear here, and it is. We can dance here together. You will be safe."

Odd these last words, especially because Aimery did not know if he was saying them more for Claire or for himself. He was only sure that he meant them.

He took his vows of chivalry seriously and had worked hard for his knighthood. It had not been given him on a silver plate. And while there had been not a few women in his past, they had all wanted him as much as he had wanted them. He had made certain of that. He could not have born the thought that he had taken advantage of anyone, and he would not take advantage of this young girl now.

What's more, he would soon betroth himself into the powerful French Royal House of Valois; he had no idea why he had not done so already. Minerve disapproved, and probably so did Huguet, but their opinion did not matter. It had not delayed him in his quest. Probably he had just been too busy, too occupied to put his signature to something that would have overjoyed his father and which promised only glory. His rationality urged it—but his instinct whispered *Claire.*

He wanted to kiss Claire, he suddenly realized; wanted to feel the softness of her pressed against him, all along his length. Wanted this desperately and unexpectedly—and almost overwhelmingly.

He couldn't do that, but he *could* dance with her. Surely there was no harm in that. She wanted to dance; Aimery saw this in the smile on her lips and in the slight sway of her body. Something still worried her, but perhaps, if he asked. . . .

But there was no point in asking.

Instead, he reached out his hand. She hesitated for a tantalizing instant and then he felt her warm fingers once again; he felt the tickle of them against the skin of his palm. The rest was easy. She followed his lead, swaying to the incessant beat of the timbrel and the flute's magic spell. Moving when he moved, pausing when he paused; dancing with him under the bright night stars.

A perfect moment; one of a very precious few, but it didn't bring Aimery the contentment he envisioned. He wanted more.

Perhaps it had not been such a good idea to bring her here. But it was done now. They were here, they were dancing, and they were alone.

The music stopped abruptly and just as abruptly Claire, breathless, moved away from him and toward the trap door. Yet, Aimery was not quite finished. The dancing had slowed him but there was still something he wanted to show her; it was the other reason he had brought her here.

"Not only is the sound from the Hall excellent but you can see through the valley from this perch, and on a night as clear as this one, you can see the Haute Savoie, the mountains that lead to my home, that lead back to Italy."

"But Montsegur is your home now," Claire said, moving beside him. "It is the castle you have always wanted."

"How do you know that?"

"Minerve told me," Claire answered. "She said a great deal about why you have come. She thinks it a mistake."

Aimery opened his mouth to question this and then thought better of it. His instincts were still as sharp as his prudence was dull. Best not to take a path that might draw him more deeply into the mystery of Claire and the strange and unexpected spell she exercised over him. Best not to ask what Minerve had said. He and his sister were close, they rarely argued, but he could feel anger boiling up in him against Minerve, pushing out any other emotion.

"Come this way," he said, abruptly, "to the other side. You can see the Roc from here."

Claire saw the lights even before she heard the voices and the screams. She saw the steady pick of torches swooping, like so many falling stars, from the village to the edges of the cliff. Towards the precipice called the Roc.

"Helene!" she cried.

Aimery reached for his sword and turned instantly towards the trap—the warrior once again, all else forgotten. "Wait here. I will send someone to fetch you."

Claire was not waiting. She matched him stride for stride.

"No, 'tis Helene," she said. "Something has happened to her. I know it has."

He turned briefly to her; his eyes narrow, his mouth hard, not used to being thwarted in his dictates. Claire had not waited for his permission.

*Helene.*

Together, they clattered down the winding stone stairway and into the castle main. Outside on the hillside the solemn call to compline prayer began to peal.

# CHAPTER 15

"She died quickly, at least there is that much." Aimery realized just how foolish and ineffectual he sounded. Words could not comfort grieving; he knew that. Claire sat huddled on a rock beside him, closed tightly inward. She had torn her tunic scrambling down the mountain toward Helene's crumpled body; its bronze splendor lay wrecked about her body. She didn't notice; she didn't care. In the bright light of the remaining torches, her face shone forlorn and shadowed and still.

A sling had already transported the Abbess's crumpled body back to the convent for its last rest, and most of the villagers had departed. Aimery had sent Huguet on ahead to calm both the castle and the village. The news of the Abbess's death would doubtless spark flames to the smoldering matter of William Belibaste and his trial. The people of Montsegur, which was widely known as a holy place of the outlawed Cathar religion, would immediately look toward the Perfect and those who might want to free him, for the cause of this atrocity. Aimery knew this and he must take steps to quell any rumor of revolt.

It was his duty to shield William Belibaste until the end of a just and fair trial, but he also wanted to protect Claire—but from what? His eyes narrowed as he stared at her. She had called Helene's name when they had first glimpsed the running torches from the castle wall. She had known the nun would be here.

*Helene!*

A shriek, a call—a knowing.

That word echoed, but any other words were useless. Claire would not be comforted, much less questioned, and he abandoned his efforts after his first, fumbling attempts. Still, there must be some way to reach her. She looked so miserable and alone perched there on her solitary rock, so vulnerable and so guilty. Yes, it was guilt written across her face: he was sure of that because he knew guilt's etchings well. He had felt them, more than once, as they carved his own face to stone. In his case, as a warrior general, they had been caused by endless battles he had ordered and by the equally endless deaths that had come in their wake. He had no idea what secrets Claire harbored; she had spoken not one word to him since they had fled the castle to arrive at the scene of Mother Helene's death. Perhaps one day she would tell him, or perhaps she wouldn't. But the memory of his own misery told him what was needed now. Impulsively he reached out to her and folded her into the protective circle of his arms. He was surprised that she did not fight him. She might later, but not now.

No tears yet, and he worried about that. For all the hurt and pain that forced them, tears were the beginning of healing and he would have welcomed them from Claire now.

* * *

The Count of Segni leaned back and tented his fingers before him on the trestle in his Great Hall. He stared over them and into the faintness of the dim, early morning light and the solemn eyes of his brother-in-law. "I've heard rumor that devil work is behind the Abbess's death. That the souls of the Cathars martyred at the Roc by the Inquisition rose up against her in revenge. No villager would have ventured there by night; the spot was said to be cursed."

Huguet grimaced at this mention of devil work. "Generally, I have found man's own capacity for mischief-making to be fully adequate. He needs no supernatural help in evil."

Aimery nodded. He had left what little superstition he possessed behind in his childhood. A man—or a woman—had done this to the Abbess of St. Magdalene; had tossed her body over the cliff and then sounded the alarm so everyone would know what had been done. Aimery wondered why, and how Claire had known. She did know something, he was certain of it. He had distrusted the totality of her innocence even from the first. Even as he held her body in the pond and danced with her last night and longed for her, he had been wary of her.

Mystery shrouded Claire, but it was a mystery he was determined solve.

Aimery rose abruptly and went to the window where he watched as an honor guard escorted Claire back to her Abbey through the faint, mauve glow of morning. She had asked to return there to be near Mother Helene, to watch with her; and he had allowed her to do so. The way was treacherous and the men still carried night torches. The light from them flickered against her shawl-wrapped body, reflecting flames against her shrouded form. *As though she were engulfed by fire.* Aimery frowned and turned away from the sight.

"Tell me what else you have heard," he said, "the other gossip."

Huguet shrugged. "The rest is not gossip. The small chapel at the convent was desecrated last night; not offensively so, but still badly enough that no one could miss it. The chalice was thrown to the floor and the altar light blown out. The door was left open to every breeze that blew through those drafty halls. Whoever did this wanted to leave sure mark of his presence. Oh, and he left a small doll, an effigy. It had been singed and then thrown haphazardly upon the defiled altar."

Aimery listened without expression, his mind already conjuring a plan. "There are no suspects?"

"None. Mother Helene fell—or was pushed—at the time of the compline bell. The nuns under her charge had been asleep for hours and thought she had been as well. They were roused to their prayers and went to the chapel expecting her."

"Someone knew she was about though," said Aimery softly. He watched as Claire disappeared from his sight. "The Abbess did not fall; I am certain she was pushed."

*And just as certain that Claire of Foix knows something about it.*

"Some say," remarked Huguet de Montfort quietly, "that the Abbess of St. Magdalene was a secret sympathizer with the outlawed Cathars, but that lately she had become disillusioned with their cause. I was told this myself by one who also was sympathetic with them and who since has repented."

"For what price?"

Huguet had the delicacy to blush. "I wish I could say that conscience alone motivated my spy's actions but, alas, your gold also played a prominent part in his recantation. He told us everything, or at least as much as he knew."

"Who is this spy?"

"No one of consequence. A peasant who was briefly enchanted by the Cathar beliefs and just as quickly disabused. Their stringent rules are mightily hard to live out when a man is confronted by the needs of his own flesh and blood. Still, this land is a legendary Cathar stronghold and the belief claimed many converts in the past. Perhaps Mother Helene was one of them; at least it appears so from the evidence we found."

Aimery turned from the window, back to him.

"We found Cathar tracts hidden in a sumter under her bed," said Huguet, "and not just a few of them, but many. It appears that our innocent Abbess belonged to a clandestine remnant. In a situation such as this—what with William Belibaste's trial and your ascension to suzerainty—there might be many Cathars who would want to tinder a fire of rebellion. At the very least, they would wish to show their strength by decisively marring your first weeks as possessor of Montsegur. The people in this land are superstitious. You've heard what they said about Belibaste's arrest."

Of course Aimery knew. "That his capture was fated and that he was amply warned of it. A pair of ill-omened magpies danced across his path as he set off; his wife dreamed badly. She begged him not to leave for Languedoc."

"She is due here soon, you know. Bishop Fournier has allowed her to share her husband's cell."

Aimery smiled ruefully. "His is such an ascetic religion and yet, even as its last known Perfect, he could not forgo the pleasures of a wife."

"And a son," added Huguet, "though an unacknowledged one. His wife began as his housekeeper. When she became pregnant he quickly married her to one of his followers, but she returned to his house in time to give birth to the boy."

Aimery shrugged. "Still, there must have been something to this religion. Men and women died for those beliefs. Maybe there was more to it than we understand."

"Or perhaps the religion itself changed, became distorted," said Huguet.

"I think accusing the Cathars in this is much too facile an explanation," said Bishop Fournier from the doorway. No one had heard him come up. "It is as though someone wants to entice us down that path so we will not look toward any other. Desecrating a church is a sign of witchcraft and the Cathars, for all their heretical ways, had no sympathy for that. Belibeste's true followers would be more interested in quelling such tales at this moment than in fanning them. It makes no sense at all for them to vandalize the convent's chapel when their leader stands accused before the Inquisition. It would only bring more trouble to them, and they do not need that now."

From the castle keep Aimery heard the sounds of early morning—the energetic crowing of a cock and the solemn pealing of a bell from the Abbey steeple. He thought of Claire.

*What role did she have in this? What was her part?*

The words ran through him before he could push them away.

"You are frowning, my son," said the Bishop. He reached out and laid his hand upon Aimery's arm. His touch felt as dry and light as autumn leaves, but Aimery, strong himself, could feel the power behind it.

"Neither Belibaste nor his followers had anything to do with what happened here tonight," repeated Roger Fournier. "They did not desecrate the chapel; I believe that Mother Helene was killed, but they did not kill her. Nor do I believe in the facile finding of so many Cathar tracts beneath her bed. Our Abbess may or may not have had those leanings—and this is not the first time I have heard those rumors—but she was much too intelligent to leave evidence of her beliefs where any spying eye could find them. No, we are dealing with a man who is both extremely cunning and astute, and it is important that we not forget that—even though he has made some mistakes."

Huguet leaned close. "Excellency, do you know who this man is?"

"I have suspicions," replied the Bishop, taking his place at the trestle table. "Only one group has been charged with witchcraft lately, and only one man managed to escape their eventual doom. I met him once, many years ago. He vowed revenge. I believe he is busily taking it now. But I must go to Paris. I must gain proof."

The three men huddled together as the bishop worked out his hasty plan.

Claire could not sleep. She did not try. There would be the day to spend with Mother Helene, the preparations to help with. For now, she would wait. Claire knew what was coming. She was standing at the window looking out at the castle when she heard the heavy wooden door to the cell slip open behind her. She did not turn around, but she knew Peter was there.

"A terrible tragedy," he whispered behind her. Though his nearing footsteps were as smooth and measured as always, Claire sensed his emotions; she felt his uncertainty, his hesitation.

"Who could have done it?" she whispered, still staring out at the castle. "Who could possibly have wanted to hurt Mother Helene?"

"Then you believe it was deliberate, that she did not fall?"

"It was deliberate," said Claire. She opened her mouth to tell Peter about the note from Helene and its call to urgent meeting, but then changed her mind. She would tell him this later, when they had more time, when they were not so shocked and grieving.

"No one would have *wanted* to hurt her," said Peter after a while. He drew near to Claire.

"Then you think what happened was an accident?" she asked him.

"I know it was. There is no other explanation."

"The others think it was the Inquisition. Roger whispered this to me when we were both near the Roc. He said the bishop found proof that Helene was a Cathar; they discovered tracts hidden in a sumter under her bed. Roger believes the Abbess was killed. They neither needed nor wanted the scandal of trying her for heresy."

Peter shrugged in annoyance. "That is stuff and nonsense. Since when has the Inquisition ever hesitated to try the illustrious? They have lit as many fires under the great as they have under the poor. It depends on what they *want*. That is all that matters. One has only to remember what happened to my own beloved Master, Jacques de Molay, and to my fellow Templars. They were all eminent men and had done much for the king and for the crown, but when Philip the Fair wanted treasure from them, the Courts showed not the slightest hesitation in condemning the lot of them to the stake."

"We may have had nothing to do with Helene's death," said Claire softly, "but we will bear the brunt of it. If what Roger said is true, Bishop Fournier will have his suspicions. He will hunt for witches."

"There are no witches," said Father Peter harshly. "It is flesh and blood men he must face, not the superstitious unknown. Poor Helene was out at night for some undoubtedly simple reason. Perhaps she could not sleep. We will never know. She took a misstep and fell from the Roc. This has happened before to the unlucky. Now, Helene has been freed from her earthly body. She is in Paradise. We should rejoice with her."

Claire opened her mouth to cry that Helene did have a reason to be at the Roc so late at night—and that *she*, Claire, was the reason. But she could not tell this to poor Peter now. He and Helene had been friends and collaborators since her childhood; together they had orchestrated the Cathar resurgence. Her death must be devastating for him, and if he chose to believe that this had happened merely because of cruel happenstance, well, then, Claire would help him do just that—for now. There would be plenty of time to face the brutal facts in the future. They would have to live with the memory of Helene and what had happened to her for the rest of their lives.

"They will want you," Peter said and nodded his head towards Montsegur. "If I know Bishop Fournier— and I do—he will take great pains to make sure there is no slacking of duty today. He will want the village and, indeed, all of Languedoc to know that neither he nor the Lord of Segni will be intimidated from their duty. Belibaste must be tried on, and nothing and no one can stop these proceedings—not even Satan himself. You must mourn and you must pray for Helene, but you must also be ready when they call for you. Our poor Helene is now dead but, fortunately, William Belibaste remains very much alive and still within reach of our care."

Should he comfort? Should he hold her? Aimery considered these questions all through his morning's many duties. He puzzled through them even as he ought to have been thinking of other things.

"Like the running of my castle," he mused aloud. For the first time that he could remember, the winning of lands and the preoccupations of his fiefdom were not the sole worries on his mind. Instead it was occupied with Claire of Foix; was filled with her.

He had reveled in her nearness: first at the pond and then on the parapet and even—God help him—at the Roc after the Abbess's death. And he was glad, truly glad, that the bishop had not halted the day's proceedings in mourning.

"We must not," Fournier had said. "We must go on."

Aimery glanced from his place at the High Table over at Claire, as she busily scribed out the day's events, with her head bowed and her pen scratching smoothly across parchment. She was dressed in a simple wool dress that he had given her; her hair, bright and clean, held back with the green silk ribbon that had been his gift to her. She did not look up under his scrutiny, but he could see the strain upon her.

"I can't agree with the bishop," whispered Huguet from beside him. "We could have stopped this trial for one day; we should have stopped it in respect for the Abbess."

"The bishop wants to reach a certain point before taking his leave. He wants to arouse no suspicions about his trip to Paris."

"But all this wild talk and accusation—it is more of a desecration than what happened in the chapel last night."

"I imagine not to Belibaste," replied Aimery. "He must know that each peasant telling a long tale against him adds moments and perhaps hours to his life."

As Aimery watched, Claire dipped her quill into the lead ink well. She did not look up at the peasant who was being so intently questioned by Jacques Fournier. Only a very little sunlight filtered through the windows but it was enough to touch a halo to her flame colored hair. Hers was the only brightness in that drab and dreary room; the only thing that remained to remind him of the festive time this place had hosted just a few hours before. Aimery felt the walls of Montsegur Castle—his life's ambition, his home now—press in upon him and he wondered if he would ever truly find peace here. Out of the corner of his eye, he watched as a black cowled priest rose from his place at the Trestle Table and turned to the witness. The drone of questioning began again, as dust swirled on the air and, upon the hearth, the castle's dogs stretched and growled in their sleep.

It was all Claire could do to keep her thoughts on the page she was writing. She dipped her quill into the well, but then droplets of dark blue ink fell upon the parchment and ruined it. She would have to do this work over again later; she could never let Fournier see the mess she'd made of it. He might become suspicious of her. But this botched and spotted scribing was the best she could do this day. It was all she could do to get through her work and keep her eyes lowered—not to glance at Aimery of Segni. She did not want to see the questions in his heaven blue eyes as they regarded her.

"And you are sure they spoke of scamperings?" asked the young priest, the latest Inquisitor.

For an instant, a frown furrowed the forehead of Yves, the peasant accuser, but then he smiled again. He remembered what he should say. "Ah, yes, the scamperings every night, I heard them and they were bold and dangerous. It quite frightens me to even think on them."

He was off now, on the Perfect; telling a tale so ludicrously invented that even the youngest Inquisitor looked on in keen disbelief. Claire concentrated on the work before her but, in a way, she was grateful for this malicious prattling. Under cover of the hoops of mirth it evoked, she glanced up continually, looking to see if Father Peter was about.

Usually she spotted him immediately, even with the hall jammed with hot and sweltering people as it was now. Sometimes he would be dressed in a prosperous merchant's spotless linen, at others in the ragged homespun of a peasant. He preferred the latter.

"No one pays the least attention to poor folk," he once told Claire. "No one sees you. No one takes notice. Poverty is the best disguise on this earth."

Claire had believed him. In those days, she had believed everything he said. Since the day they had climbed the Roc through darkness to reach Montsegur, they had been together, rarely spending a day apart—until now.

*Her second birth, he had called that night, best to forget the first.*

She had looked to him for everything. He educated her, he gave her strength; assured her what they were doing was right.

But was it? What had Helene been so determined to tell her?

Treasure, she had written. But wasn't the Cathar treasure merely a myth?

She must get to Peter. Claire made up her mind to tell him of the note. Why had she not done this before? She must have been tired, exhausted even, not to tell this to Father Peter last night. She had never withheld her thoughts from him; she had never withheld herself. And she knew she must rectify this situation as soon as she could.

Bishop Fournier raised a hand, calling halt to the day's proceedings. He stretched discreetly from his ornate chair, and then turned in conversation to the Lord of Segni. The other judges tried not to pay undue attention, but they hovered discreetly near, looking for all the world like hovering crows.

Near Claire there arose a general grumbling and stirring. It had been a tedious day after the excitement of the night. Most men had come to Court expecting to see Belibaste again led forth to the witness chair. The talk of scampering imps and little demons had not amused them; they were disappointed that Fournier had not chosen to parade him forth for their amusement and groused about before they took their leave.

A stooped peasant, hurrying forth, carelessly dropped a live chicken from beneath his coarse undertunic. In a twinkling, the castle dogs pounced. There was general screeching and squawking as the hapless bird flapped about the room, inches from his pursuers, while all about him soldiers, knights, priests, and peasants dodged, casting bets and calling insults.

Claire turned quickly away from the imminent slaughter. She could not face it; and instead gathered her quills and laced that day's parchments into her calfskin sumter.

She hurried out the door and down the long corridors, running until she passed through the heavy oak doors and was out of that enormous and stifling castle.

It was a muggy, overcast day, heavy with the summer sounds of crickets and cicadas and the heavy hum of insects. After the savageness of the hall, the fresh air felt as clear and crisp as winter to Claire. She stood alone for a moment, breathing deeply and leaning against the castle's granite stones; gathering strength to trudge again to her convent. She was lucky enough to be able to do so, and at any moment the Count of Segni might change his mind and demand that she return to the fortress. He might come himself or send his sister, Minerve. Claire had no wish to see either of them, to be close to them, or perhaps she did—and that would be wrong.

Because she wanted him; she needed him. When Aimery was near her, she felt safe and cared for and freed from her duties, and the memory of that safety lived on. Yet there was only one person she needed to be with; only one person who could help her and that was Peter. She had come dangerously close to forgetting this while she lived under the protection of the Lord of Segni, but now that she was back in her proper place, in the convent that she had always called home, she could feel herself becoming free of his influence. She just must stay away from him. That was all.

*But I want to be near him.*

She turned and hurried away from this thought and back toward the sanctuary of convent. Her pattens clicked up torrents of dust as she raced alone up the dry and dusty trail.

*Magdalene.*

The word was like a whisper through the trees. It touched the leaves above her head and shivered them, despite the heat.

*Magdalene.*

Yet it was not some strange Magdalene being called; it was she, it was Claire. Claire they truly wanted. Claire who would do all she was told.

*Magdalene.*

And in the end, what did it really matter? From the first she had fought against this; fought to stay herself; yet what had it gotten her? What had she won? Magdalene or Claire, they were both the same. They were one . . .

. . . because she knew the voice that beckoned to her; indeed, she stopped upon the path to hear it more easily and then shook her head.

"Peter, my Father," she said, as she turned to him.

# CHAPTER 16

"You loosed the fowl, didn't you, Peter? You set the dogs upon him in the Great Hall?"

Peter chuckled softly as he drew her away from the path, and into the forest. The day's gray sky soon disappeared behind a thicket of overhanging leaves.

"A clever trick was it not?" asked Peter in his turn, oblivious to the incredulity in her voice. Claire tripped and then righted herself. The old man did not offer assistance; he did not seem to notice. Gleefully, he chuckled again.

"A clever ploy upon my part," he continued. "I knew that, after the excitement of Helene's unfortunate death, the Lord of Segni's men would be in good form today, and that they would be disappointed that Belibaste himself was not brought out for show. I did not want to take the chance that one of them could have recognized me from other days and from other occasions. I dressed as well as I could to blend in with the others, but I could take no chances today that a sharp-eyed fellow might remember me. I had to see you and I needed a diversion."

"And so you provided one," said Claire softly.

*Braying dogs. Blood splashing everywhere behind her.*

Peter of Bologna was too busy with his own thoughts to notice any difference in the train of Claire's. He moved her words aside with a wave of his hand.

"It was better that she sacrifice herself to help the Perfect than that she end in some peasant's boiling pot. And I had something of import to tell you; something the Count of Segni may not have shared with you; something that you may not have heard."

Claire listened to her footsteps falling upon the forest's moist undergrowth. The air was still here. It smelled sweetly and strongly of decay. For an instant she remembered how cool and welcome the air had seemed near Aimery's castle, how she had pulled it greedily into her lungs. They reached a clearing and Claire lay her bundle down upon a hollowed log. She sat down with a sigh to face Peter, who trundled down himself.

"Poor Helene," he said with a sigh, "but there was a priest injured as well last night. Did they tell you that? Did the Count of Segni share that information with you?"

"A priest hurt?" Claire shook her head.

"Not badly hurt, but with injuries enough to raise suspicions. I believe Bishop Fournier called it an 'unfortunate incident,'" said Peter, "but then he has always been full of inane explanations."

This was not Claire's assessment of the cleric; she thought him quite wise. Yet, she said nothing of this to Peter.

"Will this bring more attention to the Cathars? Will

we be held accountable?" she asked him. "What happened to the priest, and when?"

"The incident took place this morning. It involved a priest who came yesterday from Paris with urgent news for Jacques Fournier. It is rumored that he came on the instigation of our own Helene—yet, you know the ways of gossip. Anyone will say anything, and especially of the dead. I learned of the incident from someone I know in the Count of Segni's employ. He could not tell me the reason nor what message the priest brought, only that he had been hit upon the head from behind and severely injured—'left for dead,' were the exact words. I imagine this was the reason behind Fournier's quick ending of this morning's session."

Claire nodded. She felt the earth shift beneath her feet.

"Another death."

"The priest is not dead, at least not yet."

Peter clucked his tongue and then moved to throw back the cowl of his peasant's tunic. When Claire looked at him again he was staring at her with the concerned eyes she had come to recognize from her childhood.

"This has happened to us at a most inconvenient moment. First Helene's death, now this, and Belibaste not yet freed," he said. He reached across to take Claire's hand but her writing sumter slipped and she grabbed at it, then sat with it clutched to her. After a moment, Peter drew back his own hand.

"They will think we are behind this," said Claire. "There is already wild talk about our Mother. Now they will think the Cathars are behind this as well."

"Not living Cathars, but ghosts," Peter assured her. "Perhaps not in the Great Halls of Montsegur Castle itself but through the countryside they whisper that the martyrs of the glorious Cathar era have come back to wreak revenge against the Inquisition and all its henchmen, against the Bishop himself and Aimery of Segni and Huguet de Montfort." Peter paused for a moment, let these words fall deep. "Still, we do not need people thinking badly of the Perfect, not with the last of our great priests on trial for heresy. They may start with ghosts and spirits, but eventually they will blame us for the wounding of this priest. They will say the Cathars sought revenge for Belibaste's trial and, perhaps, even for Helene, now that she has come under scrutiny. This will give them the excuse to turn against Belibaste with increased fury. This is undoubtedly something our great Bishop has taken into consideration, which is why this news is not generally known and why Belibaste was left safely in his cell today, away from the proceedings. My man says Fournier is planning to adjourn this trial and take leave for Paris. He has heard something, or suspects something, that has made this trip imperative."

"What could that be?"

Peter shrugged, an innocent gesture. "Something. Anything. But the import of all this is clear. Belibaste must be got from prison immediately; his escape must be delayed no longer. We cannot wait for the end of this trial, or for his wife to arrive to help us. We must work upon his freeing now. It is our duty; he is our only hope."

*I am Perfect. You are Perfect. Still . . . Belibaste must be freed.*

Claire nodded, slowly at first and then with more enthusiasm. For, of course, Peter was right. He was always right—in the end. She felt shame flood her that she had distrusted him.

"Belibaste's case is hampered, more so today than

even yesterday," repeated Peter. A look of bright concern shone upon his face. "One could sense it in the Great Hall this morning; *you* could have sensed it had you not been so saddened by Helene's death. It has ignited a tension that was not there before. Now, perhaps, even the Count of Segni would like to be quickly rid of him; would like to see him staked."

"Aimery would see no man die by burning," said Claire and then she caught herself. "He has always openly repeated and repeated that he is against witch hunts in this land."

"He says this, yes, but he defends them. Have you not forgotten that he is Protector of the Inquisition's priests?" questioned Peter with a small, weary shrug. "Rome vested him with this power and the French king confirmed it."

"That's not true," cried Claire. A startled bird flew upward from the trees. "Sir Aimery happened upon this turmoil. He did not create it. He took possession of Montsegur the same day that William Belibaste was brought here in chains. You know that."

"I know that you now defend him," retorted Peter, "and I *also* know that Aimery of Segni is the descendent of two malignant popes, men who led nations against our people. Through marriage, your good Aimery is now even related to the Montforts, a powerful family, indeed, and one whose fortune grew from the seeds of the Cathar destruction. Do not delude yourself of this man's virtues. There are few in Christendom as powerful or astute as the Count of Segni. If he chose, he could release William Belibaste at this very moment and there would be none to gainsay him in his privilege. He is, after all, seigneur of Montsegur; he is free to do what he wants with William Belibaste. He could free him."

"But it is important that justice be served. It is important that there be a real trial."

Even as she echoed Aimery's words, Claire heard the ring of hollowness within them. Would justice really be served in burning a man because of his beliefs? And surely that was Belibaste's fate. He would never recant, and so he would die.

"He could do something if he wanted," repeated Peter softly, and then he gave himself a mild little shake. "It is obvious that he will do nothing and that we must defend ourselves as best we may. Tell me now; have you learned nothing of him?"

*Only that he is a man and not a monster. Only that he has held me close and made me feel safe. Only that I crave that comfort now.*

Claire shook her head.

"Nothing," she said to Peter of Bologna. "I have learned nothing."

"You will." The little priest shook his head wisely. He was well acquainted with the ways of men, with their weaknesses; and he knew that Aimery of Segni was weak for Claire of Foix. "One has only to look upon him to see that he is smitten with you; and since he is charmed by you, he will naturally think that you, in your turn, are charmed by him. His kind always thinks arrogantly thus. They are too filled with pride and hubris to believe otherwise. Aimery of Segni will think he can have what he wants from you and we will use this weakness against him. Eventually, he will tell you everything you need to know—and you will then tell it to me."

The old man sighed as he swept in all of Montsegur with an expansive gesture. "Eventually—and soon now—we will have this all again. We will retake this land for the Cathar Perfect. We will spread out from this, our perfect homeland, and conquer and subject the whole of France. This place anew will be a safe haven for the Cathara and the Templars. We will come into our power once again."

"And William Belibaste will be saved?" whispered Claire.

"We will certainly save him," assured Peter. Again the wry chuckle. "He is our last Perfect. We will need him to complete our mission, as we will need you. Your mission is to learn what you can from the Count of Segni. The fates have well positioned you to do this—why, even his sister, the Countess de Montfort has taken you up. Use their interest. Get from them all that you can. Right the wrong that their ancestors did to us in the past."

One lone bird trilled away in the shadow. Claire could not see him, but she turned away from Peter to look.

"Do you still have the herbs I gave to you?"

Claire nodded. "Yes."

"Are they well hidden?"

"I keep them with me always. I did not know where to leave them."

"Then use them. Feed them to him. Make him confide in you. Make him tell you the truth. I believe he plans a journey. Go with him. Learn the truth."

Claire nodded. And though at first she hesitated, this time when Peter offered his helping hand, she took it. This was her Father Peter, after all; and they had been together from the start.

# CHAPTER 17

And Peter was right. The Count of Segni did seek her out, almost immediately, and with the very proposal that the priest had guessed.

She had come back to her convent, knowing that Helene's sacred burial would be that evening and wanting to give her Mother her prayers. Helene had been denied the Consolamentum, the one Cathar sacrament, by the suddenness of her death, but Claire could pray for her. She could watch.

She made her way to the convent's chapel. Originally, at the time of its establishment in the last century, St. Magdalene's had been a Cathar stronghold; a place where women were educated and succored and taught the rigors of the Good ways. Women were esteemed in the Cathar culture; indeed, they were revered. However, when Dominic de Guzman and his fiery Dominicans swept through Languedoc bringing Inquisition on the heels of Crusade, they had reformed all of the old convents, brought them back to the rule of the orthodox religion. Yet, when her turn came to be Abbess, Helene had quietly and efficiently taken back what she believed had been stolen. She had been a dedicated Cathar, yet she had used her high position to serve both religions. Helene had been loved and greatly respected and this was evidenced by the fact that, despite the rumors that now swirled about her sympathy with the Good, the small, stone chapel was still filled with mourners. Claire heard gentle crying as she took her own place at its rear. Peasants and merchants; nobles and nuns—all had memories of the kind woman who had justly and charitably ruled St. Magdalene's for so many years. Helene had kept her own beliefs secret from the other religious and had never tried to influence them in any way.

*"It is enough that each is free to worship as he chooses. The true Cathars wanted only that; they felt no need to force others to their way."*

Helene had repeated these words time innumerable to the child, Claire. Now Claire, the woman, grieved her great friend and her Mother.

After that, she took refuge in work. Her cell had been empty now for more than a week and was in desperate need of dusting and sweeping. Claire toted wooden buckets up the stairs from the convent's fountains and scrubbed her bed linen in harsh lye soap. She beat her feather mattress, polished her simple stool and prie dieu with heavy beeswax, arranged bright, red geraniums in an unglazed pottery bowl. Above all, she tried to love this room as she had once loved it; tried not to think of the other, larger one that still waited for her within Aimery's fortress. Tried desperately not to think of Aimery—and failed, and failed again. Dismayed, she found herself repeatedly thinking of him, even when she was not consciously thinking about him at all.

She fought it. She had just replaced the straw broom upon its hook near her door when she heard the unexpected clatter of footsteps running up the hall. Coming straight toward her.

She had only time enough to put her fingers to the doorpull before it was snatched from her hands and the door itself flew open.

" 'Tis the Knight of Segni," said Mother Fausta, second in rank to Mother Helene, and now the Abbess in her place. "I told him he should respect this cloistered, holy place but he said he has come for you. He wants to take you home."

Looking at the nun's flushed, puzzled face, Claire felt fury flash through her. How dare Aimery stomp his way into this quiet mourning? He had invaded her life, snatched her from her duty, taken over her mind. She would not give him one thing more!

"But I am home," she said through clinched teeth, "and I will not be taken from it again."

"Not this place," said Aimery quietly. He had come up, and stood behind the panting nun, resplendent in his dark mourning tunic and his golden spurs and his brightly jeweled sword. "I am taking you to your true home, to Foix. We are going back to where this all begins."

# CHAPTER 18

"The Count of Foix sends his compliments to you, and his regrets," said Aimery of Segni early the next morning, as they began their journey through the rugged, mountain country that would lead them from Montsegur to the fortress where Claire had been born. "He felt it important to go before us. Our visit was unplanned. He needed to make preparations for our reception."

"Why *are* we going?" Claire blurted. She had wanted to ask Aimery this question since he had first announced that they must leave for Foix. "Why must I come?"

Aimery did not immediately answer. Instead, he turned in his ornate saddle to survey the carefully chosen entourage that trundled along behind him. Twelve of his best knights, complete with their own entourages of squires and pages, rode along at the leisurely pace their liege lord set for them. In addition, jesters and falconers followed on ponies. His prized Parisian cook imperiously commanded three assistants and two cov-

ered wagons loaded with select foodstuffs, gifts for
their hosts at Foix. After that lumbered three pack wagons, all bearing the cream and scarlet colors of the
Counts of Segni and all jumbled within with whatever
had come first to hand. Aimery had not cared what they
carried. In truth all this pomp was camouflage, meant
to deflect attention by attracting it—and this was the
true reason he had brought Claire.

She didn't know this, and while she rode along beside him, waiting for his answer, she let her thoughts
wander back to the previous night.

"My lord of Segni has come for you," Fausta had
said, standing tall. "But you need not go with him if you
are not inclined. No one can *make* you go with him."

Strong words, but it took only a glance from Aimery
to send Fausta scurrying down the corridor once again.
One day she would rule of the convent of the Magdalene with firmness and love, just as Helene had done,
but she was young still and had not as yet arrived at the
place of authority within herself. And a scowl from
Aimery of Segni had caused even many strong warriors to tremble and quake.

He waited patiently until her footsteps had finished
echoing away from them and then he turned to Claire.

"I will not leave my convent," she said quietly. "Helene
was my Mother–Abbess—more than that—I will not
leave her. I will not return to Montsegur Castle."

Aimery shook his fair head. "I would never ask you
to leave St. Magdalene's until after your Abbess is safely
laid to rest. Do you think me that uncaring? I was the
one who allowed you to return here in the first place."

"Her burial is tonight, at Vesper time, yet I will not
come back to Montsegur even then. You do not need
me boarded at your castle. I can come to it for the

scribing, as I always have; I can complete my task well enough and still live here."

"No one is asking you to return to Montsegur, at least not yet."

A scowl traced its way across her smooth forehead. "Then why have you come for me?"

"I need your help."

Relieved by this, Claire reached back to loosen her apron. She understood helping very well. "Then I will fetch my quills and parchments. It will take me just a few moments' time."

"There is no need for them. As I said, we are not going to Montsegur," said Aimery, his eyes never leaving hers, "because I am taking to you Foix."

"To Foix? Why?"

"Bishop Fournier has suspended the proceedings, not just for today, but for at least a sennight. His official reason is to give the convent and village time to mourn the loss of the Abbess. He also declared it to be a kindness to the prisoner, giving his wife time to arrive. Neither of these are the bishop's true reason for this extraordinary step."

"And what is his true reason?"

"He wishes to go to Paris. He thinks he will find an answer there."

*To Helene's death? To why the latest priest was wounded?*

Peter had shared this secret information with her, and Aimery must not know that she knew. For all their sakes, and above all at this moment, she must be circumspect; she must be wise.

"Does it concern the Cathars?" she asked cautiously. "All of Montsegur knows that tracts were found in a sumter under my Mother's bed."

"The Cathars," answered Aimery, "and the Knights Templar."

She remembered the funeral; the memory of it played through her mind as they left the security of their mountain fortress and headed north along the main pilgrim road. And later, after all that was still destined to happen, she would look back upon the quiet grace and simplicity of the ceremony, on the way their tiny, stone chapel had been filled with all the people Helene had so loved. She would remember the flowers, the rich, seductive scent of wildflowers, and of lavender and of thyme. Mourners had placed their offerings in small earthen jugs or in ornate silver vessels or they had merely bound them together with flax string and placed them around the sconced candles at the nun's feet.

Most of all, she remembered Aimery beside her: the fresh smell of him, the brush of his arm against hers, the security of having him near.

Especially when her mind chorused the singing questions—could I have saved Helene? Would she still be alive now if I had gone immediately to the convent when I received her missive, and not waited to meet her at the great Roc? What was it she was so desperate to say to me? What was this talk of treasure?

She would never know now.

Bishop Fournier said the Mass. He wore the simple tunic of a priest and not the ornate scarlet and gold trappings of a bishop. Helene would have liked the simplicity of this, Claire thought. He spoke of Helene's goodness and not of the great convent she had ruled. Hers was a service quickly and sweetly finished.

The Vesper bells tolled dolefully as they filed out

into the evening, toward the spot where Helene would lie. Claire caught Peter's eye and he smiled at her, sadly and wisely. He was still her Father Peter, after all, grown tired and old seeing death and destruction. Now, Claire thought, he will add Helene's death to the list of those for which vengeance was needed.

Aimery was one of those who carried Helene's simple, wooden box from the chapel to the churchyard. He walked beside a peasant, the convent's gardener to whom Mother Helene had always been attached. Aimery had told Claire, at the Roc, that he would not offer condolences or easy explanations for this inexplicable death; he had not known Helene as she, Claire, had known her, and it would be impertinent and facile of him to try to force a cheery way into her pain. He may not have offered easy explanations, but he had held her close. He had sheltered her. Within his strong arms, she had felt protected. And as she watched on, it had somehow heartened Claire just to watch as that same strength gently lowered Helene, her Mother, into a place filled with flowers.

Still, the loss hurt. She wanted away from the memory of it as they plodded on towards Foix.

"Why have you brought me with you?" she asked again.

*Yes, why?* thought Aimery.

Because he loved looking at her, loved the idea that this particular woman was riding beside him?

He had sat her on a bay, one of the few gentle horses within his stables, and one of his favorites. Gabrielle, he called her; it was an angel's name and fit for Claire's mount. He had guessed that Claire would know little about riding; that she kept her saddle as well as she did both secretly surprised and delighted him.

"I had to go and I thought you might enjoy the diversion," he said mildly. *Not the real reason, but close enough.* "It is your birthplace and you are named for it. Are you not known as Claire of Foix?"

"I may carry a noble name," she answered, "but I am a peasant, nothing more."

*A peasant who could read and scribe Latin; a peasant who knew how to sit a saddle well; someone had taught her these things and many more. Aimery intended to learn who had done this. He needed to know this because this knowledge would solve mysteries, it would clear the riddles running through his mind about her. And then . . .*

"Yet, you have no idea who you really are," he said to her. They rode beside each other, a little ahead of the others. "By your own account, you lost both your parents when you were much too young to remember them, or at least much about them. I have always thought that a singular tragedy. Don't you want to know more?"

"What is there to know?" asked Claire, though for an instant her heart leapt. "They were common laborers. No records are kept of peasant births and deaths. I can know nothing of them."

"What a little snob you are, Claire. Records are kept for all souls within a parish range, and not just for nobles and clergy. Who has told you otherwise? Who has said there was no account of your birth at Foix?"

Claire kept her gaze straight ahead. "I have always just assumed so."

"Well, you have assumed wrong, my small lady–scribe. As you know, my venerated ancestors Lotario and Ugolino of Segni both served as Pope during the early days of the Crusade against the Cathar Heretics. Lotario especially, as Innocent III, was instrumental in quashing them in the last century, but he thought, as does Bishop Fournier, that all the trials should be fairly held. He watched the proceedings closely from Rome and insisted that all trial scribing be brought to him there."

A sigh of relief escaped Claire. "Then you must want me to scribe something or translate a document that might be still at Foix. That is the true reason you have brought me with you."

"Not exactly," the Lord of Segni replied, "but Innocent III had a special interest in the women of the Cathar movement. My uncle admired their strength. He believed them to be misguided, yet he admired them nonetheless. The new count said there was a Lady of Foix whose likeness is frescoed on the walls of his castle. She was a woman who both interested my ancestor and intrigues me. Esclarmonde of Foix was her name—have you ever heard mention of her?"

Of course, Claire had. "No," she lied.

"I thought not," said Aimery. "She was one of the greatest of the Cathar Perfects but dead now for a century or more. You would have nothing in common with her. However, the Count of Foix said you resemble her strongly—he was much taken by the likeness and encouraged my own desire to bring you with me to Foix."

Claire shrugged. "The count saw me very briefly and from a banquet table's distance. We have never met. How could he note a likeness?"

Yet, he had stared at her; Claire remembered that now. He had stared at her eagerly and been on his way to them when Aimery had smuggled her from the Great Hall.

"He did though," said the Count of Segni, "and, according to the Lord of Foix, the likeness is exact down to your red hair and your extraordinary eyes, and it is quite remarkable. You may take this as a great compliment. Even those who abhorred her beliefs conceded that the Lady Esclarmonde was a great beauty. She is a legend; one of the last true Perfects—and a Magdalene as well."

"A Magdalene?"

Claire's throat constricted around the words.

Now it was Aimery's turn to look straight ahead. "Mary Magdalene was the patron of the Knights Templar, the woman whom they worshipped. Of course you would know nothing of that."

She should have had some visceral memory of this place, she thought. After all, her ancestors had been burned here; her own parents martyred. She would have expected their blood to call to her; that they might even rise from the dust before her, screaming for revenge. Instead, Claire felt nothing from them as Aimery's chief squire pounded upon the great castle's drawbridge with the ceremonial staff of the Segnis and demanded entrance for the liege lord. Claire felt neither interest nor curiosity. She was too afraid.

*What did Aimery truly know? Why had he brought her here?*

Peter had said evidence was found that linked Mother Helene to the outlawed Cathar remnant. Now, for the first time, Claire wondered if it linked her to them as well.

She would know soon enough.

It was a moment before the bailiff came out to meet them. He was a tall, sallow fellow who bowed with great courtesy and said he would take word to his lord that the Count of Segni requested hospitality for himself, his knights, his men at arms—and for Claire of Foix. This was all accomplished with the precision of a

court masquerade—and, of course, that is exactly what
it was. The Count of Foix had returned straight from
Montsegur and knew full well that Aimery of Segni
was a bare few hours behind him on the road. Still,
courtesy and ceremony were as important as bread to
the people of Languedoc, and the vassals of the King
of France, who now ruled this land, were also compelled to observe its refinements. In the long moments
while they sat under the scorching sun and waited for
entrance, Claire of Foix turned resolutely toward the
enormous iron gates of her past—of Foix—and watched
them as they slowly rose, affording her entrance.


She could not shake the shelter of memory, though
naturally Claire remembered none of what she now
saw. She had been far too poor to live within this castle
and too young when she left the town itself—what was
there of life here to recall? Since babyhood she had
made her home at Montsegur and Montsegur was the
only past that claimed her.

And yet . . .

And yet, there was something quite familiar about
this strange and haunted place. She felt it as they rode
slowly through the outbuildings of the castle, where
the men at arms would be lodged alongside the fortress's
own defenders. Her parents had been killed here when
the first of the new Frankish lords of Foix took suzerainty.
She wondered if that man still lived; if it had been his
son's face that had smiled down the table at her during
the banquet at Montsegur. She wondered if she would
be forced to shake hands with a person whose own
hands had martyred her family. Peter had told her, and
many times, that they had been killed because they had
refused to give up the Old Ways and their precious reli-

gion. Fortunately he had been there to save her; to carry her away before she could be harmed. He could do nothing to save her parents. It was a source of great sadness to him—oft repeated—that he had so failed.

The old priest told this tale with tears in his eyes, and Claire had cried along with him, for parents she could not remember, for a life she did not know. And Peter had always comforted her. She would be Perfect one day, and revenge them; she would be Magdalene.

This last was their secret; they were the only two who would know. The Cathars would once again rule this land, their home.

Now, suddenly, a wave of hatred washed through Claire as she walked through this strange courtyard, toward an unknown place. It flooded out of her to sweep toward everything and everyone that surrounded her—toward the mountains and the hills, toward this forbidding stone castle and the upstart who now commanded it. And toward Aimery of Segni; Aimery who could hold her close and make her forget, for an instant, that she was alone—had always been alone—and lived in constant danger. Aimery who had brought her here seeking shelter—but from what? She turned away, gritted her teeth and, for the first time in her life, she let the anger rule her.

She was within a nest of enemies and this fact had best not be forgotten. Aimery would not and could not help her if he knew the truth about her. He was sworn to guard the interests of both the bishop and the king. And he was ambitious in his own right; his sister had said this. If the scent of heresy brushed against her and thus touched him, he would be forced to sniff her out and to send her to the Inquisition and to the flames.

No false tenderness, no floating at the pool would save her and she had best remember this.

This truth infuriated Claire. Her clear, rational Cathar mind said one thing; her deepest emotions another.

*He would leave her. She would die.*

She was grateful when the heavy doors suddenly rolled open and an elegantly dressed Count of Foix came down his castle steps to greet them. Claire had controlled herself and her face once again. She still had her mission, after all; and she had been trained to fulfill it.

"My lord of Segni," he said with great ceremony. "It is an honor to welcome you to Foix Castle."

Aimery climbed down from his horse and the other count knelt before him, placing his clasped hands within the Count of Segni's in the age-old custom that illustrated fealty to the liege lord.

"You are most welcome," he said, rising gracefully once again to his feet.

Claire took the opportunity to study him. He was younger than she expected; younger than he had appeared to be when the long banqueting table separated them at Montsegur. She was relieved by this. It helped to lift her burden of hatred. He was too young to have killed her parents; he must only have been eight and twenty at the most. His years were far too few to have allowed him to participate in the atrocity against her family. He would have been but a child back then. Relieved, she smiled at him.

And he smiled back at her. He had Aimery's short, fair hair and similarly blue eyes but the combination was not quite so appealing on the Count of Foix as it was on the Count of Segni; and this man did not appear to possess the natural force of his liege lord.

Yet the smile upon his face seemed genuinely pleasant enough as he welcomed them.

Aimery said, "Claire of Foix, I would like to present Emerico de Cabaret, Count of Foix."

If he was startled that the Count of Segni gave his lowly scribe precedence, Sir Emerico effectively cloaked his astonishment behind a mask of chivalry. His bow to Claire was low; his hand upon her waist as he lifted her from her horse was light and respectful. When she was safely standing on the gravel courtyard he turned to a small, round woman who stood within the sheltering doorway of the castle main.

"Claire of Foix, may I present Joanna of Landiwick," he said simply, "my wife."

The two women made deep reverences to each other and then walked side by side through the castle doors.

If anything, the location of Foix's fortress was even more mountainous and formidable than Montsegur's— and Montsegur had always been noted for its inhospitality to intruders. Legend murmured that Raymond Roger of Foix had continually swooped down from his isolated demesne—a Cathar stronghold—to wreak havoc on the crusading French troops under Huguet's ancestor, Simon de Montfort, only to disappear once again within the rocky aerie of his ancestral home. Raymond Roger's rebelliously turbulent exploits were the stuff of which legend was formed. One of the King of France's first concerns, once his land was brought into subjugation, was to remove the hereditary count and put a new man in his place.

Despite its jagged location, and the turbulence of its past, this castle possessed a serenity that eluded Montsegur. As Claire followed the young chatelaine through the cavernous corridors of the Foix fortress, she marveled at its wide expanses of beeswax polished wood and the embroidered tapestries that hung upon its wall. Trestle tables were littered with an impressive number of beaten silver objects and none of its carefully white-washed walls was bare. Regardless of the aridness of the mountain lands, there was still a carpet of fresh thyme strewn upon the floor, plenty of flowers in heavy gilded pots. Claire, educated to simplicity and taught to despise all worldliness, found it hard to find fault with the way in which the young count and countess kept their castle; she felt the spirit that manifested itself in the serenity of these beautiful surroundings. And she knew Aimery felt it as well.

"I imagine my lord of Segni has spoken with you of the fresco of Esclarmonde of Foix," whispered Joanna. She blushed. "It is a remarkable resemblance. I trust you do not mind my speaking of it?"

"You shouldn't tease the Maid of Foix with such things," called back her husband who had preceded them with Aimery. "She will see for herself the resemblance after a rest from her journey and a good evening's meal. The Count of Segni knows something of Esclarmonde's legend. His ancestors studied it, and he has agreed to share what he knows with us. From what I understand, though, Esclarmonde of Foix was not only a Cathar Perfect she was also rumored to be the Templar Knights' Magdalene as well—though the Magdalenes are rumored to be witches and rule demons. We will look upon the noble Esclarmonde by candlelight and see if we think her capable of such grim deeds as sorcery." He stopped, laughed. "Certainly she had the flaming red hair that is the enchanter's mark."

Servants bearing heaped trays of fruit, cheese and bread and icy silver pitchers of cold spiced wine scurried toward them as they entered Foix's Great Hall. Joanna motioned Claire to a fine chair, covered in pale blue linen.

"How goes the priest?" began Sir Emerico, and then

he glanced quickly toward Claire. "I'm sorry. I know you had not planned to tell the lady. Does she now know?"

Aimery took a draught of water before speaking. "I had not wanted to trouble her again so closely upon the death of her Abbess. But she knows now. I told her. As to your first question: he does well. He is kept under guard and I have left word that I should be sent for immediately should his condition change."

"Do you know what message he carried with him?"

"It had been committed to memory," replied Aimery. "We do not know it yet."

"Then it must have been important," said Lady Joanna. "And, unfortunately, his was not the first of your misfortunes; at least that is what we heard at Foix. This priest, the Abbess; they say there was another monk who took mysteriously sick and died the day you arrived at Montsegur to take rights to your castle."

"Yes," agreed her husband, "he was supposedly well versed in Latin and slated to scribe the proceedings for William Belibaste's trial."

Claire had known about the monk, but she had not put his illness together with his scribing. She did so now; she sat very still and she listened.

"This heresy trial has brought nothing but ill luck," said their host with a shake of his head.

His wife shook her skillful curls in fervent agreement. "We are lucky indeed the Inquisition did not choose to bring him here to Foix for judgment, or we would have had this trouble on ourselves."

She started, embarrassed, and looked about her with a discomfited titter.

Claire did not want to hear what they had to say about Belibaste; she did not want to share this part of herself with them. As the others talked and the servants scurried, she let her eye wander.

Foix Castle was indeed a grand place; though smaller, it was much more opulent than Montsegur. Even in summer the walls were lined with tapestries and the thyme upon the floor had been freshly swept. You could see patches of it that had been laid that very day and were still fragrantly green from the kitchen garden. Could all these hangings have been brought from Paris with this young couple when they took up residence, or had they been here from Count Raymond Roger's time, from the apex of Cathar power in this region? Peter had always taught her, and the rest of what he laughingly called "The Remnant", that their Cathar ancestors had lived the simple, frugal life that befitted their beliefs. He had railed against the extravagance of both the French Court at Paris and the Papacy at Rome. Yet, despite its rugged location, Foix Castle itself could only be described as luxurious, and it had been Raymond Roger's home. Its fine silks and linens, its tapestries and silver ornaments— all obviously old and well worn—bore the signet of the ancient House of Foix. Without her realizing it, Claire's brow wrinkled in thought, as she tried to maneuver these puzzle pieces into place.

"Is not that so, Lady Claire?"

She jumped at the unexpected mention of her name, looking first to Aimery and then to the others. They all stared back at her with polite interest.

"Sir Emerico made mention of the Cathars," said Aimery softly.

Emerico nodded. "There is rumor that they were behind the attack upon the priest. I heard the claim myself before I left Montsegur. That poor man—imagine, there from Paris for only two hours."

"Monsters," cried Joanna, again with a shake of her

curls. " 'Tis the second time in its recent history that they have killed at Montsegur."

This was something Claire had never heard before. "Other killings at Montsegur?"

"Indeed," said Sir Emerico as he leaned toward her. His face flushed. He was obviously eager to tell this story; a warrior warming to a battle's tale.

"The Cathars have never been as peaceful as they would have us think. One main uprising occurred many years ago near Montsegur—to be exact, in a little town called Avignonet. For you see, it was not so much the Crusade that brought out enmity in the people, as much as it was the Inquisition that followed it. There was no safe haven for the Cathars. The investigations turned father to spy against son and wife against husband. Under Crusade, the Cathars stood together; under Inquisition this unity crumbled and they were easily picked off one by one. You see yourself the fruits of such treachery in the capture of William Belibaste. Was not his betrayer also his dearest friend? Had he not even chosen Arnold Sicre as his successor?" Sir Emerico shook his light head.

He was so young, Claire thought, there was not yet even any gray mixed in his hair. *How can this man be wise? How can he know our history?*

And yet, she realized with a start, the Count of Foix was undoubtedly older than she was.

"The tragedy happened on the Eve of Ascension Feast," continued Sir Emerico, "which in that Year of Our Lord 1242 was at the end of May. Two of the Great Inquisitors, Stephen of St. Thibery and William Arnald, sought hospitality at Avignonet, a small fortified town. They were expected."

Here, his wife took up the tale. "Avignonet, as you know, is in the very heartland of Languedoc. Perhaps

you passed through it in your journey, Sir Aimery?
No? Well, it is like the rest of this land: craggy mountains giving way to fertile valleys. The town itself can
be seen from many a high place. I hear there are those
who now venerate it.

"The two Inquisitors had picked their bloody way
into this heartland through the tributaries of its various
veins, compelling and torturing confessions of heresy
in all the villages that lined their roads. Reportedly,
they kept eight scribes fully employed in writing down
disclosures of Cathar sympathies and malfeasance.
They left devastation in their wake. I hold to the orthodox faith but I have never been in sympathy with all the
Inquisitor's methods.

"It seems the Cathars, as well, decided that they had
been docile enough; they no longer wanted to participate in their own destruction. And, as fate would have
it, on this particular night, the Inquisitors brought no
bodyguards with them. They did not think them necessary. In the past, except during the time of the Crusade
itself, the Good had gone like lambs to the slaughter
and the Inquisitors showed no compassion. Fathers
were stripped away, leaving their families to die of star-
vation. Even women—and some say especially women—
were hauled from their villages, never seen again in this
world."

Claire glanced up to see Aimery studying her. His
eyes had gone a deep shade of cobalt blue, but she
could not see in them what he was thinking. She could
not see if he sympathized with those poor, doomed
people—or if he didn't.

Sir Emerico continued. "The judges were welcomed
by Raymond d'Alfaro, who sat as bailiff in that town
from Raymond VII, Count of Toulouse. Raymond was
an important person in his own right in that region be-

cause he had married the count's bastard half sister. Still, given the fact that all of his own power emanated from that of his brother-in-law, it is hard to imagine that the bailiff would have acted in such an important undertaking without the express consent of his overlord, the count. At least this is what everyone believes.

Sir Emerico stopped to glance around the room and make sure that his audience was still in his thrall. As he did, his wife leaned forward in her seat, resting her elbows upon the table and then lowering her head upon it. She smiled at him. The new Count of Foix continued with his tale.

"The bailiff played the perfect host. He showed commendable hospitality by lodging the two weary men deep within his castle's keep. Away from the bustle of the town, he said, so that they could dine in peace and sleep. He left one of his most trusted servants to solicitously attend the friars. This same servant, once he had ascertained that the Inquisitors were at their evening meal and greatly anticipating their down filled beds, left them there and slipped off to the forest."

Silence again, except for a bird's shrill caw.

"Where he was, of course, expected; six men had gathered, and when the servant carried his signal, the group of them started immediately for the castle. They knew exactly where they were to go and what they were to do. They were joined by others along the way; in fact, they formed a war party that had just that morning made the treacherous trek from Montsegur under the able leadership of one Peter Roger of Mirepoix. The band of them could have easily been mistaken for laborers coming in from the fields, but rather than scythes they carried battle axes, and there were horsemen at their rear. This was carefully planned. The Northern French had sent armies to Languedoc to guard the Inquisitors, and roving bands of knights and men at arms flocked the place. It was dangerous for any Southerner. Indeed, they were forced to disguise themselves but by the time they reached Avignonet they were additionally sheltered by the blackness of night.

"The servant originally sent to fetch them, awaited them there to open wide the town gates. Men were left behind to cover their retreat, but the main body went straight to the castle and then directly down within its keep. By then about thirty townsmen had joined them. They were frightened of the havoc that threatened their hamlet with the Inquisition, and eager to revenge their brothers and sisters and mothers who had already fallen prey to it. These local men were armed with clubs and cleavers. Their guide led both the men of Avignonet and their brethren from Montsegur through the castle's deserted stone passageways until they came to the massive oak doors that sheltered the two Inquisitors. Raymond d'Alfaro beat upon them with the hilt of his signet sword."

Again Sir Emerico stopped, glanced around him and waited for his wife's encouraging nod. "You can imagine the rest, but at least we are assured that the end came quickly. The last of the Inquisitors had barely time to invoke the Virgin in prayer before he was beaten down. They rifled through a wooden chest that one of the Inquisitors had tried to protect by throwing his body upon it. This trunk, as it turned out, contained the register of all their work: all that had been scribed by the eight men that had taken down the various trials proceedings. The marauders tore it to shreds, burned it, opened wide the window and scattered its ashes to the night winds; some traces, though, remained in that death chamber to settle upon the corpses of the two Inquisitors."

"The men from Montsegur slipped from town as quickly and quietly as they had come, leaving those from Avignonet to hurry to their own hearths and homes and finish up their evening meal—and act as though nothing untoward had happened. The men of Montsegur had accomplished their purpose. On their ride back to the city, those in the villages who were next to feel the Inquisition's whip greeted them with flowers and wild cheers. It is said that one village priest, who was not even a Cathar, rang the joyous Te Deum, announcing to the world that his people had been liberated from a great curse."

"Had the Inquisitors not been killed, they would have killed," said Claire quietly. "I have no sympathy for them."

Yet, she did. She felt it.

"I have no sympathy with them," she repeated.

Sir Emerico snorted and then laughed outright. "In a certain sense," he said, "there is no doubt that protection formed part of the murder's motive. But many believe there was a more compelling motive as well. During their inquiries, the two friars are rumored to have discovered the whereabouts of the Cathar treasure. Some say they were killed to keep the secret."

" 'Tis often the case," twittered in his wife. "The cloak may be velvet but it covers that which is base."

"Did the men from Montsegur learn the secret?" asked Claire. She did not care that the others stared at her. "Did they know where the treasure is to be found?"

"Not then," said Sir Emerico. His voice echoed with boredom now. The crux of his story had concerned the battle between the Cathars and the Inquisition. The rest was just a goodwife's rumor and he cared nothing for it.

"Not then," repeated Emerico, "but there were always others who knew of it. And they say that Belibaste knows."

His words seemed to fly up to the ceiling of his castle and flutter there amidst the banners and proud pennons of his race.

Claire heard their echoing long after the others had turned once more to the pleasure of their sweetmeats and their cooled wine.

*The location of the Cathar treasure, known by Belibaste and by few others.*

Claire wondered.

# CHAPTER 19

A look of amazement that quickly melted into shocked outrage whipped across the Lady Joanna's face before she bowed to the inevitable and agreed that Claire of Foix should occupy the chamber next to that of the Count of Segni on the noble floor. Most men, she thought, would have the courtesy to sneak in their fancy women in the night; they would not have been allowed to sleep so near a highborn, wedded woman, much less the chatelaine of a castle such as Foix. Joanna did not question that Claire was something more than scribe to the Overlord of Languedoc: one had only to look at the way he regarded her to know that this was so. Though he was discreet, even respectful, the fact of his interest in Claire was quite obvious, as obvious as the accompanying fact that her husband owed the Count of Segni fealty, and she must bow to this arrangement. Joanna did this with as much grace as she could.

The Count of Segni was not French, after all; he was from Italy and the whole of Europe knew that strange things happened there.

The one propriety she held to, however, was that she, herself, would not be made to share a chamber with this Maid of Foix. This was the custom with gentlewomen, but Claire was no gentlewoman. She might be educated and beautiful enough—Joanna only admitted this last grudgingly—but no one knew of her lineage. Emerico had said she was of peasant birth. Claire herself insisted this was true. Still, no one knew for sure and this, Emerico had whispered to her, was part of the reason Sir Aimery had insisted on bringing her here. He was determined to clear the mystery of her lineage.

Foix was a small place. Joanna thought he would have no difficulty in doing this.

"I have placed you here by yourself," said the countess now as she opened a small chamber's door, "so you will have privacy and peace. I will summon servants to help with your dressing. Send word if there is anything else you might need."

Claire nodded. She knew what this small, round woman thought and, as the door eased shut between them, the knowledge first embarrassed her and then made her laugh. As though she, Claire of Foix, could ever be a man's outside woman. She was a Cathar Perfect and had never been tempted away from that thought.

*Except when he held me. Except when I floated in his arms.*

That fleeting time was over. That sanctuary disappeared.

She wasn't safe. Not here. Not with him. She was one of the last Perfect of Languedoc, a member of a heretical sect that he was vowed to uncover and destroy. Enemies surrounded her. She must guard both her virtue and her life.

And there was more: if, indeed, Belibaste knew of a

treasure, as the Count of Foix insisted he did, then why had he not gotten word to those planning his escape? A path to his freedom could be laid with gold coins and Belibaste was certainly intelligent enough to realize this. If he knew that in the last century, before their destruction, the Cathars had buried their wealth, would he not have gotten word to them? Surely he would have told Peter; he knew how tirelessly the priest had worked to plan his escape.

There was no peace in these thoughts, and no way as yet to answer their questions. She must think of something else.

Claire gazed around her new chamber with interest. She was certain this small, out of the way space had been originally intended for members of the minor nobility; those whose rank demanded that they be given hospitality within the castle main, but whose title did not fully warrant this position. This room had been whitewashed, but not recently, and there was no fireplace, which meant that the space would stink of damp and be cold in winter. At the top of the ceiling, despite the heat, Claire could see the tracings of last winter's mildew. The furnishings consisted of a raised bed, dressed with clean linen sheeting, and a trestle desk and a small prie-dieu and crucifix. She knelt before it now. She needed its comfort. She needed to think.

Could there really be a treasure?

Father Peter had always insisted that there wasn't. Wives' tales, he called the rumors, or worse. Could he have been mistaken? She had never questioned him before, but perhaps in this he was wrong. Claire jumped up quickly, toppling a pewter jug of wildflowers to the floor. She must learn the truth behind this rumor. She sensed this was the true reason she had come to Foix;

she must learn the truth and take this knowledge to Peter. They must use it to liberate William Belibaste.

"And then perhaps we will all be free as well," she whispered.

Without thinking, Claire reached up and loosed her hair from its simple casing. She arched her neck, shook her head slightly and felt the weight of her tresses as they tumbled thickly along the length of her back.

She must ready herself. She must be prepared.

The last robin had twittered safely into his nest before Claire finished her preparations. She had never spent so much time on herself before in her life—a life that had been filled with rough flaxen clothing and harsh pig-fat soap but also with a certain peace. She felt no peace now. Nor, she realized, had she felt peaceful for a very long time. Perhaps placid was the better term. She had been placid and docile and trusting, her life mapped out for her from the day that Father Peter had rescued her from the destruction of her family. She had wanted what he wanted: revenge. She had craved what he craved: the resurrection of the Cathar remnant. Now she suddenly realized, as she sat stiffly waiting for the Count of Foix to come for her, that she did not know what she wanted, that she did not know what she craved. And that she trusted no one.

*Learn of the treasure. Use your powers.*

She frowned, shook her head, as Father Peter's words pushed their way into her mind. How could Peter be asking this of her—when he insisted there was no treasure to be found?


It had started innocently enough; at least Aimery was confident of that one thing. He had intended nothing; he had merely gifted a pretty maiden with a ribbon. Then he had taught her to float upon water, and intended to teach her to swim. He had moved her to his fortress when he sensed the danger in that flame-haired doll at the wicket gate. He had held her near when her friend died. He had brought her with him to Foix to find answers. These were all innocent gestures, harmless even. Yet, what he was feeling now was neither innocent nor harmless. Aimery of Segni knew this.

He wanted her.

He was man enough to own this as he watched the Maid of Foix weave her delicate way to the high table, just as she had woven her way through the thicket of curious, rowdy onlookers on the day he had first met her at Belibaste's trial. How different she was now. *He* had made her different.

She no longer wore the shapeless, simple homespun of a novice. Instead she was clothed in one of Minerve's best silk tunics, a deep, dark Lombard blue shot through with threads of gold. He had bought the silk himself while passing through Como, and Minerve had had it fashioned in Paris by a dressmaker renowned both for her beautiful cutting and her extravagant price. Minerve had always loved this tunic, and it said much for Claire's place in her affection that she had sent it along with her to Foix. The garment looked much better on Claire than on Minerve, he decided, and he had always thought his sister the loveliest of creatures. Claire, with her hair drawn simply back and clothed in this splendid garment but wearing no jewels, put his sister's beauty in the shade.

*Wanted her.*

He smiled ruefully at the thought, though he could not quite see the thread in its progression. He had never consciously thought of Claire as a desirable woman, but he remembered now that Huguet had teased him about her on that very first day.

*She is promised to the convent.*

*Though not yet professed.*

He'd said these last words himself and they had seemed like nothing more than simple bantering at the time. Now, he wasn't sure.

As he looked deeply into her eyes—did not look away—he saw a gossamer that linked his impulsive purchase of a ribbon to his decision to bring her into Montsegur and then on with him to Foix. Looped together, they linked his body with hers at the pool, were looped together by it as she fit easily within his arms the night that Helene had died and then later as her head came to rest so near to his heart. It was, undoubtedly, a very delicate, very finely traced thread. But it was proving to be quite strong.

Claire saw his eyes darken as he stared at her. She was startled and then slowly they captivated her. She did not let her own eyes leave his; did not slide her glance away as something in her urged her to do. She pushed through that shy thought, moved beyond it, so that she could truly *see* Aimery, Count of Segni, for the very first time.

The whole of that grand and noisy hall disappeared as they stared at each other, so close now that Claire could easily have reached out a hand to touch him. But she didn't. *Seeing* him was enough. Afterwards she would digest this instant, would pull it apart in an effort to understand just what it meant and how it mattered. Her mind worked that way—but she was finding that her heart did not. For this precious moment it just wanted to feel.

And then the spell broke. The Count of Foix hurried over to help her into a seat—Aimery was his liege lord, after all, and must be respected—while his small, round wife smiled nervously.

"Rumors," she said, "there are rumors that the troubles will start here as well."

No one needed to ask which troubles she meant. Since Belibaste's return, talk throughout Languedoc had centered upon his arrest and the conspiracy that would surely seek to free him. That he was still imprisoned did not seem to matter; fear still shivered everywhere.

"And now with all the deaths at Montsegur . . ." She lifted her silk clad shoulders with a sigh. "Everyone talks of the Cathars again and they were quite forgotten. When Sir Emerico first took up suzerainty here, no one mentioned the ancient troubles. No one even knew of them. But now with Bishop Fournier's being here and bringing the Inquisition—why, there is nothing but talk of old times. They speak of Simon de Montfort and the Templar Knights; they talk of Esclarmonde of Foix."

Claire's heart thumped in her chest at this mention of the Knights Templar and their relationship to a Cathar Perfect. It brought them too close to Peter. They might know nothing about him; must surely be ignorant of his very existence. Still it brought them near and she wanted to say something, anything, to distract them away. But Aimery spoke first.

"These are quite interesting," he said, playing with a long object he had lifted from the carefully laid table.

"They are called forks," said Emerico, plainly proud of their acquisition. "They are a Saracen invention. My father-in-law first discovered them in Jerusalem, on Crusade. They are much handier than knives; they pick the food more easily. Joanna's father is a Valois and quite an innovator. The whole family is like that. It is said you will be united with them yourself before long."

The husband and wife shot quick looks to each other and then to Claire.

"The Lady Isabeau and I have been near-betrothed for some time now," said Aimery smoothly. "Nothing has been settled as yet. I have always thought the arrangements for marriage are best left in the hands of bailiffs and Lombard bankers. Ours have not as yet agreed."

Both Emerico and his wife bobbed their heads in enthusiastic unison. They could see no harm in this; their own marriage had been arranged following these same guidelines. This also helped to explain Claire's presence. If rumor were correct, negotiations for the marriage between the widowed Isabeau of Valois and the Count of Segni had dragged on for three years now. The joining of two such great houses in holy wedlock might be one thing—a complicated question of lands and heritage and dower rights—but a man had other needs as well. And these needs might well be satisfied by a pretty little scribe like the Maid of Foix. It was known throughout Paris that, despite the question of her impending marriage, the Widow Isabeau widely indulged what were politely referred to as her "prerogatives"—and so, they both silently agreed, the Count of Segni should be left free to indulge his as well. Now that they understood this to be his intention, they smiled with new benevolence upon Claire.

This was exactly what Aimery had wanted them to do. It left the field open for his next question.

"Did you by chance know that my sister has married a descendent of Simon de Montfort?"

The Lady Joanna had been reaching for a sweet-meat—her third—but she raised a polite eyebrow and said, "Really? Yes, now that you make mention, I seem to recall hearing something to that effect. Of course, I should really *know* it, but there have been so many noble marriages lately. One cannot keep track of them all."

"Though, of course, any alliance involving your illustrious family is an important matter in the whole of Europe," added her husband hastily, in order to smooth any affront to the family pride of his liege lord.

His wife, taking her cue, agreed with him most readily.

Aimery smiled to himself as Sir Emerico clapped his hands and well trained servants scurried forth from behind the heavy tapestries, this time strutting about with beaten silver trays. They carried brimming pitchers of strong red wine. Joanna began an animated conversation about the virtues of a new glover brought down from Paris.

"The finest kid gloves anywhere," she said reverently, "and the best color—though, perhaps not the best price."

Aimery's interest was not in French glovers.

"I have heard that Raymond Roger of Foix was the most ferocious of Simon de Montfort's adversaries," he said.

"He was considered quite able," said Sir Emerico, his face grown flush from the wine. "Many thought him the most outstanding general fielded by the host in Languedoc, but, in fact, he had few rivals for the title. The Southerners were determined not to fall under the yoke of the Northern Franks, but they were generally independent mountain men and their unfettered ways carried over into their dealings with each other. They could not take orders; they could not work together. Unlike the Franks, who relied on strategy, the peoples of Languedoc trusted in what they considered to be the basic rightness of their cause. They saw no value at all in working together, and we all know the outcome of their foolishness."

"The Inquisition," whispered Claire. Aimery wondered if anyone else had heard her other than himself.

"Of course the Franks won," said the lady Joanna staunchly and with a pious wag of her head. "It was Crusade. They had the good will of God behind them."

"They enjoyed the support of the established powers," replied Aimery. "Sometimes these can be two different matters."

Joanna shook her tight curls but her husband hastily interjected before she had the chance to reply.

"Perhaps you have heard the legend of Foix?" he asked.

"Tell it," commanded his lady wife. She stabbed at marzipan with a jeweled knife. Claire counted eight rings upon the one hand alone. They glinted merrily in the candlelight. "It might amuse our guests to hear the tale," she continued. "Especially Claire, for our lord Aimery has designated her Maid of Foix. Perhaps it will interest her to hear how Raymond Roger encouraged both his wife Phillipa and his sister Esclarmonde to become Cathar Perfects?"

They were back where they'd started; Claire could do nothing about it. And perhaps it was best that she remain silent; that she stop being frightened of what Emerico might tell her, and that she listen and learn.

"They say his reasons had less to do with religious devotion and more to do with his hunger for Loba of Cabaret," said Joanna with a twitter. "She was rumored to be quite a seductress and though all of this happened barely a hundred years ago, it was safe then to entrust your wife and sister to a Cathar convent. There was no burning back then. That came later. That came with Crusade."

Out of the corner of her eye, Claire saw Aimery shift slightly in his seat and draw closer. This tale interested him as well and it occurred to her that he might well have brought her to Foix so that she could hear these local legends.

The rulers of Foix readied for their story, Sir Emerico with his wine and his wife with her sweet.

Emerico took a healthy swallow from his goblet. "They were ferocious battles, absolutely ferocious," he said. "The Christian against Christian fight against the Cathar heretics was the most bloodthirsty ever waged— much worse than those fought against the Saracens in the Holy Land. Simon de Montfort laid this land waste and lit witch fires to guide him on his way through Languedoc. Count Raymond Roger was one of the only ones to field a true resistance. The others, as I said, were too independent; or like the Count of Toulouse, they were too weak."

"A *very* weak man," repeated Sir Emerico. His words were accompanied by a dismissive wave of jeweled hands by both the lord and lady of the castle. "Raymond Roger and his son were different. They were the last of the great Cathar defenders to hold out."

"But there was very little of religion and a great deal of politics to these battles," said Aimery of Segni, whose ancestors were the ones to first foster this Crusade. "The lands were fertile and France laid claim to them, especially after the greatest heiress in this region, Eleanor of Acquitaine married the English King Henry, and laid claim for that island kingdom to share in their possession."

Again Emerico took a healthy gulp of wine. Some spilled from his silver goblet to stain the rich white linen that had been laid upon the table. A maid dropped one of the heaped platters; this brought a stern tsk-tsk from her mistress.

"It was Montfort against Raymond Roger of Foix," said Joanna with a delicate sigh. "What a contrast they made."

Her husband continued, "Simon was married to a truly wonderful woman, Alice of Montmorency, and it is said he derived great strength from his lifelong fidelity to her. On the other hand, whilst Raymond Roger loudly espoused virtue for his Cathar female relations, in his own life he was notoriously lax."

"Don't you mean the reverse?' said Claire. "Was it not Count Raymond Roger who was devoted to his family and Simon of Montfort who was debauched?"

Was this not the way she had always heard them described by Peter?

The Lady Joanna tittered at this; the new Count of Foix laughed outright.

"Oh, no," he exclaimed. "It was exactly the opposite. Troubadours sang songs about the old Count of Foix's roving ways."

"Although I think the word 'debauched' a trifle exaggerated," added his wife thoughtfully. "Perhaps exuberant might be the better term."

Emerico nodded. Claire thought them a most complicit pair. And she was aware that Aimery had leaned closer. He was interested; she could tell.

"But Montfort was not, as you say, exuberant. Alice of Montmorency was the only woman in his life," said Emerico. "I remember my father telling me that she rode right into battle with her husband; she would not be left behind in some castle to wait for his return. They were together in their marriage, hand in hand."

"The way a marriage should be," agreed his wife,

"not like Raymond Roger of Foix, with a wife convented and living openly with his mistress in his castle."

No one noticed Claire's silence.

"Though he really wasn't a *bad* man, just human," said Lady Joanna. "And with a man's human needs."

"Indeed," said Emerico. His wife smiled, as though they talked of an eccentric relation, and not a man whose lands and castle they had usurped.

"He died quietly in his sleep, and is buried here near Foix." Sir Emerico gestured outward, his arms stretched out to encompass all his recently acquired lands. "I must say that through all his tribulations with the Crusade, he managed to maintain an uneasy truce with the Church within his own fiefdom, and could be quite generous to those members of the clergy who were inclined to either overlook his excesses or provide him absolution for them. In the end, it was the Cistercian monks—the very ones who had incited for Crusade in the first place—who provided him a final resting place."

"It was the end of an era, you know," said Aimery quietly. "His passing marked the end of Crusade in these parts."

"And of the Cathar cause as well," said Claire without thinking.

" 'Tis funny," said the Lady Joanna, "how you have all been brought together again. Segni and Montfort and now this Maid of Foix. It is almost as though the old pattern of enmity has been set up again."

Claire spoke quickly. "I have nothing to do with these noble causes. I am peasant born."

"But you *were* born at Foix," insisted Joanna, "and now you serve as scribe at this latest Cathar trial."

"But now and not then," insisted Claire.

*Something was coming. She could feel the shift and*

*the changing as it neared. She wanted to turn back and rush to Peter; to the man who had always meant safety to her, to the one who had always cared. And yet she knew that she couldn't. No going back now. One step, two steps. The future pulled her forward. She couldn't turn back.*

*And she was alone and afraid.*

*Had always been alone, she suddenly realized; had always been afraid.*

Sir Emerico picked up his tale again at the point which he always found the most interesting. "Instead, Simon of Montfort had died in battle, besieging Raymond Roger at Toulouse—and winning. Toulouse was and still is, one of the great commercial centers of this region and its people, both Cathar and Orthodox, were united against the invaders. The counts fought side by side with common peasants; men, women and children fought. They all knew what would happen to them if Montfort held the day. His armies were met with any and every thing the beleaguered Toulousians could hurl down from their walls: lances, javelins, feathered quarrels, even filled chamber pots. One Dominican scribe noted that the small stones from their leather slings blackened the sky like rain clouds. The people of Toulouse fought with the desperation born from knowing that all their lives depended upon the outcome. For all his many virtues, Simon de Montfort gave no quarter in Crusade."

Joanna chimed in. "They could not possibly have won—my husband will tell you why. Indeed, it is legend now how the priests were already hearing confessions and the Perfects giving the Sacramentum when the miracle happened."

"And a miracle it truly was," agreed her husband. "The Frankish invaders had built a great catapult at huge expense. This war machine was so feared that the

Toulousians actually named it; 'Cat' they called it, Montfort's witch's familiar. And they knew if this great Cat were allowed to draw near their walls and breech them, they would all be massacred. The machine had to be destroyed."

"As usual, it was Raymond Roger of Foix who decided to dash down from the citadel one fine morning to do surprise damage. Legend holds that the very pious Simon was praying the morning Mass when his nemesis swept down upon him and he would not stop or hurry the Mass to its ending. This may only be a goodwife's tale, but many swore he entreated God for either death or victory; then he crossed himself, snapped on his steel helmet and entered the blood-fray for the very last time upon this earth."

"Guy de Montfort, Simon's brother and comrade in arms, rode beside him and within moments the tide turned against the men from Toulouse. But from nowhere an arrow found its mark in Guy de Montfort's horse's head just as a second arrow tore through Guy's groin. Hearing their combined screams, Simon leapt from his own horse to come to their aid."

Belatedly, Emerico seemed to remember the women beside him. "I hope I have not offended your sensibilities—especially yours, Maid Claire, as you are convent bred."

Claire shook her head, as Lady Joanna smiled and nodded her husband on.

"This was the act of a good man, but it doomed Simon de Montfort to his death. Someone from the fortress spied him and let fly a mangonel. They say a Cathar virgin sent it forth. The stone struck his helmet, instantly killing him. Simon fell, black and bleeding, so the story goes, and the Crusaders rushed to cover his dead body with a silk cape embroidered in his signet colors. Rumor of his death spread like a brush fire through both the Crusading and the Cathar camps. The truly unthinkable had happened: Simon de Montfort lay dead. The astonishment was so great that at first there was only stunned silence, and then a great roar erupted from the walls of the city: *Lo lop es mort! Lo lop es mort!* The wolf is dead! The wolf is dead!

"From the walls of Toulouse, chimes, church bells, drums, flutes, tabors and clarions beat out ecstatic rhythms for the rest of the day and well into the night.

"It was left to Simon's eldest son, Sir Amaury de Montfort, to gather his father's corpse and carry it out of sight of the revelers. Within a month's time, the great Cat, Simon's hated 'familiar,' was burned and the siege of Toulouse lifted. Later that year, on the first of July, the Crusaders launched one last, desperate attempt against the walls but it was roundly repulsed. Strangely it was the Cathar cause that seemed to die with him. There were no more major battles, only small and scattered uprisings." Sir Emerico paused. "At least it has been quiet until now. William Belibaste is the first Cathar Perfect to be taken in many a long year. We must see what happens as his trial continues."

He looked deliberately at Aimery.

# CHAPTER 20

"All this talk of war and mayhem," said the Lady Joanna with a delicious shiver. "Indeed, we may thank heaven that it is all in the past. Shall we see the tapestry now; the one you came to see, Sir Aimery, the one of Esclarmonde of Foix who looks so like our Maid Claire? " 'Tis truly a remarkable resemblance. I am sure you will all note it."

She led them through the corridors of her castle: past wall sconces with their torches now lighted, past tables laden with beaten silver vessels that had been filled with flowering lavender, past tapestry after tapestry—none of which was the one they sought. The four of them walked alone and without escort. It seemed, to Claire, to take forever: this silent parade through a deserted castle, the four of them accompanied only by the sound of their footfalls against the stone paving and the jingle of the men's golden spurs. She had no desire to view this likeness; indeed, dreaded the thought of seeing it, though she could think of no reason why this should frighten her. The woman was Esclarmonde of

Foix, after all, a great Cathar Perfect. Someone she had always been taught to revere and respect. Yet, even Aimery's presence beside her, walking close, could not quiet the dread that trickled through her. And since the night of Helene's death, she had come to think of Aimery of Segni as a protector, a safe haven; at least she had felt protected within the shelter of his arms.

Then.

Now he walked shoulder to shoulder with Emerico of Foix and he was once again her enemy—a danger to her and to Peter and to all of their plans. Claire sensed this peril, and sensed as well that the danger somehow stretched out from him and surrounded her.

At last Joanna said, "Here it is, in this small room. Hidden away. Indeed, we have no idea at all how this chamber was used in the past."

*As a chapel.*

Claire knew this; perceived it in the still serenity of torchlight flickering on simple whitewashed walls; could almost see the ghostly outlines of the wooden prie-dieu that had graced it; could almost smell the sweet scent of field flowers in scattered jugs. And she could feel its peace.

"There," whispered Joanna. "She stands there."

The hanging was not large, nor had it been prominently displayed. It graced a corner of the chamber and had not they lifted their torches to illumine it, it could easily have been ignored. On her own, Claire might have missed it.

"Here," whispered Joanna. "Is she not exactly like you?"

They crowded about the small tapestry. It showed a woman instructing a young girl; on the woman's lap lay an enormous, great book. Claire had once seen a tapestry like this illumined in a collection of manuscripts that had been sent to the Convent of the Magdalene from the great monastery at Cluny. That one had depicted St. Anne giving lessons to her daughter, the Virgin Mary. This one, though similar, showed something else.

"She looks nothing like me," said Claire, "nothing at all."

The others could all see the striking resemblance between the woman who had died one hundred years before and Claire today. They shared the same clear skin and high forehead, the same shine of green eyes, the same extraordinary witch-red hair.

And the look they wore was the same; perhaps this was the most troubling.

The tapestry's carefully stitched woman sat beside a window, obviously one within this very castle proper, because the craggy hills outside were clearly visible. Claire had crossed the path of them, coming with Aimery for Foix. The book upon the woman's lap lay forgotten; she and the girl, who looked like a younger version of herself, gazed out that window and the woman pointed out through it. Her hand with its slender, long fingers had been exquisitely worked in silk. You could make out diamonds upon them and the glint of a large emerald; simple jewels, really, but not what Claire had been led to expect upon the person of a Cathar Perfect. Peter had always insisted to her that the Cathars had wanted nothing from this world, neither its beauty nor its ornamentation; instead, that they looked with longing toward the next. She had believed him, everything he said.

Yet this exquisitely ornamented woman had once been the true mistress of this magnificent castle. You could sense—*Claire* could sense—that she had been actively involved in buying its beaten silver, in choosing its rich tapestries, in making sure sweet thyme always lay freshly upon its inlaid floors.

And yet she was a Cathar Perfect.

*Telling her something.*

Claire moved closer. She stared at Esclarmonde of Foix's hand as it reached out toward that replicated window, toward the path that led toward Montsegur, the path that Claire had followed on her way coming to Foix—or leaving it.

Still, it was the book that caught Claire's attention and, forgetting the others, she squinted closer at it until she saw the red, double crossed emblem of the Templars on its cover.

Linking the Cathars to the banned Templar Knights; linking this beautiful red-haired woman to Claire's own Father Peter—as his Magdalene.

Perhaps.

Startled, Claire thought she saw a knowing look ripple through the innumerable small stitches that made up the lady Esclarmonde's tapestried face—or was it a warning? Claire wasn't sure; and more than anything else this uncertainty frightened her, chilled her. She had always been so certain in the past.

"No," she said, turning her back upon the Cathar Perfect with her strangely jeweled and pointing hand. "She is nothing like me. Nothing at all."

# CHAPTER 21

*The fire engulfed her. She felt its scorching heat, heard the crackle of its searing destruction. She endured the screams of pain.*

*Maman! Papa!*

*Flames were all around her and she could not see through to them. Still, she could hear her parents, could sense their presence. Yet, she was so small, what could she do? How could a young child help against so powerful a foe?*

*And the fire came for her as well, reaching out for her, blistering her small feet as they danced upon the floor—of what? For an instant the adult Claire stood beside the child Claire in the dream and she saw . . .*

*But the fear of really seeing was too intense. It drove Claire back into the nightmare of her child body. Again she was small and tiny, breathless from the smoke.*

*"Maman! Papa!"*

*Just a whisper from her swollen throat.*

*Gone.*

*No answer.*

*No hope now.*

*"Run! Run from him!"*

*Was that her mother's voice? Claire stopped, looked around. Could not tell.*

*Flames everywhere now. Surrounding her. Laughing at her with their licking red lips. Almost too late.*

*She saw the man then. No, she did not actually see him, but felt him swooping her up. Carrying her away. He held her close, pressing her cheek against the coarse comfort of his homespun robe—so close she could smell the smoke upon him.*

*Then the man started to run. He carried her into the forest; he took her away from the flames. Claire gulped in the fresh, clear air. When she vomited, the man gave her cold water to drink*

*"Our Esclarmonde," he whispered. "Our Magdalene. You will forget this life and every thing in it. We will care for you—Helene and I and the others. We will teach you and see that no bad thing, no fire, comes near you— no, never again. You will be happy. You will be Perfect."*

*The child Claire clung to him.*

The adult Claire woke screaming.

# CHAPTER 22

He knew he could not have her. Aimery, Count of Segni, had not ridden the hard path that led from poverty to prominence by following paths that led nowhere. And Claire of Foix would lead him nowhere. He knew that. He had fashioned a life around duty and obligation and he wore the rewards of this life with proud satisfaction: his suzerainty of Montsegur, his sister allied in happy marriage to a great family, and himself . . .

He looked around him as he walked briskly through Foix Castle. Emerico had already achieved exactly what he himself wanted. He had rebuilt this fortress, made it grand and mighty and strong. He held this land for mighty France. And the Count of Segni knew he would have this same magnificence, even more, once he betrothed himself to Isabeau of Valois.

Yes, once he finally did that.

He had no idea why he'd put it off so long. The excuse he'd always given, his facile tale of Lombard bankers and their machinations, was just an excuse. He knew that. He was the only one to blame for this delay in pledging his troth to one of the most eligible heiresses in Christendom. And for the life of him, he could see no reason for his delay. True, Isabeau was no saint. She was a widow, and an active one; even in the Holy Land, tales of her various escapades had reached him. Gossip and rumors, he had called them publicly, though he easily read the truth in them. Still, Isabeau was rich and noble enough to do what she liked. The tales told about her had never troubled him in the past. No one else seemed to mind either; she could take her pick from eligible names and fortunes. This was the privilege of those who, themselves, claimed name and fortune. Aimery thought of his father, something he had not consciously done for some time now. Remembered how he'd craved power and glory; called them the symbols of a life well-spent. Nothing else had mattered to the elder count of Segni. But, perhaps, other things were starting to matter to his son. Perhaps this was the reason he had never finalized betrothal plans with one of the richest—and most licentious—women in France.

Impossible, thought Aimery. He even smiled at the thought. He wanted no virgin, never had wanted one; pure women came at too high a cost. Instead, he could unite with Isabeau and she would continue to live her own life as he would continue to live his. Their lives would be as they were now: he in one part of the country, she in another. He admired the type of marriage his sister had with Huguet, or Simon de Montfort had shared with Alice of Montmorency. But he wanted nothing like that for himself. It was too confining.

Aimery paused in both his wanderings through this castle and his thoughts and looked out an arrow slit onto the small, formal gardens of Foix. Claire sat there, still as the stone she rested upon. Her hands cupped beneath her chin; her face clouded with thought. Aimery wanted to know what she was thinking. He hungered to know this. Yesterday, she'd heard those stories of Crusade; she'd seen her strange and striking resemblance to Esclarmonde of Foix. And there was more to come, he planned more—more that would piece together the mystery of her life. He seemed more interested in solving this than she was. Watching her, he wondered suddenly and inexplicably if she was frightened.

If she could hold herself still, thought Claire, if she could but withdraw deep within herself and listen, she might find peace. But she was too agitated. She could barely hold her body still; she could not quiet her mind. Yet, when she walked around this quiet garden, her fear grew worse. The gravel on the garden paths bit through her thin shoes like flames. So she sat quietly, hearing every sound: the buzzing of midges and bees among the flower beds, the cooing of doves in the espaliered trees.

She heard Aimery as he drew near.

"I thought we might go down to the village."

He might have offered many masking reasons: a stroll to sample the last offerings of the market, a visit to the Cathedral. Instead he told the truth and Claire was grateful for it.

"The Lady Joanna says there is an old woman living at its outskirts, near the brook. She said it will not be difficult to find her. The woman is rumored to be a witch; this probably means she is well-schooled in being discreet and in holding secrets."

"Secrets?"

Claire had been well-schooled in holding these as

well—wearyingly so. She hesitated for an instant, then gave Aimery her hand and followed him.

As they walked side-by-side, she said to Aimery, "I was told that my parents were killed by the Inquisition, burned because they were Cathar Credentes, which means this was my heritage as well. I have always believed this, and I still do. But lately . . ."

Aimery said nothing, but Claire felt his interest, his patience. She remembered how safely he had tucked her within the shelter of his arms, and she suddenly realized that she longed for that safety again.

Claire took a deep breath, began again; recognizing her true thoughts only as they came out of her mouth. "I never knew differently." No, this was wrong and she changed it. "I never really *wanted* to know differently. I had my life in the Convent. I had Helene. I had . . ."

She stopped herself in time. For some strange reason she trusted Aimery and knew she must tell him the truth, or at least as much of it as she could without endangering the others. But she couldn't tell him about Peter. Not yet. However, there were things she could tell—needed to tell—about herself.

"To me the Cathars believed essentially as Christians do: a simple life lived correctly now ensures a glorious future. And in both there are strong temptations that might seem to block the way. From the little that I know, one belief might seem very much like the other. Indeed, once the Crusade against the Cathars was finished, the great St. Dominic himself set about changing their women's monasteries into convents for the conquering Christians. This did not take much effort on his part."

"But there are differences," insisted Aimery quietly. "You are an educated woman. Someone must have taught you that. The Crusade has been finished barely one hundred years. Everyone still knows the differences in the

creeds. Considering what is known of your parents—
or, at least what is thought to be known—the nuns should
have protected you with this knowledge. You were
young when you were taken, but still not an infant. You
could have already learned something of these mistaken
beliefs from your parents. It seems strange that a knowledgeable woman like Mother Helene would not have
taken great pains to ensure no heretical belief endured
within you."

"I was not interested," said Claire quietly. "And because she believed in them herself."

If what she said surprised him, Aimery gave no indication of this. "You didn't question what had happened
to your parents—or why it had happened or when?"

"It did not concern me."

And Claire realized that it hadn't. She had been
busy with her life and with her studies; too busy to actively mourn parents she had never really known.
Instead, she had plotted and planned with the others to
revenge them and in this way—by keeping their beliefs
alive in Languedoc—somehow restore her mother and
father to her. An impossibility and she knew this.

"It is different now," she continued slowly as their
feet trod a path through the midsummer dust. "I knew
only the convent before. I did not question what Helene
taught me. I had a life purpose; that was enough."

That Helene had taught her not to question the
Cathar doctrine was something Claire could not tell.

*Only lately have I come out of the safe cocoon of my
convent to see the world for myself.*

They were near the village now but Aimery turned
them into a side way that led within the forest. The trail
narrowed and grew steep, and Claire was glad for the
bowering of the trees above her that blocked out the hot

sun and its midday heat. The air smelled of pine and the richness of earth.

Aimery seemed to accept this, seemed to understand. He said, "I cannot judge you harshly for this. Sometimes, lately, I wake thinking that I am living my father's life and not my own; that it was only his ambition that brought me over the Haute Savoie and away from Italy. Yet, Montsegur is a grand place and I am happy in the mastering of it—or I soon shall be."

He patted her hand, an encouraging gesture. For an instant Claire could not tell which of the two of them it was most meant to reassure.

She almost missed the Wise Woman's small cottage, *would* have missed it had Aimery not seen the way. A small, squat structure, covered with green vines, it blended well into the forest that surrounded it. It was a lovely, wooden home, as beautiful in its own simple way as Foix Castle, or even Montsegur. And peaceful; Claire could sense the peace that radiated from it. She was transfixed and it took an instant for her to pull her gaze away toward the neat path of herbs that grew before its waxed oak door or for her ears to pick out the sounds of water running through a distant brook bed.

An inviting picture—but suddenly Claire was not invited by it. Instead she was afraid, filled with the terror that had screamed through her late-night dream. And she would have turned and scampered back up to Foix Castle, but Aimery was beside her and she had to go on.

A very old woman moved out from the shadow of a tree. Dressed in flax cloth, she had a thick coil of snow white hair, and skin tinged brown from years of summer sunshine. She said nothing at first as she examined Claire through clear, dark eyes. Then, still without speaking, she turned and beckoned them to her home.

*She has lived here for many years. She will know.*

At the door, the woman turned back to Claire and her smile was brilliant.

"You look like your mother," she said. "I would have known you anywhere."

# CHAPTER 23

Ever afterwards, in happier times, Aimery would never quite be able to tell just what had happened and when. He would ponder the sequence of events, never quite sure when they had spun out of his control and taken on a life of their own. Yet he realized exactly which pricked stitch had begun the swift unraveling. Yes, he realized that fateful moment fully and completely.

He had kissed Claire.

She had kissed him.

Events had moved on from there.

At least he could honestly say that he had planned nothing and, certainly, he had not seen a wish upon Claire as they emerged from the Wise Woman's cottage into the dense, ripe forest air. Not that he ever viewed this as an excuse. He needed none.

Claire said only, "If she will come, we must bring her to Montsegur with us. William Belibaste's wife will have arrived by now. They must be told. Everyone must know the truth."

Aimery nodded; he, too, knew that this Wise Woman and her knowledge must be carried to Montsegur.

Claire looked at him a moment, her eyes clear and bright, but hiding something. Aimery was convinced of this. He was too instinctive and experienced a warrior not to know when a secret lay hidden behind a maiden's guileless face.

He also knew she had no intention of confiding in him, at least not yet. Still, they had grown close and she considered it. He saw the small shake of her head as she thrust the thought aside. There would be no secret sharing. Claire clearly had other weighty matters upon her mind.

He guessed that the Wise Woman's story had come as a revelation to her, though not as a total surprise. As the woman spoke—slowly and precisely, remembering everything—Aimery had watched understanding etch its way across Claire's forehead with the precision of dominoes falling into place. For his own part, he had never believed that tale of Inquisition burning. The Crusade was a hundred years over now and only flared to life occasionally, even here in Languedoc. The trial of Belibaste had attracted wide attention *precisely* because it was an aberration, something that did not happen every day.

The woman, whose name was Jeanne, ended her tale by saying that Claire's parents lay in the small churchyard behind the Chapel dedicated to St. Anne. To Aimery, this was her most telling disclosure. Everyone knew no burned heretic could be laid to rest in hallowed ground. Their ashes were scattered; their souls consigned.

\*   \*   \*

"An accident," said the woman as they left her. Her voice filled with sympathetic understanding. "A tragic accident."

Claire nodded. She knew better.

"May I take your arm?" she asked him.

Aimery held it out to her and her light touch thrilled him, and brought with it a stern chorus that reminded him of his duty to his family and his name; of his vows as a knight to protect this woman, not desire her.

"They thought me dead," said Claire, walking beside him, once in a while brushing against him on this warm and fragrant summer's afternoon. "They have me buried in the churchyard with the others. I had a brother. Did you hear that as well?"

"Do you remember him?"

*Andre. As dark as she was fair, laughing up at her, reaching out to her.*

"Sometimes. Sometimes, lately, I do."

"Would you like to visit them? Would you like to go there now?"

Claire nodded.

For all the grandeur of its castle, the village of Foix itself was actually quite small; and for years now the Wise Woman had lived just outside its shadow. She knew the place well. The directions she gave to the churchyard were both clear and direct. Aimery and Claire made their way there without misstep. Only children and small animals were not occupied during this busy, pre-harvest day and they were the only ones to stare at them as they walked past. One small boy waved.

The graveyard was old, ancient even. Claire even saw a few tumbled down stones at its far end. Small weed patches sprouted here and there. Still it was a lovely place despite its evident decay. It was still a simple place, meant for peasants and the few village merchants; the nobles of Foix lay safely and eternally at rest within the Cathedral Main. She was from peasant stock, she had always told him that; now he could see for himself.

They knew just where to go. Jeanne's directions remained explicit. They walked silently to a far corner, along which the graves hugged a wattle fence. They approached slowly, Claire beside Aimery, holding his hand.

"It is not what I expected," she said to him. "The only tales told to me—false tales, if what the Wise Woman said is true—involved my parents in a horrible end. The Cathars were said to be peaceful people, but when I thought of my parents, I thought of violence. I wanted vengeance."

*But had she really? Or had she only wanted Belibaste to go free?*

She could not say this to Aimery, not until she heard Peter's explanation. Not until her Father could make her understand.

*The Inquisition burned your parents, but I saved you from it. I brought you safely here and I made you our Perfect and our Magdalene.*

"I never thought they had found rest in such a peaceful setting as this."

Yet they were here, buried beneath four small crosses, placed close together in a shady spot that smelled of fertile earth and growing herbs. She knew she was in the right place. For the first time since coming to Foix, she felt she had come home.

\* \* \*

That night, Claire walked silently through the still halls of Foix, anxious to be once again within the quiet of her own chamber. She walked surrounded by an honor guard of four torch carrying squires and men at arms. Aimery of Segni was not with her; he had stayed behind after the evening meal to discuss the castle's affairs. Claire had been dismissed; her scripting talents would not be needed until the morrow. Yet, Sir Emerico had insisted upon this show of respect. Since the wounding of the priest and the other troubles at Montsegur, no one took chances—even within the solid walls of Foix Castle. The Crusade and the Inquisition had brought more than enough bloodletting to Languedodoc; they did not need more.

*I must get back to Peter. I must hear what he answers to the Wise Woman's tale.*

Her mind trembled under the weight of it, under its difference from what she had always been taught. Peter had always said her parents had died willfully at the stake, not that they had perished through the accidental firing of their small wood cottage. Father Peter and Helene, no—not Helene. It was Peter who had always instructed her; Peter who had fired her hatred of the Franks and the Inquisition, who had insisted on the rightness of the Cathar cause.

But had he lied to her and, if so, why should he do it?

*He tells the truth. He tells the truth. He tells the truth.*

Claire's small feet beat the rhythm of her words through the empty stone halls of Foix Castle.

She remembered what Peter had always told her. The Franks were bad. They were killers and plunderers; they had wreaked a century of horror upon the Cathars before annihilating them. She, Claire, could avenge what they had suffered. More importantly, she could put an end to their suffering forever. She must help Belibaste. She had only to . . .

*Find the treasure! Snatch it for us!*

Peter's voice plucked at her memory.

*The treasure . . .*

That he had always insisted didn't exist.

# CHAPTER 24

"Running a castle is the most boring work in Christendom," grumbled Aimery of Segni to his host. Emerico of Foix was in perfect agreement. They were both warriors and had won their castles through battle. Now they were deeply into the peaceable, but still hazardous, work of settling Foix's accounts. The parchments inching upwards from the floor threatened to engulf their kid-booted ankles.

"'Tis always torture doing these accounts," grumbled Sir Emerico. "I'd much rather be out facing untold hordes of Saracens or at least hawking about."

"But a torture we'd best get used to," said Aimery, looking bored himself. "What have we worked for, if it was not to obtain our castles?"

It was barely eleven by the bells ringing from the steeples, but the day's work had already pitched Sir Emerico well into his second tankard of fine wine.

"The obtaining was one thing," he said, "the living with will be something else again."

"Fought and schemed to obtain would be more like

it," corrected the Count of Segni with a grin, "at least in my own circumstance. I determined upon Montsegur from childhood; within my family it has always stood as a great symbol. I took service with the French king in quest of it."

"And now it is all yours," said Sir Emerico, "just as Foix is now all mine."

"Indeed," said the Count of Segni softly. "Indeed."

He glanced at the leaded window just in time to see a gyrfalcon take flight into the clear blue sky.

Claire sat beside him, her fingers busily writing and then correcting the sums and notes as they were given to her by Sir Emerico.

"Not that there is really much danger in Languedoc," said Emerico with a laugh. "No Saracens, no sieges; this mild speculation of a belated Cathar uprising over William Belibaste seems the only trouble that threatens, and it will pass."

"Bishop Fournier thinks it something more than a menace," replied Aimery mildly. "After the Abbess's death, he considered the matter sufficiently serious to seek answers in Paris."

"And he should soon be back, bringing his puzzle pieces with him." The Count of Foix took another deep gulp at his wine and then shook his head as he turned back to the financial matters at hand.

Claire's quill stopped and then began to scratch its way across the parchment once again.

The boring recital of sums, this time for the selling of the castle's cheeses and honeys, recommenced.

"At least you have the lovely Maid of Foix to help you," said Emerico. "I have but stiff stewards and bailiffs to attend to my matters. Capable, yes—but perhaps with not so pretty a hand at writing."

Claire nodded and smiled briefly, because she was expected to do so. The Count of Foix was lord of this castle and she was his guest. But her mind returned again and again to her parents, to the puzzle of their death and, when it left them, it turned to Peter and Helene, and what they had known and what they had hidden from her. Finally, she thought of Aimery. As she conscientiously recorded the figures for wheat sales and the various tithes from Market Day Faire, she thought of him.

And wanted him.

She realized that she wanted to kiss him; longed to kiss him, and more. Ah, it was too late to want him now and Claire knew this. She had taken certain vows, had professed certain beliefs.

*Not my choice.*

But she still could not tell why it wasn't and really could not understand this voice at all.

After their short meal break at midday, the Lady Joanna wandered in with her ladies and suggested a turn through the orange grove. Aimery had no use at all for another walk with the Countess of Foix, but he happened to glance down and see Claire's slender ankle peeking out from beneath the green silk of her long tunic. The dress was large for her and much too formal for the occasion; it was obviously something that Joanna had discarded because it soured her complexion. But the green was perfect for Claire. It brought out the color of her hair and brightened her bewitching eyes. The dress reminded him of the ribbon he had gifted Claire with and he wondered what had become of it.

He turned to the Lady Joanna and smiled. "I would love to see your orange groves, my lady. It is exactly what might refresh me most."

In fact, he could hardly have come up with a better idea himself. It was not as difficult as he had thought to dislodge himself from Emerico and Joanna. Once she had assured him that although the tress might have originated in Sicily, the gardener who had so skillfully espaliered them had accompanied her from the more fashionable Paris, she was content to leave them to their wanderings.

"We allow the children from the village to come once a week to gather the fruit," said Joanna with an airy wave of her hand. "They can only take what has fallen but you, of course, Sir Aimery, can take whatsoever you like."

"Thank you, my lady," said Aimery of Segni, her liege lord. "You are indeed kind."

Her husband weaved a little bit, an effect of both the wine and the heat, and he needed tending. Joanna bustled him away, leaving Aimery to trail behind with Claire. He took her arm and escorted her to the low brick wall that overlooked the valley. Green and bushy trees lined the graveled walks and oranges dotted their leaves. The perfume of summer hung heavy on the air.

"Beautiful." They neared the precipice and Claire breathed deeply. She did not loosen her light hold on Aimery's arm. It made him feel—protective of her. He knew what was coming, sensed the danger in it, and knew that she did as well. But he did not want to let her go.

Languedoc spread itself below them, a tapestry of granite cliffs, green hills, deep valleys.

"If you look closely enough you can see the mountains that arch down into Italy," Aimery said as he pointed them out to Claire. She still held on to him and he could feel the decided warmth of her body, smell her scent blending into the day's sweetness as she looked up at him.

"Your face lights when you mention Italy," she said. "You must miss it."

"As I imagine that you would miss Languedoc if you were taken from it?"

She paused for a moment, still looking toward the south and Aimery's homeland, and then surprised him with her answer.

"I don't know that I would miss it," she said slowly, "because I've never imagined leaving Montsegur. I never thought I would come even as far as I have come to Foix. Montsegur has always just been a part of me, a part of my duty. The convent of the Magdalene is the only home I've ever truly known and Helene the only mother. I think I would have been the most loathe to leave her. Now that she is dead . . . Of course, there is Father Peter."

"Father Peter?"

"He is one of the priests who ministers to those of us at the convent," she said, but her smile faded.

Aimery briefly wondered about this priest and wondered why the mere mention of him had turned Claire somber. He found that, without knowing him, he resented him for this. Claire so rarely smiled, but when she did, it dazzled Aimery. He wanted that smile again, plotted what he could say next to bring it—and was totally unprepared for what she said to him.

"I want to kiss you," she said, her eyes upon his; not smiling at him, but not looking away.

She surprised him so that for an instant he stepped back from her but then he smiled, held out his hands, heard himself say, "But why?"

Claire hesitated for just an instant, still looking into his eyes, still holding his hand. "Because I want to kiss you. I *choose* this kiss—and more."

Aimery didn't question, didn't answer. Instead he reached across and drew her near him. She felt warm against his chest, so soft, so fragile. She came willingly into his arms, throwing her head back just a little so that her loose hair brushed against her spine. He tangled his hands into it, lifting her head more, pulling her even closer.

Then his mouth was on hers, his lips brushing softly against hers, his tongue tantalizing. And then he was kissing her. She tasted fresh, of cloves and mint and her tongue was soft as silk against his. He felt her heart beat beneath the faded green cloth of her hand-me-down dress.

Kissing him came naturally to her. It was as though, for the first time, her body moved out and enveloped her mind. She felt her arms reach out and draw him near, felt her own hands mingle in the velvety froth of his hair, felt her pelvis tip into him.

"Claire." His voice came to her from a great distance, either deeply from within her or from within him. It didn't matter because he was kissing her, tracing his mouth along the smooth column of her neck, caressing the heartbeat in it. He moved his hand away, hovering near her, and she felt him hesitate. Without thinking, she reached up and pulled his hand down to cup her breast, and pressed it to her as her nipple hardened beneath his gentle fondling. She caught his tongue tentatively at first—and then she drew it deeper. And all the while she exulted because she knew that she, Claire the Cathar Perfect did this—felt this—and that this was her choice.

Their kiss seemed to go on and on, reaching out,

lasting into eternity but really only a few moments could have passed. When Aimery finally released her, Claire slowly became aware of the same hot sun shining down on her, heard the same buzzing midges. In the distance she could see the Lady Joanna walking beside her besotted husband, still holding him up and quietly scolding him. Above her the birds still twittered and the smell of ripened oranges and fresh lavender hung heavy on the air.

Only Claire had changed—deeply, fundamentally—and only she knew it.

# CHAPTER 25

Peter sensed the change upon her. For many years, since the disbanding and burning of his brother Templars, when he had been the only unrepentant left alive, he had depended upon a keen sense of his own preservation. He owed his continued existence to this gift and it had made him good at discerning even a small shift in the wind. He felt one now. From his perch high on the walls of Montsegur, he heard change ringing through the peel of Claire's laughter as the great castle drawbridge clanged down to welcome her and the Count of Segni.

Stealthily listening, hidden from view, Peter suddenly realized that he had rarely heard her laugh before and the sound of it now, coming so close upon Helene's death and Claire's own unexpected journey to Foix, caused the priest's brows to pucker. He wondered what had caused this sudden change. But then, laughter meant nothing. He of all people should know well that a jovial face often masked a treacherous heart. Claire had changed, but he would make no assessment of this change until he had the chance to speak with her, question her, watch her. This was his Claire, after all, and he had guided her and raised her from a child. She would tell him what he needed to know—even without intending to.

And there was nothing that could ever make her turn against him and their Cause. At least of that much, he was certain.

He shifted his position and watched as Claire's pony frisked beside Aimery of Segni's powerful warhorse as they led his honor guard of knights through Montsegur's great portcullis. Peter counted—one, two, three, four, five—sixteen knights, a great number; and then he saw the tiny huddled figure on the back of a small mule. Again his brow puckered; he wondered who this might be. All in good season; he would learn soon enough. Again Claire laughed and the sound of her happiness continued to echo up to him long after the gate had clanged shut once again, closing her within the castle main, with the Count of Segni.

*What had caused this change?*

Peter of Bologna, the great Defender of the Knights Templar, pasted a smile upon his face. He fixed a twinkle in his eyes. Whatever the news from Foix, it could wait. It *must* wait. He could be patient—at least until he saw Claire. At least until they had their words together. After much patient coaxing, William Belibaste had finally told him that the trail of treasure led from Montsegur to Foix—and Claire had just returned from that great fortress. Here she was, smiling and laughing with whatever news she brought from it. Peter could be patient. He had learned this life lesson well in the dungeons of the French King, as he heard the cries and moans of his tortured brethren; as he had cried and moaned himself. Yes, he could be tranquil. Something would happen. It always had in the past.

In the end, she waited to come to him by night, as he had been almost certain she would do. Up the stairs, round the dark corners, just as she always had in the past and just as he was certain she always would do in the future. Peter smiled to himself as he heard her light footsteps, pushed aside the slight uneasiness he'd felt this morning watching her enter Montsegur, laughing and smiling at the young Count of Segni—his enemy, *their* enemy. But then nothing could ever come between him and Claire. He had raised her openly—at least among their brethren—to be the Cathar Perfect, and secretly he had taught her to be the Templar Magdalene. It was too late to change this now. No one could do it.

She slipped silently into the room and Peter smelled the scent of flowers upon her. Roses, he thought, another novelty. He examined her in the dim light from the sconced wall torch, looking for other signs of change. There were few, but these few were significant: the absence of a wimple, the nice dress of blue stuff that she wore, the bright green ribbon that tied her loose hair back. He noted all of it, but not with concern. He was merely curious. After all, she had come, just as he had known she would.

She hunkered down beside him. He opened his mouth to question her about Foix, about what she had learned there—if anything. It had all happened so long ago. He felt no fear. Who was left to remember the death of peasants?

Instead she was the first to speak. "Have you seen Belibaste again? Has his wife arrived?"

Peter had not expected this question; in fact, once he had learned what little he could of the treasure, he had given very little thought to Belibaste while she was away. His wife was of no interest at all. "I have not *seen* him," Peter said testily. He was not used to being questioned. "It is dangerous to go too near him, or to show too much curiosity. His wife is here; Bishop Fournier sent for her and she sees our Perfect."

"I would like to see him as well," said Claire.

"But why, child?" Peter placed a mighty hold both upon his curiosity and his temper. "I've said 'tis dangerous to be near him and if the Count of Segni were to find out, or the bishop . . ."

She drew herself straighter. "I must see him. There are things I need to ask him."

"Why not ask me? Have you not learned everything from me in the past?"

"Yes, I have learned everything from you," Claire repeated. She was silent for a moment, as though considering something. When she spoke again it was only to repeat, "I must see Belibaste."

Peter felt a first small frisson of misgiving. "I will arrange a meeting," he said. "The task will not come easily or cheaply, but it can be done."

"And I must meet his wife."

"She lodges in the village. All know of her there."

"Then I will speak with her," said Claire. She turned away from the priest, moved slightly, stared at the dark walls. "It is urgent that we find a way to free her husband, and for that we will need her help."

Freeing Belibaste had become the most important thing in Claire's life. Indeed, it was the only thing she thought about, or that she would allow herself to think about. She could not dwell on her parents and why Peter might have lied to her about their deaths; she

could not think about kissing Aimery. Since leaving
Foix, Claire had forced herself to wake with the thought
of Belibaste in the morning and to go to sleep plotting
his liberation at night. He must be freed; she must see
to that. It was what they had planned and worked for;
what, she now suspected, Helene had died for. Besides,
it was much easier to think of Belibaste than to let her
mind wander because invariably it rested upon Aimery
and the security of his arms around her and the yearn-
ings, deep and primal, that he aroused in her. Or she
might think of Peter and the darkness that was beginning to swirl around him.

*But why?*

Why would Peter lie about how her parents had
died? If Jeanne was to be believed, her mother and father and young brother had not been killed at the stake.
They had died when their cottage caught fire and
burned down round them. For all its tragedy, their
deaths had been an accident and no grand conspiracy
of an all-powerful Inquisition to stamp out the seeds of
Cathar revolt. Perhaps her parents had not even been
Cathar; there was no proof that they had been. Jeanne
had not thought that they were.

Yet Peter had always insisted that her family were
Cathar Credentes and that those who opposed their beliefs had sought to ground them out and had not
minded grinding her family with it.

He had lied to her; it was that simple. And if he had
lied about such an important matter as that, what other
lies had he told her through the years? What other lies
was he telling her now?

If only she could take this to Aimery. If only she
could talk about it with him.

Yet, that was impossible. Peter might be turning into
her enemy, but that did not make Aimery of Segni her

friend, nor did the fact that they kissed affect the very clear difference between them: she was peasant, he noble; worse, she was a Cathar Perfect and he had been commissioned by the pope and the King of France to put down heretical revolt in Languedoc. If he were to discover the truth about her, if he were to learn her secret, he would be forced to hand her over to the Inquisition and the stake.

No, she could not tell Aimery. Kisses they had shared were not enough to change his mind about his duty to his liege lord and the vows he had taken. He was too honorable a man to let this get in his way.

But she wished that she could confide in him.

Oh, God, how she wished that she could.

Or that the kissing might stop. But it didn't; it couldn't. She wanted those kisses as much as he seemed to— perhaps more so—because to Claire they were novel and vital. With the threat of death hanging over her, they made her feel alive. They made her forget William Belibaste. Aimery's lips upon her brought her back from the loftiness of her Cathar mind to explore the new intriguing intricacies of her own earthly body. She marveled at the way his leisurely tongue along her arm raised gooseflesh and made her shiver in the summer's heat; that his hands running through her hair could intoxicate her; that his lips upon one part of her body could strike such a cord someplace else.

And she was as eager for these kisses as he was. Every chance they were alone, she reached for him, came to rest within the shelter of his arms. Gloried in the fact that she could besot him.

Kissed him.

Loved him.

But not with her newly awakened body.

"Not that," whispered Aimery, as this new and puzzled Claire stared at her reflection in the glory of his eyes. "Not yet."

Claire blinked as she came into the gloom of the Great Hall. Linen hangings had been placed against the windows to keep the late afternoon heat out, but they withheld the light as well. As usual, there were knights and men at arms about, playing at dice, talking, seeking sanctuary from the outside heat. Aimery stood upon the raised dais talking, his bright hair shining through the shadows. He stopped when he saw her, smiled, moved to come down to her. Claire shook her head just slightly; she must first see Minerve, and then she must seek out William Belibaste.

The Countess de Montfort waited for her on the tiny lady's balcony above the Great Hall, surrounded by her children. If anything she had grown more enormously pregnant, though Claire would have thought this impossible.

"Come sit by me," Minerve said, whisking her neglected needlework from a low chair. "We've not had a moment to ourselves since your return. My children long to see you and I must know exactly what you thought of Foix and the Knight Emerico and his fine lady. Is he still as fond of wine as he used to be, or has being in Languedoc proved a curing?"

"Hardly," replied Claire, settling herself. "If anything, he is fortunate indeed to have so many new vineyards at his disposal."

Minerve laughed her merry laugh. "You always put things so delicately. It must be the benefit of a convent education. I'd have called him a drunkard and been done with it."

Claire took the nearest rosy cheeked baby onto her lap. "Then you know him."

"*Knew* him," corrected Minerve, "in Paris before his marriage."

Claire nodded. "His wife seems to be a very great lady. Together they've turned the castle of Foix into a place of marvels."

"It is doubtlessly exquisite," replied Minerve, wrinkling her nose, "but also probably very boring."

"That is precisely how your brother described it," said Claire.

"I imagine he would." The Countess de Montfort's eyes narrowed. "And yet theirs is the life he is preparing for himself. Isabeau of Valois will bring polished silver aplenty to their marriage; intended, of course, to make up for her tarnished name." Minerve shrugged and then unconsciously stroked her large belly. "I'm sure Foix is a lovely, well-ordered castle, but I have no intention at all of seeing it. I should turn green with envy at having actually to witness its well-run and efficient munificence with my own eyes—let alone have my husband see it. Why, Huguet might decide to put me aside!" She laughed at this notion and then continued. "I have tried my best to do well by my brother and his new possession, but you can see the mess I've made of it. My own holding is managed no better. It is overrun with children and people and pups, all coming and going—in short, a terrifying mess."

"I imagine most people would say that Foix is perfectly managed," said Claire thoughtfully. "The plate is polished, the servants in livery, the meals served on time."

Minerve lowered a chastened head then mitigated this by raising a comically cocked eyebrow.

"I was always worried at Foix," continued Claire, "and tread its floors lightly, constantly aware that few peasants like myself had ever been allowed to sleep upon its noble floor. Montsegur is much more welcoming. I have been welcomed here."

Only as she said the words did Claire realize just how absolutely true they were. From the first day she had walked into its grandness, when she had come to commence her work scribing Belibaste's trial, she had felt welcomed here; as though this were truly her place and she belonged.

"At least that," said Minerve with a laugh. She waved an arm that included her children and the airy chaos that surrounded them. Both women laughed as they picked up the castle's needlework and mending. Just as they did, Minerve's youngest child fell over chasing one of the others at knight-play and the two women rushed to shush and quiet him. By the time this was accomplished everyone had completely forgotten the well-functioning tidiness of Foix.

"Has the bishop returned?" asked Claire, innocently enough, as they settled to their stitching once again. She kept her gaze studiously upon her piece of linen.

"Not yet," replied the Countess de Montfort, "and I, for one, am glad of it. His absence means that this absurd trial is stopped as well. Not only does this mean I will not have to share you with it—and this alone pleases me greatly—but I have always felt that this man's inquisition was not only unfair and unjust, but that it also came at a particularly unhappy moment."

"Unhappy for whom?"

"For all of us, but most particularly for my brother," said Minerve. Her thread caught and she paused for a moment as she fiddled it through the tapestry. "It is difficult enough for him to come into possession of a castle with such a clouded history, but to do so right at the beginning of another heresy trial . . . Why, this is bound to call forth comparisons; to bring the thought of what had happened here before freshly again to everyone's mind."

Claire studied her needlework. She knew Minerve would continue on without encouragement. What she didn't know was whether or not she wanted to hear what the Countess de Montfort had to say—and if what she would learn would help her to help William Belibaste.

"They say those who have been killed unmercifully haunt the place where they died," continued Minerve with vigor. "In this case Montsegur, indeed, all of Languedoc will be alive with an idea of vengeance. It is a terrible thing that William Belibaste has been brought to trial. I know many say he is receiving simple justice and that heresy must always be stomped—but why drag a man across two kingdoms to try him, just because his beliefs differ from those normally held? There is something terrible happening here. Huguet senses it and I think Aimery does as well. It is almost as though the both of them are being called back to answer for their ancestors' sins; as though my husband and my brother are being sentenced for something *they* did not do. Only a madman would want this type of witching trial, and I hate it."

Her words seemed to shake the pennons hanging from the rafters of the Great Hall. They rustled above Claire in a breeze she could not feel. Yet, she saw Aimery's cream on scarlet move and another knight's gold on black; and still another's faded blue against silver that was so old and time cracked that its true hues had turned almost white. The combination of standards and colors seemed endless, all hallmarks of the noble families who had laid claim to Monsegur—for a day, for a week, perhaps even for a few seasons—only to lose it in the end. Below her, servants scurried to and fro under the Count of Segni's direction, working mightily to bring the gleam of Foix to the crumbling grandeur of Montsegur. She wondered how long it would be before the Segni colors, too, began to dim and be forgotten.

But at least Bishop Fournier had not returned. She still had time to save William Belibaste. She may have lost everything else, but she still had her mission.

Yet, Minerve could not be forgotten.

"And perhaps," she said, "it is not coincidence that the three families, who were most instrumental in the troubles here last century, have been reunited once again. My husband Huguet, is directly descended from Simon de Montfort who brought the Crusade against Catharism to Languedoc; my brother and I are Segnis and so was Innocent III, the pope who authorized the warring. And you, my dear, are related to Count Raymond Roger of Foix and his sister, Esclarmonde, the Cathar Perfect."

"Impossible," said Claire. A chill slithered through her, as once again the pennons rustled overhead. "My parents were peasants. I saw their graves at Foix. They were simple folk, not nobles."

"Nonetheless, it is bound to be so," replied Minerve. She, too, stopped her needle and turned the full intensity of her gaze upon Claire. "You must be related to the Defender of Languedoc; your presence here makes no sense otherwise. With all of the aggressors represented, then the defender must be recognizable as well. You are related in all of this. We just don't know the how and way of it yet."

"My parents were not heretics," said Claire. She looked away from Minerve now and down to the simple linen stitch she worked. It seemed to absorb her full attention. "They are buried within St. Anne's Churchyard at Foix. They died, by accident, in a fire. They perished within their own village. They were not Cathar—and so neither am I."

As soon as she was certain of the trees' leafy coverage, Claire stopped her lonely amblings and ran. Ran deep into the forest. Summer hung heavy all around her, making the air so thick and heady that she could barely pull it into her lungs; making the earth beneath her feet so rich with mould that it tried to suck her in with every step. It couldn't, though; she flew over it.

To Aimery. To their secret place.

*You are related in all of this. We just don't know the how and way of it yet.*

Minerve could have been right beside her, still whispering her earnest words. They had gone on to speak of Foix again, of the children, of Minerve's pregnancy and the imminent birth of her baby—"A girl. I know it"—but through it all, Claire could not wait to be away. She needed the peace and quiet of the pond and the surrounding forest. She needed to think.

Almost on their own, her feet brought her to the place where she and Peter had met so often in the daytime. She saw the rock he always sat upon and the little indentation amidst the fallen leaves that had been her place. She did not stop there today. She ran on, and over the pounding of her footsteps she could hear the echo of her destination reaching out to beckon her through the still, moist air.

And then she was there.

It was so hidden, this secret waterfall. She had stumbled upon it only by accident when Mother Helene had sent her to pick wild berries in the forest and she had lost her way. It had startled her then, just as it did now— an unexpectedly beautiful, serene curtain of water that shimmered from the rocks above her into the glistening pool at her feet. The convent rules had been strict and her life quite circumscribed within its walls, but still over the years Claire had managed to sneak from her duties to seek this place and to be alone—except that Aimery had found her here.

He would find her once again. She knew it.

She doubted that anyone else even knew of its existence. Or if they did, it was a fantasy she held that they did not. Certainly she had never seen evidence of another's being here; had never seen footprints in the ground or a trampling of water grasses along the pool's edge. Instead, it had always been like this: the shimmering water; the soft enclosure of the rocks and the forest; a bright blue, cloudless sky overhead. The pond itself was tiny; it had always reminded her of a miniature lake, though it was barely the span of three grown men from one side to the other.

For some reason, she had never told Helene of this place, nor Peter. It had been the one secret that she kept from them. She didn't know why she'd done this, still she was grateful, now, that she had. It meant that she was alone. No one knew where she was; no one could find her, except Aimery—if he looked.

And the pool invited her; just as it had the day she had floated on its surface in his arms.

She kicked off her soft leather pattens and dipped a toe into the water. It was cold and crisp as silk against her skin, just as she remembered it. She could settle into it and find oblivion, and she wanted that oblivion. She wanted—needed—to stop thinking. For the first time in her life, she needed to *be*.

Claire quickly undressed, hung her simple garments on a low tree branch and waded into the water with long strides. The hairs on her arm bunched in shock at the cold but she was grateful for this. It pushed everything else but the thought of this place and this moment from her mind.

The water was so clear that she could see beneath the waterfall's bubbling on its surface, to the rocks and plant life at its bottom; and it was so deep she could lie quite still upon it and be carried along by its soft eddies. She lay back on it, the way Aimery had taught her, and let herself be caressed; looking up through incredibly green leaves to an impossibly blue sky, with just the barest tracing of white clouds upon it. She heard the splash of a fish and felt the ripple as he passed near her. She smelled lavender and rich earth and from somewhere far away, the deep, wintry scent of pine.

She floated.

Another fish; another ripple. She caught its silver streak in the sunlight and as she looked down, she caught sight of her own body, cool and white, resting on the clear water. She looked away quickly, as she had been taught to do. The body was not to be regarded, not if she was to be a Cathar Perfect. She must look up and beyond.

*Not my choice.*

But she was not a Cathar Perfect anymore, and perhaps she never had been.

It took effort but she forced her gaze down to look through the clear water and at her body. She looked at the small rounded shape of her breasts, at her arms stretched wide, at her hands splayed out beside her, at her legs, at her ten toes. She looked at the tangled, small nesting that marked her woman's entrance. It took a surprising effort to do this—to watch, to look, and to learn. More than once she had to push through her own strong resistance in order to really see her own body, to see the changes in it—as she thought of Aimery. Certain parts of her hardened: others grew soft and pliable as wax. The upper part of her thighs actually seemed to melt and become as transparent as the water.

The thought of him did this to her.

But he was *real*—whole and strong, a man—and so his actual presence did more.

She missed that presence, as she thought about the feel of his mouth upon hers, the gentle touch of his tongue against the heartbeat at the base of her throat. Claire caught her breath, and remembered how she had caught it once before, when first his arms had encircled her; remembered how she had felt safe here with him as her body warmed the water that nestled it.

*If only I could tell Aimery.*

That was a dangerous thought and she knew to put it firmly aside. There could be no telling Aimery. He might kiss her; she might kiss him; but there could never really be trust and communication between them. If she told him one thing she would have to tell him all the others. She would have to tell him about Montsegur's secret Cathar cell and her place in it; she would have to tell him all about Helene and the mission they shared; she would have to explain about Peter and expose him. And she could never expose Peter until her suspicions became certainties—and perhaps not even then. He was her Father, after all; the only family she had left. But most of all, she would have to convince Aimery why William Belibaste must be freed. And she knew that no kiss from a peasant could ever make the noble Count of Segni see the necessity for this. The force of his name and his responsibility would compel him to do as his ancestors had done before him, so he would burn Belibaste for heresy and all the hidden Cathar cells throughout Languedoc would rise in rebellion against him. Peter had told her this and, although she was beginning to have her suspicions concerning him, Claire knew that Peter had not lied about this—because Peter wanted the bloodshed.

She knew this suddenly and without question, and the truth of the realization made her long for Aimery once again. The skin on her arms crawled together and she was frightened—oh, so frightened.

No where to go.

No one to trust.

Except Aimery—and Aimery, Count of Segni, was her enemy. It would be his duty to burn her on the stake beside William Belibaste if he knew what she truly was, and what she truly prepared.

The sky had deepened toward nightfall by the time she finally made her way to the bank and walked through the high green weeds that hid the pond. As she reached for her apron to dry the drips from her hair, she thought she saw movement, the flash of silver. But when she looked around there was nothing. A trick of the light, she decided.

She held her head back, shook it gently and relished the feel of her own hair against her own spine. For an instant, she closed her eyes, thought of Aimery; then she reached for her tunic and her other garments and put them on slowly, one by one, smelling the sweet scent of roses that clung to them and loving the woman she had become.

She had turned toward the path and was almost upon it, when she heard movement again. Felt nearness.

Claire whirled to the sound and the feeling. And there was Aimery before her.

He was smiling, and holding out a very ripe peach.

Claire surprised herself by smiling back—and reaching for it.

# CHAPTER 26

"I probably should say I've just arrived and that, of course, I didn't see you in the pond. It would have been wrong to look upon you. Not chivalrous." Aimery paused. "But if I said that, I'd be lying. I've been here for quite some time now—watching you; though reveling in you might be the more accurate way of putting it. At first I thought that I should just slip away; failing that, the least I could have done was make myself known. I did neither. Instead I watched you."

They stood face-to-face at the edge of the pool. Claire shook her head a bit to shake the water dampness from her hair, and to give herself time to think. But she couldn't think, at least not clearly; she was too captivated by Aimery's eyes. They were so clear, so brightly blue that to Claire they looked as though they might shield heaven.

"I wanted to see you," Aimery continued quietly, "the real you. Not what has formed you and made you what you seem to be."

"And what do I seem to be?" She was curious. He

didn't answer and after a moment she tried again. "But do you think you managed? Did you really see *me?*

"I saw enough," he said. And then, "Are you offended?"

She thought for a moment.

"No," she said finally. "Sometimes I think I'd like to see *me*, too."

He smiled at this, just a little. "You are such a mystery, my Claire," he said. His voice was low, husky even, and he was standing so close to her that Claire could feel the sweet whisper of his breath against her cheek. Something told her to move away, to put distance between the two of them. But she didn't.

Instead, she held her breath, closed her eyes, stayed where she was. Being near Aimery was like being within the pond once again. The constant fear left her, and all the confusion and turmoil. She didn't worry about what she should do or what she shouldn't do when Aimery was with her. She didn't consider her mission; she didn't think about being Perfect. Life became very simple when she was with Aimery. She breathed. She lived. She became happy.

She reached out toward that happiness now and then checked herself.

"May I have some peach?" she said.

"Of course you may," he answered.

He spread her discarded apron beneath a willow's shading, settled her down first and then himself and then pulled his jeweled knife from its sheath. The blade glinted in the last of the day's sunshine as Aimery raised it and sliced smoothly and effortlessly into the peach's warm flesh.

Claire reached out cupped hands to catch the fruit

before it fell onto the forest floor; but Aimery shook his head, drew it back.

"No," he told her. "Close your eyes."

She shook her head, instantly alarmed.

But he said, "Trust me." And she did.

Claire eased her eyes shut and as she did, her moist lips parted.

For a tantalizing moment she felt—nothing. The earth stopped and there was no motion, no sound. She was tempted to peek through her lashes, to whisper for Aimery, but instead she stayed perfectly still.

Then she felt his fingers ply gently at her lips with the peach's sweetness. She opened wider and felt the ripe fruit dissolve within her mouth; felt its honey coat her tongue and slip down the inside of her throat.

Claire smiled.

"More?" asked Aimery.

He bent to take his knife to the fruit again but Claire stopped him. She laid her slim hand upon his arm. "My turn," she said.

She took the knife and easily wedged out a small piece of fruit.

"Now 'tis your turn to close your eyes."

She saw Aimery hesitate just as she had done. But in the end he lowered his lashes and parted his lips—just as she had.

Claire ran her finger over the fruit then slowly brought it closer to Aimery. She placed it delicately beneath his nose; ran it back and forth, not touching his skin with it but coming very close. She was having fun with this, playing; but he surprised her, swooping up to take both her hand and the moist peach into the recesses of his lips. Claire yelped, then laughed outright and the sound startled a nestling flock of starlings into the sky. But Aimery did not release her. His hand moved up to capture her wrist and he held her fingers firmly to his mouth while his tongue lapped the fruit's juice slowly from all five of them.

Claire couldn't help herself. She moaned.

"You are a mystery," he whispered.

Claire shook her head. No more mystery and no more hiding, at least for this instant. She wanted to be known.

He smelled fresh and warm as he drew near her; like sunshine should smell, she thought, only better. But by now she had kissed him often and was familiar with the rich aura that emanated from him—a mixture of fine soap and rich leather and man. And something else—something new, something hinted at before but never really there.

*Love. He loved her; she could tell.*

She nuzzled nearer; wanting to fill her nostrils and her being with this new element of Aimery, but he hesitated. Drew back.

"Claire?" he said. His voice was puzzled but she refused to open her eyes to see this puzzlement upon his face. She didn't want him pulling back, wouldn't have it. This was finally her choice. She wanted Aimery and she reached up, her eyes still tightly shut, and drew him near.

She parted her lips so that Aimery's tongue could find its home within her mouth and—God!—but he tasted good. His lips smooth as silk; his breath warm and still hinted with peach. She arched closer; she could barely have enough of him. Never, before Aimery, had she ever felt like kissing a man, like loving him; but this felt so right.

*Loving him.*

"I love you," she whispered.

Again she felt him hesitate. Still she refused to look up and see that hesitation in his eyes.

"I love you," she said, "I didn't say that you had to love me."

"It's not that," he said. But it was and Claire knew it. It didn't matter to her though. Being with Aimery made her feel safe and secure; made her feel special and not Perfect. Perfect could wait for another day.

*This* was her choice. *This* was what she wanted.

"Just this once."

Instinct, old as time itself, made her move her hands along his spine, made her draw his hand to her breast. Now it was his turn to moan as he traced his fingers lightly across her damp clothes until they could both see her nipples harden and reach out to him in the twilight. His tongue followed his hands as he gently removed her tunic and her undergarments one by one. She gloried in the feel of his body, the length and hardness of it, as it pressed against hers. His touch enlivened her, made her a new person—more complete, more whole, more aware. She was acutely aware of the waterfall tinkling into the stillness of the forest's pool. As his lips caressed the heartbeat of her throat, she could hear the drone of insects in the grass around her; and when his hands slipped downward, deeply downward, she briefly opened her eyes to the star-filling sky above her and to the heady perfume of lavender and honeysuckle and new grass. If she listened, really listened, she knew she could hear it stretching up and out from the earth.

When she looked down she saw the whiteness of her own skin gleaming against the forest's deep, night-muted greens as she lay molded against Aimery and as she felt his touch.

She heard a moan and it was a moment before she

realized that it had come from her, that it had erupted from some deep, secret part and that it was the result of his hands upon her body. It had come from the part she had been taught was most shameful, but she gloried in it now, just as she gloried in Aimery's soft encouraging words.

"You are so beautiful," he whispered. "I could be with you forever."

Claire, the Cathar Perfect, reveled in the hardness of him; gloried in his manhood as it pushed against her thigh.

"Beautiful Claire." He kissed the words over and over again into the delicate flesh at the crook of her arm. "As clear and fresh as sunshine."

"I never knew that anything like this could exist before," she answered back and the words caught upon another rush of ecstasy as his fingers moved down to probe deeply into the niche of her womanhood.

"Claire, are you certain?" His question rasped against her cheek and he hesitated, would have stopped, but Claire drew him back again.

"I have never been so certain of anything before in my life." And it was true. She wanted Aimery, wanted him desperately. She had her mission; she had to free Belibaste but the strength she felt when she was with him, and the security, were her shields in the night. It was her mission—but Aimery was with her. She felt that, and when all of this was over, maybe she could tell him then. Maybe he would understand.

But for now she could be with him, become one with him in this glen with the sound of the waterfall playing behind them, and the busy chatter of night insects, and the soft stroking of a breeze through the leaves overhead.

"Certain," she repeated.

"It might hurt you," he whispered. "I don't want to hurt you, but I may."

"You could never hurt me."

He didn't. He entered her slowly, gently; for a long while lingering with the tip of his manhood teasing pleasure from her secret parts. Claire, lost in the honey of her own passion, instinctively raised herself, drew him in deeper, and then moaned with pleasure—over and over again, all the while Aimery drove deeper into her womanhood and into her heart.

Until suddenly she felt the earth move without her and within her and her body shattered into a million scintillating pieces, as bright as the stars she saw above her when she opened her love-drunk eyes. Then once more Aimery was kissing her, bringing her back together again, making her whole once more.

"And I am whole," she whispered, into his shoulder, "I am home."

And it was perfect.


Afterwards . . .

She must have slept for a moment, maybe longer, but she awoke to Aimery leaning over her, and his face in the starlight was so anxious that she knew what he wanted to say. Claire raised her fingers to his forehead and smoothed out its wrinkles with her own hands.

"I wanted it," she said. "My choice."

"You don't understand, Claire." His voice had the earnest tones that he probably used when explaining some particularly hazardous moves to his men. Claire smiled to herself. She wasn't one of his men. She was a woman now. He had made her one.

*My choice.*

Aimery continued, his words whispering through

her splayed fingers. "You were a virgin and I took you. I've wanted you. I love you. But I should never have taken you here. I should have thought . . ."

She couldn't have him ruin this for her; couldn't let remorse or should have beens get in the way.

"No, Aimery," she said, and she was surprised by the fierceness in her own voice. "We aren't going to think. I am not a child. I know what I am doing, and loving you is what I choose to do."

"I love you," he whispered. "I don't quite know what I should do with that, or what it should mean. But I do love you. I pledge you that. And I will let that light lead me."

Claire nestled close against him, held him to her heart.

And for the first time in her life she realized that she felt safe—safe within Aimery's heart where nothing could touch her. He had been honest with her; not promising her the moon or marriage but giving her his love.

For right now—and maybe forever—that was enough.

As she lay on her apron that smelled of roses and the scent of their lovemaking enfolded her, Claire felt whole. For one precious moment there was no William Belibaste. There was no deceit.

# CHAPTER 27

Yet Belibaste must still be saved.

It was just past midnight, the usual time when they met with the others, but Claire and Peter were alone in the dark Cathar cell.

"So he has kissed you," said Peter. He looked closely at Claire and suspected that more had happened—very much more, and in the last few days—but, as usual, he kept his keen observing to himself. She was changing, and changing swiftly, though the transformation might prove useful to him in the end.

"Where are the others?" asked Claire, ignoring what he had said to her—another sign of change. "You sent word that we would plan for Belibaste's escape. You said we should all be here."

"As indeed, we are," said the priest. He waited for his meaning to grow clear. "We are all that is left. The others have been frightened away."

"After Helene's death?"

"Before it, actually," said Peter truthfully. "William Belibaste's capture and his trial have proved to be—unnerving, shall we say. It has plucked the courage from a great many who only vowed to follow him through hell itself. However, now that Helene has died and Belibaste's death seems imminent once the bishop returns and the trial continues, it seems that martyrdom is not the blessing that it once appeared."

Claire sat across from him, dressed once again in the simple, white nun's clothes she had always worn. Only the flash of her loose, red hair marked the difference in her since those first balmy days of summer that had witnessed the beginning of Belibaste's Inquisition. But the changes in that time had been considerable and were not limited to a freeing of her hair or the reversion to old habits. Peter, the great Knight Templar, knew this.

"I thought I would have seen more of you since your return from Foix," he said to her.

"He has kept me busy." Claire looked up at him and then quickly away. *Doubtless, grateful, thought Peter, that any guilty blushing is hidden by this dim light.*

"The Count of Segni keeps me occupied," she continued, "with scribing the changes he wishes to make to the estate. He knows I speak the peasants' dialect and he finds me useful in making certain they understand his instructions for the farming and for the use of the lands. That is all. He says he means to keep me busy with these matters until the bishop returns."

"This is as it should be," said Peter. Even his voice seemed to contain a benign twinkle. "But has he mentioned anything about the trial? Has he said when exactly the bishop will return?"

"Bishop Fournier sends word that he will return directly, within the next few days. My lord of Segni tells me that he is investigating a connection between the trial here and the outlawing of your own Knights Templar.

He seems to believe there is some connection between the two."

*Was she studying him? Was she looking for a reaction?*

Peter smiled, forcing the same smile into his voice. "There is no connection. What happened to my beloved brother knights destroyed both them and our Templar cause. I was the only one left alive who did not recant, the only one to escape. Fournier is foolishly wasting his time if he tries to make some connection between events here and what happened so many years ago in Paris." He paused and listened for a moment to the slow drip, drip of hidden water oozing through the walls. "But our bishop is a sly one. I have never trusted him."

"We do not need to trust him in order to free Belibaste."

Peter of Bologna looked up at this. "And are you still interested in William Belibaste? Do you still mean to help me free him?"

"I have never faltered in my determination," she said quietly. "It is the one thing that remains true for me."

Peter strained slightly forward, but, try as he might, he could not read her expression through the cell's gloom.

"I wondered . . ." he said musingly and then he shook himself slightly, made up his mind. "His wife is here; she waits only for the bishop's return to make herself known. She sees him though. She has told me of his condition."

"May I see him as well?" asked Claire. "Can you arrange it?"

"Her name is Yvonne," continued Peter, after a lengthy pause. "She is shy, keeping to herself as you might imagine. She is frightened that the witch fires might eventually burn for her as well. But, yes, I will arrange for a meeting. Leave me to it. In a day, two at most, I will bring you together. Now run on to your prayers and your sleeping, my dear child. You must stay fresh around Aimery of Segni. We are the only two left now and we must know all that we can in order to effectuate the Perfect's escape."

Claire nodded and began to gather her skirts and to rise from her low stool. Suddenly, Peter reached over to lay his gnarled hand upon her fresh young one.

"I am so glad you have not deserted me," he said to her. "I am so glad that we two still mean for William Belibaste to be freed."

But was she still with him?

Peter sat back in his wooden chair, his face knitted in thought, long after the sound of Claire's footsteps had finished echoing back to him.

Clearly, she still had great interest in seeing the Perfect freed but she had said nothing of the Cathar revolt that should accompany it, and they had plotted and dreamed of this together through all her young life. Now she seemed to think that Belibaste's liberation would be the culmination of their goals, instead of only its beginning. Once they had effected the spectacular escape that he, Peter, envisioned, then the Cathar cause would indeed be strong again in Langeudoc. Not only would the recently defected return to them, but they would bring others with them, thousands and thousands more. Peter was certain of this. He was so close now, so close to finding the key to it all; all he needed was the clue he was certain Fournier would fecklessly bring with him, and then he could find the Cathar treasure and with that William Belibaste would be spectacularly freed.

Failing that, if William Belibaste were to die . . .

Peter stopped, cocked his head, listened attentively to the dripping of the water.

A novel thought, that—Belibaste's dying—and one he had not explored before but perhaps it might prove useful. He had only envisioned his ends served by the means of Belibaste's escape and a subsequent revolt. But circumstances had changed drastically since those early planning days. First Helene and now Claire . . .

Peter shook his head, amazed at the weariness that overtook him. Helene was one thing, a nice woman, useful even; but Claire was something else again. She was his secret Magdalene, destined to be the greatest of all the Cathar Perfects. Through many long seasons, he had religiously groomed her for this role, for her place in the world that waited for them. The thought that she could so easily give up all he had striven for through so many cold, hard years pierced through him like a knife. For an instant he hated Aimery of Segni, hated this usurper with a passion he had not felt in years; indeed, that he no longer thought he possessed. However, Peter soon got hold of himself once again. Hatred was a white hot emotion; revenge was something bitter cold. And he was used, now, to the cold. He would deal with Aimery of Segni eventually, also with Claire.

He smiled. She would be his Magdalene once again. Perhaps no longer a Cathar Perfect, but the original Magdalene had been no virgin. Peter smiled at the thought. It was not too late. They could still conquer and then rule, but before that happy time there were still many things that needed attending. He rose slowly from his wooden chair and made a careful way to his waiting bed. Outside the Abbey's peaceful walls, a cock crowed a welcome to the dawning day.

Jacques Fournier lingered on in Paris as one hot August day melted into another. Claire, as Aimery's scribe, received many folded parchments from him, red sealed and signeted with the bishop's ring of office. She passed these on immediately to the Count of Segni. She did not want to know their contents. He told her anyway.

Jacques Fournier had discovered a link between this case and a most mysterious man. He would bring the information with him when he returned. He hoped that all proceeded well in his absence, that daily affairs at Montsegur progressed and that there had been no more violence.

"I, for one, am doing very well indeed, at Montsegur," Aimery whispered into the halo of her hair, into the long white column of her neck.

He seemed to glory in her, and Claire had never been gloried in before. She allowed herself to enjoy the strangeness of it, and the sensation. She knew they would be brief. Once Belibaste was freed, she would have to run away, have to start a new life in some village far from Languedoc. There would be no choice about that. By freeing the Perfect she would lose Aimery for certain, but she knew with a deep knowing that William Belibaste *must* be freed. It was the one point of certainty that she brought from her old life into her new. Quietly, secretly, and without the need for further death, Belibaste would be liberated. The way to accomplish this would present itself if she but waited for it, and watched. Claire felt this in the depths of her heart. His liberation, her first mission as Perfect, would also be her last.

Afterwards . . .

Afterwards she would know what to do as well.

But for right now she would love Aimery; love him dearly and passionately. She would glory in his body, as he gloried in hers, and she would find safety in his soul. She lived for the moments they could be together at their own special place beneath the trees and with the waterfall singing in the distance. She had no idea what he felt for her and did not want to know. Once or twice, after they lay content and satiated, he would lean upon his elbow and trace her lips with a blade of grass and he would try to broach the subject of his feelings, of his plans. Claire lifted her fingers, placed them upon his mouth. She did not want to know.

"You are the strangest creature ever I've met," he said more than once as he looked down upon her in the dappled sunlight. "Usually 'tis the first thing a woman wants to know—if she is loved or isn't."

"It doesn't matter to me," said Claire, and she meant it. "Things are as they are; you are noble, I am not. This cannot change."

"But you should let me state my feelings," he said and there was just the trace of annoyance in his bright eyes. His irritation puzzled Claire; she wondered where it came from. But she shook her head anyway.

"Let us leave things as they are."

How could Aimery love her if he did not *know* her? And Claire could take no chance of revealing either herself or her plans to him. She must keep these within herself, hidden deeply inside. So instead of responding to him, she kissed away Aimery's questions. She had spent her life living other people's choices. Freeing William Belibaste was her own choice, her own responsibility, and she could not share it with another. Not even the man she loved.

She would always recall these full, slow days of August before the bishop's return from Paris with wonder and with love; and she had the added pleasure of knowing that they were special even as she lived them. A new universe was opening to her, a universe abundant with scent and feeling and being. She had never paid much attention to the world in which she lived and now she was finding that it contained heaven.

The warmth of summer enveloped her and the strength of her relationship with Aimery. They were rarely separated, meeting near the waterfall after he was done with his duties as Montsegur's seigneur and she had finished with her tasks as its writing scribe. He would come to her from the kitchens with a willow basket filled with cold chicken or roast meat and bread, wild greens and sweetmeats. They would dip a silver tankard into the icy stream and Claire would watch the waters condense upon it and then lick the small, melting droplets with the very tip of her tongue. They would pick fruit from the tree and Aimery would slice it for her with his jeweled dagger and slowly feed it to her, just as he had done the first time they had come together.

And they would make love. Over and over again, they would make love.

He would run his tongue and his hands along the curve of her body, his touch dissolving her and forming her anew. At first, she lay passively beneath his touch not knowing quite what she was expected to do. Aimery guided her with his voice and with his hands and Claire proved an apt pupil. She concentrated upon him, listening as his heartbeat quickened, thrilling to the intake of his breath. Rejoiced as his cry joined with hers as together they found union and release.

For the first time in her life, Claire felt powerful. All the strength that Peter had promised would be hers as he rigorously educated her to be Perfect, she now discovered in the love she felt for this one man.

And he loved her, she knew it, *felt* it with some deep, unschooled knowing; but she never questioned him about his feelings for her. She did not dare. These glorious days would all end soon enough and Claire wanted—*needed*—this time of abandonment and feeling. It must last her for the rest of her life.

He had bought manuscripts while on Crusade in the East and he showed them to her, bringing them out in their leather satchels, unwrapping them one by one and spreading them out before her. There must have been twenty of them, at least. He brought them out of their trunk and shared their rich colors and their perfect calligraphy and the infinitude of knowledge that he knew they contained.

"And I have more," said the Warrior Aimery of Segni. He looked shy, as though his own interest in such a peaceful and beautiful enterprise both surprised and baffled him.

The intricate beauty of the Oriental manuscripts fascinated Claire, the Latin scribe.

"I've no understanding at all of Arabic," he continued, encouraged by her interest. "None at all. I carted them back because I found them lovely. That was my only reason."

He did add that Isabeau had thought their carting a waste of space.

*Better used for perfume or gold ornaments, something of value, she had scolded.*

Instead Claire said, "Oh, indeed, they are beautiful. I only wish my work were half this grand." She examined his treasure with care and awe.

Aimery heard the pleasure in her voice and he smiled

up and into the sunshine. She could not know, and he would not tell her, that he planned every one of their encounters. Late at night, as he tossed upon his soldier's bed, thinking of her, longing for her, he framed within his mind the small things he would do for her, all to place a smile upon her serious face, all to hear her laughter. The gift of a peach, the picking of a flower, she was grateful for everything and she told him so— told him so and meant it. He knew. So he planned each moment of these blessedly free days that they could be together. He planned the food they would eat, the walk they would take, the long banks of flowers along their path. He searched out a secret narrow pleasance that overlooked the whole of the valley that led outward and away from Montsegur to Foix, and another that Haute Savoie, the gateway into his beloved Italy.

Once he discovered her love of his manuscripts, like a great mummery master, he meticulously plotted these out for her as well.

They sat beneath a spreading oak with sun dappling down through leafy branches onto a parchment discourse on Saladin, which was Aimery's favorite of them all. It concerned the Eastern ruler's close relationship with his enemy, Richard Lionheart. And you could individualize them both so well: Saladin the Oriental prince and his English counterpart, both in rich blue samite with the sun and moon embroidered upon them in gold and silver threads.

"They were so much alike," said Aimery to an attentive Claire, running his long, elegant finger along the smooth surface of the manuscript. "Both were cultured men who looked upon even war as a chivalrous action. They shared the same essence; they looked out at life with a shared wonder and goodwill. I remember reading once, in an old manuscript in an abbey library in

Jerusalem, that the Turks called the Christian soldiers iron men and hated them for the invincibility that their armor seemed to give them. But Saladin, their ruler, did not feel that way. He wanted to learn from the foreigners. He wanted to take in everything he could."

Claire looked through the manuscript until she came upon archers and knights whose silvery armor glimmered back on the page. She said that it was odd to see these foreign images of such a great crusade, such a western undertaking.

"Richard Lionheart and Saladin were enemies with less in common than William Belibaste and Bishop Fournier and yet the two rulers managed to respect one another and to build a type of friendship," she said.

Aimery opened his mouth, ready with a quick explanation as to why two princes, though of differing beliefs, could build friendship and yet a bishop and a peasant, who shared the same basic religion, could not. But he realized suddenly that was just exactly what they were: quick and ready explanations, which had little to do with the simple truth. Instead he heard himself say, "Bishop Fournier is a just man. He will seek justice here. This trial may be wrong and it is certainly wrong to want a man such as William Belibaste locked away forever, but we must wait for the bishop's return. We must hear what he has to tell us."

A dirty and weary court messenger arrived at the next day's dawning with word that the bishop would reach Montsegur upon the morrow. A second missive that the messenger, a Cistercian monk from within Fournier's own bishopric, was secretly delivered to the Count of Segni later in the day. It told of an interesting link that Fournier would explain upon his arrival. He

begged the Lord of Montsegur to grant him an early in-
terview.

But, for Aimery, this would all take place upon the
morrow; today—this last free day—he would spend
with Claire. He was determined upon this.

He sent formal word to her convent requesting the
Maid of Foix to join him at the wicket gate after midday prayers; this was their usual time together as the
knights slept off the effects of their noontime wine and
the village and its inhabitants lay sluggish in the heat.
But he and Claire had their pool to cool them and their
combined bodies to warm them. Afterwards, they
could walk along their pleasance and look out and
away as they always did.

He got through his business quickly and was waiting for her as she walked up the pathway from the convent. He sighted her from some distance away and
enjoyed watching her small steps raising clouds of dust
and seeing sunlight captured in the glorious aureole of
her hair and blazing out from it. She smiled shyly as
they fell into step together and he thought, suddenly
but yet again, how different she was from Isabeau who
would have greeted him with a wink and slyness after
what they had shared. Not Claire. It was as though
their lovemaking had not touched the pure core of her,
though he knew he had gone more deeply into Claire's
being than he ever had into that of his near betrothed.

Bishop Fournier had noted an interesting postmark
to the brief missive sent to Aimery announcing his return. The South, Acquitaine and all of Languedoc, must
still be brought into submission to the Crown of Paris
once and for all. The king was determined upon this, as
was the pope in Rome. There could be no more threat
of insurrection and revolt. It was Aimery's duty to see

that this happened, said the bishop in a short but telling postscript. He must wed the South to Paris, if he meant to keep the suzerainty he had striven for. He must marry Isabeau without delay. Without realizing it, Aimery grimaced at the thought.

"What's wrong?" asked Claire as they laid their ornately embroidered linen on the grass. Aimery shook his head. He felt the guilt of it, but this was not something that he could share. Of course she knew of his intended betrothal—everyone did—but he could not tell her the secret of the conflict it raised within him. She would not understand. How could she? Sometimes he had the damnedest time in understanding it himself. Isabeau was everything, represented everything, which he'd always wanted.

*But I love Claire.*

The thought was no surprise. It had been building within him, becoming clearer with each passing day. Aimery knew this as they took their usual places—he with his back to the huge trunk of a gnarled oak and she with hers against a slating of rock—and began to eat their usual simple meal. But he had not bought the leather sumter of manuscripts with him. This was their last, free day together and they should talk.

Above them the sky was so blue and cloudless that it appeared to Aimery as though it might stretch from them all the way to Italy and home. He thought it strange that he still thought of Italy as home, but there was nothing to it. He did. Hardly a romantic, he still somehow felt that if he were able to just look hard or long enough he might make out his own town of Segni, shining in all its splendor somewhere beyond the Haute Savoie.

So deeply was he into his own pleasant musings that

at first he did not hear Claire's words. She had to repeat them; her clear, intelligent eyes staring directly into his.

"Why don't you just release him?" she repeated.

For an instant Aimery's handsome face squinted together in perplexity and then he realized whom she meant.

"William Belibaste? But he is under process by the Inquisition. He must be tried and found either innocent or guilty by it. I have no jurisdiction."

But Claire was having none of this easy explanation. She pressed toward him eagerly.

"You could free him, though. You know you have the right. You, Lord Aimery, are Seigneur of this place; appointed by both the pope and the King of France. They would listen to your ruling on this matter and they would give you *droite de Seigneur*—the right of a First Lord to choose. Bishop Fournier would support you in this. He shows little enough enthusiasm for these proceedings. I think he is actually tired of burning peasants for foolish beliefs."

"You know I don't agree with witch hunting." Aimery shook his head. "The trouble is that Belibaste does not believe his ideas to be foolish. He has daily been offered the chance to recant and he has daily refused it. He stays his own course; no one forces him to it."

Still, Claire was right about one thing—he was tired of the proceedings and the bishop was as well. The thought of William Belibaste and his newly-arrived wife living their lives beneath Montsegur, waiting for judgment, was not the welcome Aimery had envisioned in his lifelong dream of attaining his fortress. It blighted Montsegur for him, and he wondered if he would have liked this place at all had Claire not been with him.

"I cannot go against the mandate that has been given me. I cannot go against the Inquisition."

Still the seed had been planted, and as he reached for Claire and held her to him and kissed her, a very small, still part of him wondered if this was still true. If indeed, Belibaste could not—*should* not—be freed.

# CHAPTER 28

Bishop Fournier returned the next morning, almost hidden within an accompanying flurry of royal pomp. The king had spared Sir Valois de Bonne to lead the escort. Sir Valois was widely respected as a First Knight of France, indeed he was the Queen's own champion, and his presence lent import to the bishop's entourage. The lilies of France flitted importantly, overshadowing the knight's own pennant and quite overpowering the indifferently colored banner of Fournier's bishopric. The king was known for guarding his own best interest, and the bishop obviously had become one of his concerns.

Claire stood beside Minerve, setting out a screen of peaches for drying, as the entourage thundered through Montsegur village. At the end of a long parade of knights and men at arms, the bishop rode alone in a small, unadorned, flax-covered wagon. As it passed by, he stared out at Claire, met her gaze with his. She could read nothing in it.

"The trial will resume now in earnest," whispered Minerve.

"Yes," agreed Claire as she watched the heavy, stone walls of Montsegur Castle swallow the men from Paris. "And we will each be forced back into our own alliances."

Minerve reached over and squeezed her hand.

Father Peter also carefully watched the warriors as they thundered into Montsegur from the North. There were thirteen golden spurred knights now, including Aimery of Segni, his friend, Huguet de Montfort, and Peter, The Templar Knight, himself—one more than was necessary. Twelve was the perfect number; it had always been so. In a far earlier life, Peter had been quite superstitious and the irony of his present situation was not lost upon him. He found it delicious.

Claire did not flee to Aimery that afternoon. Instead, she played upon the Lady's Gallery with the Montfort children so that Minerve could rest.

"Not that I need the special attention," said her friend. "After five pregnancies, I know much more about what to expect than any midwife. And I am positive my time will not arrive for at least a few more weeks. The birthing woman is wrong to think it otherwise."

Claire had insisted on staying. Frankly, she agreed with the concerned midwife that the newest Montfort child might make his appearance sooner than expected. A local woman renowned throughout the region for her skill and aware of this, the midwife had insisted that the Lady de Montfort could not remain even a few more days in this advanced condition. The woman would stake her career upon it.

For Claire, there was also something earthy and fertile and primitively beautiful about Minerve in her expectant state; something Claire found amazingly and unexpectedly wonderful—much like the kisses she shared with Aimery. Still, Minerve did tire in her condition, even she admitted this, and Claire was eager to help with the care of the many Montfort children. Different from most other offspring of the nobility, they were not given over to the primary care of nurses and servants. Much to her surprise, Claire found she actually enjoyed playing with them. She had known so few children in the past; the convent was not conducive to their liveliness, but Claire found that *she* was as she romped and played and laughed.

Thus, she was on the Lady's Gallery, looking down in the main Hall, as Aimery entered it with his honor guard. As usual, the Hall was filled with people awaiting the seigneur's formal entrance. Knights and men at arms and disgruntled peasants all mingled together, jostling each other for a high point in line. Aimery looked up, briefly caught her eye and smiled before making his quick way to the raised dais and his carved Lord's Seat.

Claire could almost feel the weight of authority settle onto his shoulders as he became, once again, Aimery, Count of Segni; Envoy from the Papal Authority and champion of the King of France; pledged to take this land and to hold it and rule it. Claire saw him spare one last, fleet glance towards her and the Lady's Gallery before giving his full attention to the business at hand.

This was her Aimery—and this was where he should be—where he had always wanted to be.

* * *

"Good heavens, it jumped!"

With a short shriek, Claire snatched her hand back from Minerve's distended belly.

"Not it, *him,*" corrected her friend with quiet complacency.

"How do you know that?"

"I am the mother and so I know," said Minerve regally. "That is enough."

She laughed as she reached for the tumbler of milk that a servant sat beside her.

" 'Tis a boy for certain," she repeated as she wiped the milk from her mouth. "It does not bump around enough to be a girl. Contrary to general belief, females are always the most active in the womb."

Claire nodded. Her years within the walls of St. Magdalene's had left her with few opinions about children and Minerve, with her brood, seemed to be an expert on the subject, so it was best to heed her notions. Minerve read this in her bemused acquiescence and laughed again.

"You will see yourself one day," she said. "After you've birthed your second child you will know all that is happening within the confines of your own body. It will no longer be a stranger to you. You will have become familiar with yourself."

*As though she, Claire, would ever have children; as though she would ever give birth.*

"I am promised to the convent," she said to Minerve as she looked away. "I shall never give birth."

"Oh, my dear, I am not so certain about that," replied Minerve. Before Claire could challenge her, the Countess de Montfort had flitted onto other subjects, talking of her youngest son and putting Claire's hand to her jumping womb once again.

She knew that things had changed for them, and that now he would come to her at night. She stayed on in her small room at the castle, dressing carefully and well in a russet silk tunic that Joanna of Foix had given her. She had laced gold ribbon through her thick hair; she had bathed and touched herself with rose oil. The perfume of it dizzied her; it made her think of what was coming.

She knew.

Claire held her fingers close for a moment so she could inhale their rich scent before touching them to the affluence of her hair. Finally, she was ready. She knew what she wanted—and she continued to want it, all through the rousing feast that had been planned to celebrate the bishop's return.

Aimery walked with a determined step through the dark, stone corridors of his fortress; the jingle of his golden knight's spurs the only sound near at hand. The last sounds of music and laughter faded out rapidly behind him and his castle grew silent. He could have been its only inhabitant—with Claire.

He hurried to the noble floor, but he stopped at one of the slender arrow slits that lined the winding stairwell. He saw a small trailing of red roses growing, miraculously, against the castle wall. Claire might like flowers; he'd never thought of that. Quickly Aimery of Segni, normally the least romantic of men, retraced his steps and went in search of them. He cut a small bouquet with his jeweled knife, careful to gouge out any thorns; then on impulse he went round to the kitchen gardens and gathered bluebells. He remembered that she had once remarked on these, so he picked bluebells for her and fresh rosemary.

Inside his castle once again, he surveyed his handiwork in the light of a sconced torch and frowned. Somehow, in the dark, he had managed to choose every dying rose upon the vine. The bluebells had not yet recovered from the day's heat and the rosemary, though still pungent, had lost a good deal of its beauty to seed. He guessed it didn't really matter; Claire would like them. Still, he wished his present had been a bit better. He wanted everything perfect for her this night.

There was no lock upon her small chamber door. The heavy latch felt cold to his touch, but it gave way easily enough—perhaps too easily. The absolute impropriety of his actions did not occur to Aimery until he was well within Claire's door. He hesitated for a moment as he moved from one dimly lighted space into another. Even though the room was not large, he could barely make out the scene before him. Gradually his eyes adjusted and he saw the bed and her slight form upon it.

"Claire," he said.

She didn't answer; instead she sat slowly up in her bed, pulling the linen sheeting around her. Against a backdrop of many pure white pillows, she shook her head—just once. Yet, this was no negation—at least not of him—and Aimery knew this. He moved closer.

"Claire?" he repeated, and this time was rewarded by her answering, "Aimery." Hearing his own name, prompted him further into her room.

He was right beside her bed. "I've brought you these," he said as he held out the flowers. For an instant their scent intoxicated him; he felt himself surrounded by fields and fields of herbs and flowers, by mountains of roses. Claire perfumed him as well. The gold ribbon was still threaded through her hair, though it had loosed a little and lay strewn on the pillow behind her, tangled amidst the magnificence of her hair. He was near enough to see her clearly now, to smell the hint of her.

"I was waiting for you," she said simply.

Of course she would be. They had grown so close together in so many ways. If he thought to come to her, she would sense the thought; know he was coming. He had started taking things like this for granted.

There was a small pewter tumbler on the table near her bed. He picked it up, poured water into it from the matching pitcher, and then nestled the flowers within. They had seemed such a sorry sight in the hallway, but Aimery forgot that now. They served their purpose. They showed that he had been thinking about her, and she knew it.

"Thank you," said Claire. "Come nearer. Please."

"Why?"

"Because I want to love you."

He smiled now himself, yet again irritation bubbled underneath. Would she never talk of their future together? Would she never say what she expected from him?

"And what of your convent scruples?" he questioned. "What of your idea to keep yourself perfect?"

"All gone," she answered, and though Aimery sensed a certain sadness about her, he could detect no regret in her voice.

"Finished?" he repeated. "Are you quite sure?"

"That life was over for me from the first day I kissed you. I wanted you from the beginning. You were my choice. From the very earliest moments my relationship with you had everything to do with my choosing and nothing to do with Father—"

"With Father?" he prompted.

"With you." She changed. "It has only to do with you—and with me."

She let the lace of her linen sheeting fall just a little from her shoulder and this motion precluded anything else, at least for Aimery. Outside the small, leaded paned windows the clouds shifted, letting the full moon break through. Bright and powerful in the night sky that surrounded it, outshining by far the faint twinkle of the stars, its light flowed into the chamber, illuminating Claire.

*He should stop—She should stop—They should stop. At least until some plans were made; some future settled.*

But Aimery couldn't do it.

"No promises," she said. "Just once more. Tonight."

Aimery felt the soft caress of her fingers against his cheek. He reached up his own hand and held it against hers for a very long moment. He looked into her eyes and saw the clarity in them, recognized the welcome. He saw the importance—for both of them, and perhaps for the first time in either of their lives—of not living in the past and not living in the future, but of taking this moment.

It was important that they live *this* moment.

Again she moved just a little, exposing the soft roundness of a breast and inviting him in beside her onto the bed. Still fully clothed, Aimery lifted her fingers from his cheek and pressed them to his mouth. He ran his tongue along the softness of her inner hand; that same hand that could so skillfully illuminate the intricate workings of an Inquisition trial. Behind him—unbeknownst to him—the full, fat moon moved directly to the center of the window and shed its light within.

* * *

Claire saw it. Right before Aimery moved his lips from her hand to the sensitive flesh that lined her inner arm, she saw the moon halo him. And she sensed it illuminate something within her that she still thought to be dark; something deeply hidden that might jump out and hurt her in the end. It didn't matter. This was her choice. She embraced it. This was her wanting; this was her doing. She was woman enough now to accept that fact. She no longer had to be Perfect.

And then there were no thoughts, no words. There was only now. There was only sensation.

Somehow he was beside her and nothing came between them. His clothing—his light tunic, and his breeches and his under linen—had all disappeared, as had her nightdress and the sheeting. They were together, skin to skin, and there was nothing left to separate them—at least for this moment. Claire's body knew exactly what it craved and Aimery knew exactly how to fulfill her. He was very gentle with her, and he was very slow. First, his mouth pressed kisses into her mouth, and then began its delicious exploration of the rest of her body. She felt his lips as they moved to rest against the heartbeat at her throat, lingering because he knew she loved to feel him there. She felt her body as it grew languid and then rose to meet his. He moved lower, first to fasten upon one breast and then the other, and the reaction of her body to his touch thrilled her. She looked through moonlight and candle glow to see her nipples harden and yearn out to him. His manhood hardened against her thigh and her legs opened to him. She was not shy. This was Aimery, her friend and now her lover, doing these wonderful things to her; calling her body to life in places where she had not even known it was dead.

And all the time, he talked to her; encouraged her. Murmured sweet words to her—gloried in her beauty and his need of her. This seemed a continuation of their talks together, of their being together. It had that same naturalness. Claire felt her body harden, draw within itself and then it was as though moon beams gathered and then crystallized and then exploded from her, reaching out to him, embracing him, as she called his name over and over again, "Aimery, Aimery," and then again, "Aimery."

It seemed to Claire that only this word had the power to settle the earth back in its place once again.


They came together again as the moon settled sedately into the night's sky. Aimery reached for Claire and loved her and savored the moment. He held on to it by holding tightly on to Claire and kindling her with his touch, by branding her with his kisses and his seed.

As the new day dawned and he lay beside her, he knew that he had made a false promise. He could never leave Claire for Isabeau. Not now—not ever again.

# CHAPTER 29

"His name is Peter of Bologna," said the Bishop solemnly, "and he is a Templar Knight."

Claire saw the puzzled furrow etch itself into Aimery's forehead. "I thought the Templars disbanded and their lands and titles forfeited to the Crown of France."

"He is a renegade," continued Fournier. "One of the few to escape and he is dangerous—in some ways as dangerous as Satan himself."

Claire kept her eyes lowered, her quill busy. They were the only three in the Great Hall. The bishop had requested this special audience and had stipulated that the castle scribe be there. He wanted a clear record of what would be said.

"Of course you know of the Templar trial?"

Claire sensed rather than saw Aimery's puzzled nod of acquiescence. "How could I not know? The story of their disgrace and fall is common knowledge throughout the whole of Christendom."

"Unfortunately, the disgrace belonged not only to them, but is shared with the rest of Christendom as well." Claire heard the creaking as the bishop tried to find a settled place in his small chair. "*That* was a bad business from the very beginning; started from greed and not from goodness—but, of course, that is just between us."

"Initiated by Philip the Fair, if I am not mistaken," said Aimery, "and if my history does not desert me."

"A recent history that commenced with this century and is already well on the way to becoming one of its main markers. The record shows that Philip and his henchman Clement V—the first schismatic pope to sit at Avignon—together accused the Templars of every abomination thinkable to man, starting with witchcraft and going on from that horror." Claire glanced up the see the bishop arch his brows in sad suggestion. "The underlying rumor was that both the king and the pope cared less about the Templar's ephemeral, immortal souls than they did about their very real and very material treasure."

"The ship of French finances has always listed," replied Aimery mildly, "but no more so than that of other major states. There is no system of taxation and the lords are forced to depend upon warring and plunder to furnish their treasuries—and yet money to wage war must be found as well."

"A point well taken by Philip," continued Fournier, "who lighted upon the Knights Templar as the perfect answer to this conundrum. Although they were exempt from taxes as well, they had made many enemies and few counterbalancing allies. Unlike their brothers, the Knights of St. John Hospitalier, they did no charitable service. Instead they housed riches for kings and nobles and rich merchants, and lent this money out at exorbitant usury to the many, that had been forbidden by Church edict, from having commerce with the Jews. The Templars, who had begun their life during Crusade as an order of warrior monks set to defend the Holy Land, proved themselves to be able and canny businessmen. They soon grew fat and prosperous and powerful, taking up residence in Paris in their formidable citadel, the Temple."

"Did they not think to purchase protection with their power and money? This is the usual way."

"They were knights, warriors; and basically they were uneducated men. They grew quickly intoxicated by their own power and their connections to high places. The last Grand Master, Jacques de Molay, was godfather to the daughter of the king himself. You know, Sir Aimery, that very few knights share your education. The vast majority of them remain unlearned to this day. Not only was Jacques de Molay ignorant of letters, he seems also to have been equally as oblivious about his own peril. He sat blissfully at dinner with King Philip as the first raid upon his beloved Temple took place. Within hours both he and his knight–monks had been rounded up and placed in the dungeons of the Louvre. They would not see the light of day again for many a bleak year and would never again draw a free breath."

"Were they not tried?" asked Aimery. "That is the law—the right to a free hearing for all men."

"Of course there was the semblance of a trial," said Fournier, a trifle impatiently. "Trial is insisted upon by both the secular and the religious laws of this land. Even a poor, miscreant peasant such as William Belibaste cannot be sentenced to death without judicial examination, much less a powerful man like Jacques de Molay. After torture and forced confessions, the Templars were brought before the king in his Great Hall at the Louvre to be publicly accused and tried. Perhaps it is this semblance of trial that holds the clue to our present danger."

They were all three silent now, and for a moment the only sound in the huge and drafty chamber was the caw of a crow coming from just outside its glazed, lead windows.

"You recall," continued Fournier, "that I mentioned the lack of education within the knight's ranks. Perhaps I should also have mentioned that the Templars, though vowed to celibacy, were monks. They were not priests. Very few of them were initiated into Holy Orders."

Aimery nodded, leaning close.

The bishop went on, "One of their brothers was a priest, and he was educated. His name was Peter of Bologna, from all accounts a most intelligent and learned man, and he was appointed to defend his fellows before the pope and king. "

"I imagine this a thankless task," said Aimery, "at best."

"In actuality I think it was much worse than either of us could imagine," continued Fournier. "Imagine being the only Templar with a full grasp of the situation and how it was to end. Imagine knowing that your brother knights depended upon you for their defense, and sitting day by day with them at the interrogation table, realizing that they faced certain death—and knowing the true reasons that they could not avoid this death—and knowing also that your fate was linked with theirs, and that there was no hope for any of you. This would have driven any man mad. It seems to have done this to Peter of Bologna, who was goaded to insanity by grief and disappointment, and by fear."

Aimery's clear eyes clouded. "Poor man! And was he eventually carried to the stake with the others?"

"Oh, no," said the Bishop. "Peter of Bologna managed to escape."

"Having seen the Louvre in Paris, I find it hard to believe that anyone could escape from its dungeons. One has only to observe how carefully Belibaste is held in this outpost of Montsegur to realize how infinitely more difficult it must have been to escape from the king and the pope," said Aimery. "The Templar trial took years. Surely Philip and Clement were prepared for the eventuality of flight."

"Peter of Bolognia just—disappeared," said Fournier. "And believe me, his absence caused great consternation."

"Because he had escaped?" inquired Aimery. "Because the court would have difficulty in finding another who could take over the defense?"

The bishop looked over at him fondly, patted his hand. "My son, for all your warring and conquest, you have remained quite naïve. Nothing has yet managed to dim your native goodness. Who would take time to care about the right workings of justice"—the prelate paused and took a breath—"when there was so much treasure involved?"

"Treasure?" Now Aimery was genuinely puzzled. Claire could see this written on his face and she loved him for it.

*And the treasure is the only thing that matters, she realized sadly. It has been that way from the beginning.*

"The hallowed Templar treasure," replied Fournier, "and something more. For it seems that when the Temple coffers were opened, they contained much less than what was thought. This was part of the reason that Jacques de Molay and his brothers were so tortured. Philip and Clement wanted the riches; indeed, they needed them. It seems that they were outsmarted in this by the old Grand Master. He never told them his secret—but he told it to Peter of Bologna."

Aimery nodded. "The same Peter who escaped."

"The same Peter who Jacques de Molay *helped* to escape," corrected the bishop quietly. "The Grand Master was an old man even as his ultimate ordeal began. Once the exigencies of his torture began, he knew his days on this earth to be numbered. He was still surrounded by his earnest brothers, but they were uneducated. What could they do confronted by the power of the Church and of the Crown? Where was the man among them who could replant the seeds of their Order once the persecutions had inevitably died down? Jacques needed someone like Peter of Bologna, a man rumored to be cunning as well as intelligent, and also unquestioningly devoted to the Templar Knights and their sacrificed cause."

Silence again—but only for an instant.

"But where would Peter go?" asked Fournier quietly. "Where could he find the ideal place to replant the seeds of his Order and revenge its martyrs?"

"He could go nowhere in Europe," replied Aimery. "The Templars had been disbanded throughout the rest of Christendom as well."

Fournier nodded. "There was England; a small segment of Templars remained in known seclusion there in Cornwall. But why go so far afield? What happened to his brothers had happened quickly; persecution had fallen upon them like lightening from a clear sky. We must remember this in order to understand how Peter of Bologna must have been thinking at the time. The

Templars were given no time to organize anything resembling an opposition, a revolt. Yet, there was a place—and right here in France—where opposition to the King and the organized religion had been brewing for more than a century, a place where it still simmered."

"A place where there had been Crusade," said Aimery, "against a people who had never been totally crushed."

"The Cathars." Fournier stretched his cramped legs and got slowly to his feet. "And remember also, my lord of Segni, that there has always been rumor of a Cathar treasure. Supposedly, it was brought down from this very fortress by Esclarmonde of Foix and buried right before Simon de Montfort brought siege."

Aimery shrugged his shoulders with instinctive dismissal. "Languedoc is rife with rumors about the Cathars and their treasure. One always hears some such talk but I have never taken it seriously. It seems mere superstition."

Yet, even as he thought the words *superstition, magic, happenstance*—words he normally would have spoken with idle conviction—he realized that he no longer quite believed in their comforting reassurance. Something simmered about him; bubbled wrongly in the pot. Instinctively he looked over at Claire, only to see her bent earnestly at her own task.

*Claire. Something about Claire. Something about his pure and innocent Claire.*

Too many things had changed during his short summer at Montsegur and Aimery realized, suddenly, that he had changed as well. He would explore these changes later, fathom their depth and their import, but now his duty lay before him. He must protect his suzerainty; he must do as he had pledged.

"Peter of Bologna," he repeated. "I feel somehow that he is near."

"Oh, yes, quite near," replied the bishop equably, "near, and set upon his revenge. I know this. I have seen him."

# CHAPTER 30

Father Peter smiled down upon the two women before him. They each made a quick reverence and then settled down again on the stone stoop of the village hut. Peter had not been able to survive his own scourging torture and the eventual death of all he held dear, his escape and the dangerous secret life he now lived, without the aid of strong intuition—and this intuition now told him that the wolves nipped close about him and he must act with care. Carefulness, to him, had always meant that he must change tactic; this had never failed to loose the enemy from his scent.

And they knew he was near. Peter had instantly read this knowledge upon Bishop Fournier's face as the royally protected company thundered through the massive gates of Montsegur. Peter of Bologna had been carefully mingled within the crowd of peasants out to see the pageantry, but for one brief moment his gaze had met that of the bishop and, in that brief moment, the Templar Knight had recognized the truth.

Still, smug in his conceit, Peter doubted that Fournier

had recognized him for who he really was. In fact, he chuckled at the thought. Fournier, Huguet de Montfort, Aimery of Segni—all their kind were lions on this earth. And he was a flea. But, one by one, a flea could join with other fleas until together they were able to torture the lion down.

That is what he had planned. Now . . .

Peter looked upon Yvonne, the aging, graying wife of William Belibaste, and then upon Claire—*his* Claire—and his old man's eyes rimmed with pain. Perhaps Fournier had not caught the link—*perhaps* this was still true—but somehow Claire had found it. Peter knew her well enough to know this. And she would have to be sacrificed, as her family had been sacrificed before her, so that the might of his duty could live on. It *must* live on. For a moment, the pain of what he would do overwhelmed him and though he continued to smile, the sense of it lacerated his soul and, suddenly, he was young again—not the old, stale murderer he had become—but a youth, bounding off to unite his life with a just cause, filled to the brimming point with youthful notions of hope and faith in right order and goodness.

That was before the torture had started. That was before he had been changed.

"Will I see my husband today?" asked Yvonne Belibaste. Her words compelled Peter back to his duty. The day shone in gorgeous splendor all about him—sunny, clear and hot—with bees buzzing languidly in its brightness.

Peter realized again that he must use the goodness of the two women before him if he was to succeed; and he must succeed. There could be no doubt in either heaven or hell about that now. Nothing could stop him. Lately, Claire had started to question, to disagree with him, just as Helene had done. Well, Helene had been dealt with and this new nuisance with Claire would be dealt with as well—one way or the other.

Now, he turned eyes bright with sympathy to the soon-to-be widowed Yvonne Belibaste.

"My dear," he said. "Of course you will see him today. Why are you so anxious? You must never give up hope."

"But Bishop Fournier has returned from Paris." The face of William Belibaste's wife drew together in fear. "And my lord of Segni has asked the Maid Claire to be ready to scribe again upon the morrow. They are to commence right after first light; I have never heard of a trial beginning that early. It may be a sign of their determination to be speedily finished with this matter."

"And it may be a sign of nothing at all," replied Peter at his most soothing. "We must not give up our hope. We must not let these infidels influence our good sense."

"But so little hope remains for William," cried his wife. "The bishop's stated purpose in going to Paris in the first place was to find proof against my husband, to link him to the Cathar conspiracy. He wanted to consult with some learned Dominicans upon the faculty at the university there."

"What makes you think this?" asked Peter, perhaps a trifle more sharply than he would have liked.

He saw the subterfuge as it flitted across Yvonne's face, but he was even more interested in Claire's heightened color.

*My Claire. My own splendid Magdalene.*

It had been years since he felt such pain.

"Because my lord of Segni told me this was the bishop's purpose," said the Maid of Foix quietly. "He told him that he wished to consult with some experts, with someone who might know. He had some idea he might find a linkage with what was happening here."

"Did he tell you which experts?"

"Historical experts," replied Claire. She raised her head a little and shook her loose hair. "Men who might be able to tell him what had happened with the Templars."

Peter stopped the pretense of regarding Claire secretly from the corner of his eye and deigned her his full attention. His pain had softened, and he was furious with her for this breech of confidence and realized that in the end, she would get only what she deserved—as they all would.

"Why did you not mention this to me before?"

"He said it in passing."

It was a smooth lie but Claire was no liar. She blushed as she purposely led Peter astray—or, at least, attempted to.

Peter knew she was not telling the truth, though he could not quite distinguish if she kept back all the truth or part of it. He would find this out later, for right now he must turn his attention to the wife of Belibaste.

"Yvonne," he said and the word was a caress. "We have not forgotten your husband. He will be freed one way or the other. I have promised you that in the past. I promise it now, once again. But our circumstances have changed and I fear we must change with them. We must free Belibaste now, quickly. He must be set free and the two of you must make your escape."

The woman's gray eyes grew troubled. She fastened her worn hands close together around the stuff of her flax tunic.

"The Bishop still promises him a fair trial," she said doubtfully. "You yourself even said, sir, that we should wait until my husband could plea for his own life before the court. You said we should not make hasty action."

Peter did not need his own words quoted back to him, especially by this peasant, but he kept his temper close in check.

"The mere fact that Bishop Fournier has requested that the proceedings recommence means that he brings new proof from Paris—proof that may be found fatal to your husband's interests and to our cause. We can take no further chances."

"Then you believe we must free William by force?"

"Only if it is necessary," answered Peter soothingly. "We cannot let them defeat us now as they did in the past. We cannot participate in our own destruction by remaining idle."

"I know my husband well," protested Yvonne. "I have spoken with him about this. Under no circumstance would he want blood shed on his account. He remains true to his Cathar ideals."

And yet, he has taken you as his cottage-wife, thought Peter, but he kept the smirk from his lips.

"I, too, hold with his Cathar beliefs," said the priest, "and I want no innocent blood shed. It will be easy enough to avoid this. Claire can get the key to Belibaste's cell for us. Lord Aimery trusts her now."

And, indeed, so it proved—at least as regarded the getting of the keys themselves. Aimery did not hold them, but Bishop Fournier, as Grand Inquisitor, personally kept the iron slag to Belibaste's prison. And he, too, trusted her. It was easy enough to come in while he was going through his parchment, to sit upon her small stool and pretend to be busy about her own illuminations; to watch and wait and snatch the key from the many on his great chain while he was gone.

Easy enough to steal; harder to live with what she had done—and what she planned to do.

*For Belibaste, she thought, to see him free.*

And it was for all of them—for Yvonne and for Huguet and Minerve and their children; for Aimery, dear Aimery, and for herself—because he would see them all dead. All of them, and without showing mercy; just as he had killed her parents and the original scribing monk; just as he had murdered sweet Helene. Peter was mad, she knew that now. That he was had become plain to her now. But why? What had done this to him? That question still rankled.

Claire knew she would find that answer as well. It would all come to her—as she set William Belibaste free.


Claire reached out her hands toward Peter, knowing this would be the very last time.

"I have it," she said, as she lifted the great rusted key to the light of the one wall sconce. "It is night now—no one watches—we can set Belibaste free at last."

The old man tried to mask his consternation, but Claire saw it in the instant that it flitted across his face. She knew him well.

"Free him?" Peter's words echoed through the empty Cathar meeting cell—a place used to furtive meetings and to secrets. It was deserted now. Their whispered words were the only sounds in the room.

"Isn't that what we wanted?" Claire's eyes narrowed and though the key was held out to him, she kept it clutched firmly within her own hands. "Since I was a child, the Cathar principles were all that I heard. We must love freedom; we must honor life and protect. We must live simply, preserving ourselves. We must always remain holy and good. We must always love peace. Isn't that what you taught me Peter? Isn't that what you said?"

"Of course." He was tired now and could not quite keep the impatience from his voice. "Of course peace is what I wanted."

"Is it what you lived?"

Claire's words seemed absorbed in the very walls around them. Peter's eyes narrowed. "What do you mean?"

"Oh, Peter—I think you know."

Suddenly he *did* know; realized that Claire had discovered everything. For an instant, he felt the world wave beneath his feet and he wanted to clutch on to anything until the roiling went away. But he was Peter of Bologna, after all; he had lived through worse than this. He had done worse than what he now planned to do.

Perhaps she still did not realize everything—not quite.

"You think you know," he said quietly. "Yet you have no idea. Not by half."

"You killed my parents." Her voice faltered but she caught herself, started again. "You killed them, and you killed my younger brother. You killed the monk. You killed Helene—sweet, kind Helene, who really believed in the ideals you only mouthed."

"And what about the doll upon the wicket?" His voice was mocking. "You forgot to list that with my great sins."

They stared at each other for one long moment, then Peter looked down at the key clutched tightly in her hand.

*Peter. My Father.*

"Make me understand," she said.

And if he could . . .

Suddenly, Peter felt that his whole plan might spring to life again, that it still wasn't too late—if he could just make Claire, his Magdalene, understand.

But he was tired. It was useless. And pride in what he'd done mastered him.

"You stupid, foolish chit—you have no idea what I have accomplished. You have no idea what *you* could have become."

He chuckled. Drew straighter. "It did not start with your parents, and it will not end with you—or even with William Belibaste for that matter. I imagine they have told you of the Templar trial."

Claire nodded.

"At least they told you what they believed: how I was chosen to defend the others." Peter paused. "How their fate was in my hands."

His eyes clouded as they looked past Claire toward something she could not see. "Jacques de Molay was my Grand Master, but he was a stupid man. Uneducated, illiterate, he could not see past the scope of his own danger. He could not see that what they wanted for his life would destroy us in the end."

"The treasure?"

"Oh, yes, the treasure." Peter's voice took on a mocking, sing-song ring. " 'What does the money matter to us when we can save our brothers from the rack and the flame?' You should have heard the old man bluster. As though Philip the Fair would have spared him—any of them. The treasure was only the first part. He wanted them dead."

"But Philip and Pope Clement offered Jacques de Molay clemency. They were all friends. Had the Grand

Master only pleaded guilty he would have saved himself from the pyre in the end. It was he who chose his martyr's death."

"He chose it."

Something flat and lifeless in Peter's last words drew Claire closer.

"You did this?" she asked.

"He chose it," repeated Peter, "but he was helped along in his fancy. You see, dear Claire, he had not the depth for leading—but I did. I could see the end. What did it matter that all my brothers and even the Grand Master himself were sacrificed—as long as our Great Temple lived on? I promised certain men in the King's Court—men who were envious of the Grand Master, or who stood to benefit by his downfall—that I could deliver him into their hands. My price was thrifty enough—my own freedom. There were those eager to pay it. After all, I was a very small fish in a very large pond. I had been tortured and racked; my body broken and nothing had provoked useful information from me. I had none to give, or so they thought. My only value was that I could persuade the Grand Master to anything. He trusted me."

"Even unto death," Claire whispered.

Peter deigned a hard look. " 'Tis easy for you to judge me, young Maiden. Or dare I call you Maiden still, after Aimery of Segni has had his merry way with you."

"It was my way, too. I chose him. For the first time in my life, I fixed my own path."

"Over your pledge to be the Cathar Perfect! Over your duty to become the Templar Magdalene!" Peter spat the words. "Just like Jacques de Molay and his kin. 'Save my brothers! Give Philip the treasure!' But I couldn't do that. The treasure was all I had to begin our great Temple once again."

"But you never got it," Claire mused, "and somehow or other that is what brought you here. Even after you betrayed the others, you could not get your hands on the treasure. It eluded you."

"They had sent it on." Despite himself, Peter was pleased by Claire's astuteness. He had created her, after all; had seen the Magdalene's gleam in that young peasant child and brought her here and groomed and educated her until even her own parents would not have known her—had they lived.

"They had sent it on," he repeated. "Jacques de Molay and his first lieutenants. It seems they distrusted everything about Paris; thought they could bargain better if they sent the treasure South for safekeeping. They knew a safe place for it, a secret. It seems that, coming back from the Crusade in the Holy Land, Jacques de Molay traveled through Languedoc. He learned of secrets here, things buried. It seems the Cathars, too, had hidden treasure. Esclarmonde of Foix, their Perfect, had hurried them down the Roc as Montsegur lay under siege from Simon de Montfort, to bury what they had. The Cathars had ruled this land for generations. They had ties to all the leading noble families and the sect had become rich on tithes and death-leaves. The location was passed down from Perfect to Perfect, but it seems the Grand Master learned the secret. I imagine he was trusted; the Templars were always powerful, but without true friends. What remained of the Cathar remnant could easily have anticipated the persecution that was soon to befall the Templar Knights. I have no way of knowing. I only know that the treasure disappeared and that it is buried with the Cathar riches somewhere here."

"And you think William Belibaste knows the location?"

"Why else would I have scented Bishop Fournier upon his trail?" he questioned mildly.

"You did that as well?"

"Indeed, the traitor, Sicre, was just a ploy. *I* plotted the whole thing. I sniffed William Belibaste out and sent the Inquisition on his trail."

"Because he is the last Perfect," said Claire

"And he will know the secret."

He lunged at Claire then, his hands outstretched, nails digging into the delicate flesh of her wrists. But she was quick and young. She managed to pull her hands away from his and, still clutching the key, ran for the heavy oak door. She felt him clutch the fullness of her skirts, but she yanked them away and fled out of the chamber, slamming the door just a half step before he reached it. He threw his weight against it again and again; snarling like a baited wolf caught in a trap, but Claire was able to hold it shut long enough to bring the latch home. Once she had, she stood back, catching her breath.

The sound of the latch homing must have brought Peter to his senses. He stopped his ranting and listened with the cunning of a trapped mouse.

"Claire," he said. "My dearest child. You are foolish to do this. Do you think Aimery of Segni will overlook this? Do you think he will want to bed you again once he discovers your secrets—once he knows that you are Cathar Perfect and that you mean to free the object of this Grand Inquisition? Or are you like most women, do you think that because he has bedded you, he must love you, and that in the end this love will overcome all that has meaning in his life and all he has worked for? Do you, indeed, think that because you know your Latin, he would chose to place you in the same room as his near-betrothed?"

Claire, halfway down the dank hall now, turned back at the words that wafted to her on the cellar's sweating walls.

"I have no pretensions of love from Aimery of Segni," she said so softly that Peter had to strain to hear her words through the thick door, "but I have pledged that William Belibaste must go free."

# CHAPTER 31

"It is the only thing that remains to me," she said to Yvonne Belibaste as the two of them darted through the dungeons under Montsegur's main keep towards the cell where the Perfect, William Belibaste, lay waiting for them.

"What?" asked Yvonne sharply. She had not heard what the young scribe said; nor did she care to hear. A miracle had happened; she was on her way to free her husband. This was all that mattered. Already Claire had told her where a tethered donkey waited for them, piled high with provisions in flax sumters and with a crude map that would lead them over the mountains and into Andalusia once again. "Hurry, mistress. Please hurry."

There was no need to prod Claire on. She was close upon Yvonne's steps, following as she led the way to Belibaste's cell. They met no one, their footfalls the only sound in the whole vast dungeon. This mystified Claire. Where were the guards? Where were the people?—but she would have time to puzzle this out in the future. She would have plenty of time, years and years of it, once she had completed her mission, once she had faced Aimery with what she had done. And once William Belibaste was free.

"This one! Here it is, mistress!"

The key jammed in the lock and Claire had to prise it out, start its turnings once again. It turned the second time and, with Yvonne's eager help, she managed to push the heavy door open, to step inside the cell.

It was full daylight and so Claire had not thought to bring candles or torches and she missed them now. It took some time for her eyes to grow accustomed to the gloom. She found the cell to be not as bad as she had imagined. There was straw upon the floor, a sliver of blanket, even a rough chair near a slimed wall. She would welcome this chair later, she knew. She could rest upon it as she waited.

Finally she saw Belibaste. His wife had found him even in the gloaming, had gone directly to his side, and they stood together, clinging to one another.

Yvonne said, "The scribe has come to set you free." Claire heard the clotted tears in her voice.

Belibaste nodded, he motioned Claire closer.

It was strange, but she had never really looked at him before. Even though he was the object of her mission, she had kept her eyes lowered as she took down the proceedings of his trial. For some reason, she had not wanted to look upon him. She looked upon him now.

He was an ordinary man of medium height, with salt and pepper hair; a trifle frail perhaps, but nothing that could not be cured by solid food—and by freedom. There was nothing about him that was special, nothing Perfect. Except, perhaps, the way he held fast to the woman beside him and the way she held fast to him.

"Hurry!" whispered Yvonne urgently. "We must hurry away from here."

Belibaste nodded. He seemed not at all surprised by his reprieve, by his good fortune. He seemed not to question it in the least. But his gaze crackled toward Claire and he did have one question.

"You know of Peter?" he said.

Claire nodded. "And you do as well?"

"Almost from the beginning, even before I came here. I knew that he had traitored the others. I knew he would traitor me."

"And yet you came anyway?"

"I had my mission," he said simply, "just as you have yours. And we—each of us—must see our quest out to its end. Have you no interest in the treasure?"

Claire shook her head.

"I thought not." Belibaste chuckled dryly. "And that is just as well, because there is no treasure."

"William, we must go!' His wife grew insistent.

Belibaste patted her hand. "It is a myth; all gossamer-woven fable. The Cathars invented theirs; Jacques de Molay invented his. Nothing behind the tales at all. And yet Peter of Bologna schemed and betrayed and traitored and murdered—all for nothing."

"He says he did it for an ideal—to keep the Temple alive once the Templars were gone."

"Nothing," repeated Belibaste. He could have been talking to himself. "Nothing at all."

"William!"

This time the last Cathar Perfect heeded his wife and headed with her toward the entrance of his prison cell. He paused and turned back, puzzled that Claire was not with them.

"Aren't you coming?"

She shook her head. Tried to smile. "No. I've something still to do."

"Tell the truth?"

She nodded. With a wife and a life of indiscretions behind him, William Belibaste was a strange candidate to be Cathar Perfect. Yet Claire, bathed now by his kindness, felt that he was a splendid priest.

"You have committed treason in freeing me," said Belibaste softly, "and no one—not the Count of Segni, not even the Inquisition's bishop—has the right to absolve you for that. You will take my place upon the pyre. Do you realize that?"

Claire laughed shortly, sadly. "I have no desire to die, but I must tell them the truth. I owe them that much at least."

"William!"

"I will not join you in your foolhardiness. I have had enough of prison and Inquisition and the threat of the stake. You are foolish to remain. And yet, sometimes . . ."

Desperately, his wife pushed him to the door before he could finish the thought. The last sound Claire ever heard of William Belibaste was the patter of his bare feet running up and away toward freedom.

Claire never saw or heard of him again.

But she did hear Aimery, as she knew she would. Heard the slow jingle of his golden spurs against the hallway's smooth stone paving, heard the jeweled hilt of his unsheathed sword as it beat against her chamber's door. Others came with him, she was certain of that; but Aimery was all she heard. All she really wanted to hear.

She opened the door to them and then stood away from it, letting them in. She noticed with some surprise that two pages carried torches to light the gathering night. Claire had not noticed the darkening. She had sat alone upon her bed waiting, trying to still the voices that urged her to offer an explanation; to put the reason for what she'd done into words. Yet, there could be no words and no attempt at explanation. The heretic, William Belibaste, had been liberated. His liberator remained. That was all anyone would hear.

She could not blame them.

She didn't want to, but she forced herself to look at Aimery as he led the others into her chamber. His eyes met hers but briefly and she saw hope flash through them—hope that he could not repress; as though somehow she *would* have an explanation for why she had traitored them, why she had used and betrayed him.

She had only the truth to offer him and there was no hope in that.

Bishop Fournier slipped in behind them. The two pages, previously instructed, placed their torches in wall sconces and then edged out. They did not look at Claire. They did not acknowledge her in any way.

"We know what has happened," said Bishop Fournier as soon as the door had closed the young boys out. "We received a note from your confessor."

"He was Peter of Bologna," said Claire. She forced her glance from Aimery to the bishop.

"We know that, now," said Fournier, "though we found it out too late."

Claire nodded. "He is imprisoned in the convent's cellars."

"No longer." Aimery spoke for the first time. "It seems that William Belibaste was not the only one to escape this day."

"Would you like to sit, Claire?" asked the bishop.

She shook her head.

"Well, I would," he continued, lowering himself onto

her small stool. "I am old and weary. The time in Paris was difficult; the trip home worse. I will take rest now where I can find it."

Aimery waited until the priest had settled before speaking. "We went immediately in search of him, once we received your missive. We searched him out even before we set the alarm for Belibaste himself. But he had gone—escaped somehow though the door was still bolted. He left a written account, though, of what he said had happened." Aimery's voice was low, without emotion. Though he spoke to her, he no longer looked at Claire.

"He blames you," said the bishop.

Claire looked up, not quite as startled as she might have been.

The bishop continued. "He was canny enough to confess to the murders of your family and of Mother Helene—he could not easily have charged you with these crimes. You were with my lord of Segni when the Abbess was pushed and, of course, you were far too young to participate in the killing of your parents. But he said you knew of these things and, worse yet, inspired him to them."

"Because I was his Magdalene."

"The Templar's saint—or idol." Fournier nodded. "According to what I learned in Paris, it is a designation that has been passed down since the time of Mary Magdalene herself. Legend has it that she fled Bethany with Lazarus and that she fled to France. The myths around her seem to have started from there."

Claire shook her head. "He only told me the barest parts of what was meant by the Magdalene legend. We talked about the Cathars. We spoke of rebuilding what had been lost."

Still without looking at Claire, Aimery stepped forward and took the parchment from the bishop's hand. "Peter of Bologna's accusations would not hold in a court of law. It is only his word against hers."

"But we are not talking about legend and myth," replied the bishop. "We are talking heresy. Tell me, child, were you Cathar?"

"I was," said Claire. Her voice trembled. She caught herself and began again. "I was. I was brought up that way."

"And did you plan rebellion?"

"I planned rebellion."

"And did you free William Belibaste?"

*She thought, I must breathe. I must keep breathing.*

"I freed him," she replied. "I took the key from Peter of Bologna. I found Belibaste's wife and together we went to his cell. But I was the one who freed him. I take the responsibility to myself."

"Why?" said Aimery. Claire, looking away, was caught by the pleading in his voice. She turned to him, not wanting to. "Why wouldn't you tell me this? You knew my mandate here. You knew my responsibilities. Why?"

"I had promised that William Belibaste should go free. I had given my word."

"No wonder you wouldn't . . ."

He stopped himself, remembered the bishop.

Bishop Fournier slowly glanced from one to the other. He cleared his throat. "Eventually I must take responsibility in this matter. The Maid of Foix has committed a treasonable offense in freeing a prisoner of both the French and the Papal thrones. But the fact that, even given the circumstances, she plotted with the Cathar revolt is graver still. She will be required to answer for this before the same Inquisition Court that

tried William Belibaste and, like him, if convicted she
will be sentenced to the stake."

Claire felt her heart scud. She blinked rapidly but
she had been expecting this. She knew that if she freed
William Belibaste and did not attempt to escape with
him, she would hear these words, she would face this
murky future. But there had been something she had to
do; something she *still* must do.

"May I speak with my lord of Segni?" she asked the
prelate. "Alone?"

Fournier seemed actually relieved to quit the chamber. He hurried forth, his simple, dark robes swishing
against the rush and thyme upon Claire's floor. Once
the door closed him out, however, Claire could not
think what to say, how to explain.

Instead it was Aimery who finally said, "I imagine
you planned this from the very beginning, you and
your good friend—your *Father*—the Templar priest."

Contempt laced his words tightly together, leaving
no space for Claire's explanation.

*As though I have one. As though he cared.*

"From the very beginning," Aimery repeated. He
was standing so close to Claire that she could see remembrance flash across his face and dim his eyes. "He
told you what to do, didn't he, and you obeyed?"

Claire nodded. "I chose to do that. I wouldn't make
the same choice now—of course, I wouldn't, not
knowing what I know. Still, I believed then. I thought
he meant to do a good thing, to bring back a time of
honor and grace; I thought he meant to empower the
Cathar remnant once again."

*And I thought the Inquisition and not Peter of
Bologna had murdered my family.*

She couldn't remind him of that, couldn't use it as

an excuse. No matter the reason, she had done what he accused her of doing. Indeed, she had done that and more.

Dust danced about in the sunlight streaming into her chamber.

"I planned William Belibaste's escape," Claire said clearly. "From the moment he was tricked into returning to Languedoc I was part of the conspiracy that planned to free him."

Aimery whirled on this. "I imagine you've not heard that Peter of Bologna actually told the bishop the hiding place of your Perfect. At least we imagine it was he. A missive arrived with a detailed map and the name of Arnold Sicre, as willing a traitor as ever I've encountered. Fournier had searched through many seasons for news of Belibaste. How fortunate he was to, eventually, encounter someone as eager as he was that the Perfect should be turned over to the Inquisition."

Aimery's words came as no surprise to Claire. Her parents, Mother Helene, and now the betrayal of William Belibaste—was there no ending to Peter's treachery? And for what?

"For what?" she asked Aimery now. "Why would he do this?"

"I imagine he wanted the treasure."

"Yet, it was only a myth. William Belibaste told me that in the end."

The Count of Segni smiled but his was not a pleasant gesture. "I think we both have learned how easy is making, how one can build a dream—plan a life—around something that never really existed."

"I love you," said Claire.

"How convenient," he said. "You've said that only once before. You could lie in my arms night after night, fill yourself with me, and never once ask about our future together. Even knowing I was betrothed to Isabeau of Valois—you should have wanted something from me. You should have wanted to be with me. You never did."

Claire felt tears sting her eyes and she hated herself for this weakness. She could not cry now, not when she had so much that needed saying. "I wanted to be with you—and I *was* with you, heart and soul. Yet, I had this duty. It was the only thing left to me. I thought by liberating William Belibaste I would end one phase of my life. I could begin again then I could be free."

Claire saw suspicion cloud his clear eyes; and there was another emotion with it, one she did not want to recognize. One that turned her away.

"Why did you not come to me?" he repeated. "You knew I did not want this man murdered as a heretic. You know I would have done my best to help."

"It was my battle," said Claire simply.

"I think you may have had another reason."

He moved closer to her, almost close enough to kiss. But there could be no kissing between them, thought Claire, ever again.

"Another, more telling reason," he repeated.

"What?" she whispered.

"I think you planned this out from the very beginning; or, rather, I think you planned it out with your good friend Peter of Bologna—your Father. I think you both decided it would be easy enough to enthrall me, to put me under a witch's spell. Was sorcery not the most damning of the charges imputed against the Knights Templar? You were the Magdalene. Peter must have taught you something." Aimery paused. "Given you herbs."

Claire blushed scarlet. "He did give me something. I never used it. I had forgotten they were even there."

"I wonder," said Aimery. "Yet, if I believed that you

had bewitched me, this would remove all responsibilities for my own actions from my shoulders. The fact is that I am as culpable as you. Even if led, I went willingly enough to the slaughter."

"I led you nowhere," said Claire. "I loved you."

"Easy enough to say those words now." He turned from her then, toward the window, toward the sunlight. "The fact is, I cannot let you burn, and you will surely burn for what you have done. Belibaste's flight, before sentencing, brands him as everything the Inquisition accused him of being. That you helped him, marks you as a traitor—at best. You heard what Bishop Fournier said as clearly as I. Of course, you are too pure, too much the Perfect, to care that you perish in a heretic's fire."

From behind him, Claire said, "I do not want to die."

"At least you tell the truth about that. I can hear it in your voice."

Aimery was silent for a long moment, still turned away so that Claire could not see his face. "I think—"

"I think," said Claire, startled by the strength in her own voice. "I think you should turn around and look at me. I think whatever we have to say to each other should be said face to face."

# CHAPTER 32

No longer good. No longer Perfect.

Claire felt the power in her own anger as it waved over her, and then rolled out to engulf Aimery of Segni. She didn't know where this new power came from, had no idea what had started this torrent. She only knew that she felt released.

"It was *my* choice to save William Belibaste," she said. "It was my choice and my commitment, and I will take the consequences of my actions. 'Tis easy enough for you to tell me sweet words of love now, Lord Aimery, but what exactly was the life your pretty promises evoked? You were to live your life married to another, living openly with her. I was a mere peasant; an educated one, perhaps, and skilled enough in Latin, but not the type of person you would want to bear the illustrious name of your forebears—your *father's* name."

Claire saw Aimery's face turn white, saw his jaw clench, sensed the warning—but she did not stop

"You offered me a life of subterfuge and hiding—

the very life Peter offered me but this time bent to your cause rather than to his. You are to marry Isabeau of Valois—a woman you despise. You are to rule Montsegur—a fortress you hate. And who would help you do it? Who would be the mortar that would keep this jumbled life from tumbling? Why, the little Maid of Foix, as you called her. *I* would be destined to do it. You are a great lord, a rich a powerful man, and I should be thankful that you deigned to honor me, to elevate me. My children should be thankful to be your bastard sons. Well, I don't think so!"

She closed the distance between them in two long strides.

"I don't think so at all. I see no difference in the life you offered me and the life that I shared with Peter. I would be the same instrument; I would be looked upon to play a part and nothing more. Perhaps I have chosen death by freeing William Belibaste. Perhaps, as you say, I will take his place upon the stake. Yet, I will do it through my own choice, not through yours. I will not meekly give my life over, never again."

Aimery, Count of Segni and First Knight of France, was not a man used to brooking rebellion from men, much less from women. He had come to Claire with vague plans for her freedom—he was, after all, lord of this castle and, in the end, could do with its inhabitants as he wished. He had expected her to be suitably impressed. That she realized this and seemed not at all grateful, angered him more than he could have imagined.

"As you wish, my lady," he said, giving her a crisp, low reverence. "I will interest myself no longer in your welfare and we shall next meet again upon your judgment day."

\* \* \*

Of course that would not happen. Aimery's own anger, though fueled enough to drive him like a madman, first to his Great Hall and then upward from there to the heights of Monstsegur's tall donjon, was not enough to have him leave Claire to the stake.

"Not Claire," he said aloud as he looked toward the high mountains that shielded his home from his view.

No one, not even the Grand Inquisitor, would want this fate for her. Fournier would know that a live and liberated William Belibaste was better for everyone than the tried martyr would have been. It was Peter of Bologna who had wanted the sacrifice. Peter of Bologna who had orchestrated the Perfect's capture and eventual trial, Peter who stood to gain from a revolt by the Cathar remnant. Better that the Cathars be hidden again, free to practice their old ways if they wanted or not to practice them, as they chose. Better that there be no more sectarian bloodshed on the Roc, or anywhere at Montsegur or in Languedoc ever again.

Claire did this, he thought as he looked out toward the rough, craggy mountains that surrounded him. And this was the beginning of his healing.

He stood there, staring south as the day melted nightward from blue to mauve to pink and as he did so, his mind formed a plan. It wasn't perfect yet; he was still too roiled by his emotions to know exactly what should happen, exactly how this should end. Much still needed sifting.

Yet, at least he had something. At least he had hope.

The first star had begun to twinkle from beneath a sickle moon before Aimery turned back toward Montsegur; toward his desire and not his duty. Claire would not accept his help and he would not offer it. But there was someone she trusted; someone who could and would help.

Somehow, as his footsteps echoed through the deserted corridors of Montsegur Castle on his way to his sister's chamber, the jingle of his golden spurs against the paving hearted Aimery of Segni.

They sounded of hope.

# CHAPTER 33

*Segni, 1333*

Iolande, Countess of Segni, squinted as she looked expectantly down the roll of the hill and then waved at the woman hurrying toward her.

"I can't see as I once did," she murmured to herself, "but I would know Claire's step anywhere."

As if in answer, the approaching woman took off her wide straw netting hat and brandished it back and forth in the air like a pennon. She pointed at the gaggle of children who tumbled up the rise beside her and then waved again as she quickened her step. Iolande waved again, encouraging her forward. For an instant, she wondered if she should share the messenger's news—it was good news, after all—but then decided against it. She thought it best to let the day's happenings unfold for themselves. A change had come over Claire, peace had finally settled, but they were both new and fragile. Claire questioned her eagerly about news of Minerve de Montfort, but in the eighteen months she had lived in his mother's house, Claire of Foix had never once asked after Aimery of Segni.

Yet, it had been Aimery who had sent her here for safekeeping, and Iolande had no doubt that, secretly, Claire knew this. Segni was like this, after all. War might rage and battles threaten, but this safe place remained serene.

*Fortunate for me that he sent her here. Fortunate for me that she came.*

Not wanting the younger woman to see how much of an effort this had lately become, the Countess of Segni struggled up from her woven willow chair and started out slowly to meet her. Iolande didn't mind the pain; she was looking up. It was a lovely day, not a single cloud fretted the clear expanse of sky overhead and only the very slightest of breezes ruffled the grove of fig trees that sheltered her.

*What a perfect day for my son's return.*

The missive had been precise and very clear, though it bore the sticky thumbprint of one of Iolande's numerous grandchildren. *We are coming,* Minerve had written, *all of us.* This last had been especially significant.

Iolande knew the de Montforts and their children would arrive directly at the small stone castle that crowned the fertile fields of their Italian homeland, but she also knew that Aimery would not. She was his mother, after all; she knew exactly the place her son would visit first. She knew his sanctuary.

Again, she waved. Claire was so close now.

Many years ago, Iolande, too, had come from Languedoc. She had left its sharp crags and its reckless splendor for this soft land of rolling hills and green fields. She had loved Italy from the beginning, knowing that this rich land would nourish her, and she had not been disappointed: the fertile fields of Segni had always comforted. They had sustained her as, helplessly, she watched her husband fall victim to his own thwarted ambition, and they had continued to do this as this same ambition tried to take possession of her son's soul. These timeless hills had encouraged her to continue to hope and she had done this. And now she sensed love had won. Iolande was not quite sure how yet, but she knew the "how" didn't matter.

Iolande smiled as she opened her arms wide to the young woman who hurried into them. In the short time she had been here, the Maid of Foix had lost her pallor and her sense of being somehow faraway, ethereal. She now seemed rooted—to this place, this land, and its promise. Gone were the nightmares that had wrung night-screams from Claire at the beginning, the cries of fear before someone named Peter, and the longing for her parents and a nun named Helene. Gone, too, was the hunted looked she had worn when she came here, and the quick, sharp glances of distrust.

Instead, Claire had become radiant; she had found her true light. Iolande's body might be failing her, but she could sense this as she held the younger woman to her heart and listened to the giggles and happy chatter of the children who always seemed to follow in her wake. The hills were heavy with harvest and reaping-time would soon occupy everyone on Segni, no matter their rank, but for now the children could play with their new mistress in the sunshine.

*For Claire will be mistress of this place.*

Iolande knew this with a Wise Woman's intuition, and with this same good insight, she knew that she must not hurry heaven.

"Dear child," she said, "tell me all you have been about."

They linked arms.

"Well," said Claire, "we went through the olive groves, seeing which should be weeded. Mario says there are trees here that have borne steady fruit since Roman times but I cannot imagine this is so! Yet this is such an ancient land—the children are forever finding coins and shards of pottery that the Etruscans made. But an olive tree from Caesar's time—it sounds far too magical for me."

And yet she wanted to believe the truth in this, Iolande could tell. Claire wanted so desperately to believe.

The Countess of Segni smiled to herself as she drew Claire nearer.

"I need you to go to the brook," she said. "The summer cress grows fine and strong there and I would have some for my evening's meal. Would you bring some for me? And go yourself, alone. It is time for the children's siesta and afterward they must go the orchard and pick the last of the summer figs. I see them wasting on the ground."

Claire nodded, kissed Iolande on the cheek. There were servants aplenty at Segni to see to the household's needs but Iolande gave only a perfunctory nod to class distinctions. It was one of the things that Claire loved most about her. Whoever was available to do a task did it; Claire had seen the Lady of Segni working side by side with her peasants in the vineyards during the *vendemia,* the wine pressing, and in the fields for the main harvest of wheat and the smaller ones of olives and fruits and medicinal herbs. With something like awe, Claire had even watched as Iolande donned netting to gather honey from the midst of swarming bees and then, encouraged by the countess, she had waded through her fears and gained the courage to do the same thing herself.

One day soon she would have to leave Segni and move on. Claire felt change upon the air, smelled it on the morning's dew, heard it in the starling's cry. It was inevitable. She could not go on here forever as she had been. She had changed; her world must change with her. But she no longer feared a shift in her circumstances. Valor was another of the great gifts of this land, and this place, and its people.

Claire nodded, started out to the woods.

She was happy, deeply and visibly happy. During her early months here, Claire hadn't recognized the feeling for what it really was; she had experienced lightness and peace as loss probably because so much had been irrevocably lost to her: Mother Helene, the Convent of the Magdalene, the fight to bring the Cathar Cause back to its homeland—and Father Peter. She found it strange that she could barely remember her parents at all, but she could remember Peter.

By rights she should hate him, and certainly she had hated him at the beginning, just as she had been filled with anger. She had gone to bed with hatred of him at night and her anger had wakened her in the morning. She had lived it during the day. Even now, as she walked safely through the cool, green woods of Segni, she felt the pull of the fear she now knew had always linked her to him. But its cold grasp had been loosened by the warmth of the love she felt here, by the connection she had forged to this land and this place.

And to Aimery.

At first, even here at his home, living with his mother, Claire had not been able to think of Aimery without that strange anger bubbling up again; she could remember nothing but their arguments, the cruel things they had said to each other at Montsegur, at the very end.

Claire imagined he had long since married Isabeau of Valois and lived securely at Montsegur, safe in the knowledge that it was now his true possession and that he had fulfilled every dream his father had ever dreamed for him.

"And I was never one of those dreams," she said aloud. "He never promised me anything. I meant nothing to him."

Then gradually this rage stilled as well, though she surprised herself by wanting to hold on to it, by wanting to keep Aimery alive at least somewhere in her mind. Once she realized this, Claire let her anger go. Aimery was no longer near. He was no longer hers—if, indeed, he ever had been. This was something else that she needed to face and she did it.

Yet, she found that she had Aimery still.

He haunted her on days like this, as she tromped through woods and felt sunlight reach down through lush green leaves to dapple her and heard the sing of a brook as it made its way to a nearby pond. He came to her, unexpectedly, especially when her mind was not occupied and her hands were not busy. Claire found herself thinking of him, even when she wasn't consciously thinking of him at all.

"After all," she murmured, " 'twas Aimery who first taught me to swim. That was my choice, something I had always wanted to learn."

And, even as bitter emotions roiled in her, she diligently practiced the strokes he had taught her until she had grown strong and proficient and skilled in them.

Even the insects seemed to sleep on this hazy, slow day. She thought of the cress she must gather, and thought they might also have small quail and birth Sicilian oranges with their dinner, and she looked forward to that. Claire didn't know how long she stayed at the forest's edge, listening—but not hearing Aimery as he approached her. Not hearing the sound of his footsteps upon the land of his home, not hearing the flowers as they clapped their hands together in the light breeze. There was no singing, *Aimery has come home.* Nothing warned her.

But there was the clear sound of a waterfall just ahead and Claire heard splashing in it. A swan, she thought, or a small deer. Animals came here often to cool themselves from the late summer's heat, and she loved animals, loved coming quietly upon them as they played. Another splash and she hurried onward, her feet barely touching the wooden bridge that spanned the stream.

She paused, looked down the water's length, and saw Aimery—as the world held its breath, as the birds and the midges seemed to halt in mid-flight.

He didn't see her, at least not at first.

And so she was free to watch him, to gaze upon him unseen, much as he must have stared at her on that first fateful day when he had taught her how to swim.

Since then she had practiced often, had improved, yet she wondered if she would ever be as masterful at it as he was. She watched as his arms sliced through the water, watched the strong column of his neck as his head moved swiftly from side to side, stared at the lean muscles along his back—the way his thin linen tunic rippled along them, the way its fine texture showed more than it concealed.

It had been many months since those arms had held her, since he had embraced her and she had felt safe. Aimery had enticed her with the idea of swimming and she had practiced. All alone, hidden away in this very stream, she had taken this knowledge he'd given her and made it her own.

His arms sliced the still, clear water with the ease of a sharp knife cutting silk. Claire closed her eyes, lifted her head, and could feel the cold water gradually warm around him, just as it always seemed to warm around her. And then she was beside him, right beside him in her mind, and in the water with him. She floated and his hands were beneath her once again as he had started her along the path to the skill she now possessed. And other skills, resolutely suppressed memories of their sweet days together at Montsegur surged once again to the surface of her mind.

Remembered longings. Very carnal. Very real.

Her eyes flew open and the sunlight, which had seemed so harsh and bright, was somehow softened as it sifted through the lush green of Segni's Mediterranean pine and cypress. And while it was true the illusion was gone, still Aimery remained, and when Claire opened her eyes, she found that he had stopped his swim through bright waters and that he stared at her. Even from this distance she could see the sun glinting diamonds around him, could feel the warmth of his bright, intelligent eyes.

*I love him.*

"I love you," he said, though she might have been mistaken. A stretch of gurgling water separated them now, and a lifetime before that. How could he love her when he was married, by now, to Isabeau of Valois?

Still, she stood motionless as he emerged from the water, the sheer, wet, linen tunic clinging to his body. She watched him shake the water from his body then disappear behind a tree cluster. When she saw him again, he was coming toward her clad in breeches and light boots but still wearing the same linen shirt. Water droplets still sparkled like diamonds in his hair. They twinkled at the corner of her vision as she stared at him.

All the time, she did not move, barely breathed, did not think; she would not think of this man married. It hurt too much.

"I've just come," he said as he neared her, "with Minerve, Huguet, and their children. Did my mother not tell you we were coming?"

Claire shook her head, and knew instantly that Iolande had planned this. But why? she wondered as Aimery drew up close beside her. He hadn't changed during the months that had separated them, during the separate lives they now had. His face looked older somehow; the lines around his eyes had deepened, but the eyes themselves were still as blue as heaven and his hair still haloed his face with gold. When he stopped, he stood erect and so tall over her that the length and breadth of him—his sheer size—made her feel protected in the world. It always had. And he looked so good and he warmed her, much like the sunshine itself.

His marriage had not changed him. There was no new harshness to the lines of his mouth and dissipation had not settled into his face. All things she had expected to see upon him, she realized suddenly, if ever she had seen him again.

*Isabeau of Valois might have him, but she will only change him for the worse.*

Claire realized now, with some shame, that this is what she had half wanted and wholly expected. Isabeau of Valois might have this man as husband but she would never have the man Claire loved; she would never know Aimery as Claire knew him.

She smiled ruefully at this thought as they trudged along, close but not touching, as Aimery took her forgotten basket into his hands. Claire's own hand burrowed into her apron pocket to touch the green silk ribbon he had once given her. It had been his first gift to her, the first thing of his that she cherished, now fingered to shreds.

Though now, of course, he was no longer hers. She could not even pretend that he was.

"My mother did not tell you?" he repeated.

"Your mother said nothing," Claire replied at last. "She did not mention even Minerve and the children, much less . . ."

"Me?" Aimery smiled for the first time as he fell into step beside her on the path. "I imagine she wouldn't. My mother would not want to spoil this surprise."

Claire nodded. It was true, Iolande would hold it secret.

Without a word, they turned together and walked silently back towards the forest—Aimery stopping to untether his palfrey at the waterside and Claire paying strict attention to the birds as they twittered overhead. They were funny, she thought, still as bright and cheerful and energetic at the close of day just as they had been at the beginning. She smiled at the thought of this wonder and kept her mind on the sweet neutral subject of birds for as long as she could.

Finally she said, "You say Minerve came with you?"

"We are all here," he answered simply.

"Including your wife? Including the Lady Isabeau?"

Well, she'd said out loud what she'd inwardly wondered and there was no way to bring back the words. So she plucked up her courage and faced him, though her cheeks burned scarlet and she felt as though her body radiated the heat of her embarrassment, afraid that the heat radiating from her might scorch him.

"I have no wife."

The words came so softly that at first Claire did not hear them. She shook her head slowly, negating what he said but not taking her gaze from his.

"It was the Lady Isabeau's own considered decision," he said. "Once it was pointed out to her that, with a king as uncle, she could do as she liked, she was quick to see validity in the claim. They call her uncle the "found king" because his claim to the throne is so tenuous. A man like that can easily be manipulated by the threat of scandal. A new king, trying to maintain his position through makeshift and untried alliances, can easily be manipulated by the threat of scandal. For one in her position, an advantageous life could only be lived in Paris and the fact that she could have the king's immediate permission, and eventually that of the Pope, to marry whomever she chose—well, she was quick to grasp the benefit of seeking as spouse the man she truly wanted."

They turned back to the path, Claire now staring straight ahead.

"And who pointed out these things to her?" she said. "Was it Minerve? Your sister never truly fancied Isabeau of Valois as your betrothed."

Aimery did not pause, kept walking. "It was I who convinced the Lady Isabeau of the advantages, and the power, that chance had newly placed in her small hands."

"You?" cried Claire, so astonished that her cry startled starlings from their rest. "Marriage to Isabeau of Valois was the culmination of all you've ever striven for. How could you give her up? How could you give that up?"

He stopped her, his hand warm upon her bare arm, and forced her to look at him. "I think the better question might be, how could I possibly marry her once I had met you—once I had come to love you?"

Claire let these words linger in the back of her mind,

did not quite know how to let her mind and her heart venture near them.

"But Montsegur," she whispered, "what of that?"

"I have given it over to Huguet and his children. They are French, and it is within their heritage. Huguet's ancestor, Simon de Montfort, died trying to take Languedoc by force and lost both his life and the land in the undertaking. It is fitting that now his grandson will have that same land and can rule it in peace."

Still, she would not fathom what he said to her, could not fathom it. "Yet, Montsegur was the fortress you have always wanted," she protested. "I—we all—know how much you have always craved it, and the sacrifices you made to secure it once again."

Aimery stopped now, faced her. "Indeed, I wanted Montsegur, even craved it as you say, but the 'choice' of it was never mine, and I came to see that. It took months and much work, yet I did come to see that though I still don't know what my choices are, I think you may be one of them. At least I hope you are. I hope you still care for me."

Claire nodded slowly, feeling the warmth of her heart on her face.

"And that you might come to love me," he said, "as I have always loved you from the first moment I saw you making your way to me as I sat upon the Inquisitor's chair."

He would have said more. Through the veil of her happiness, Claire heard him whisper words extolling Segni as a home, telling how happy his own French mother had been there, setting a near date for their marriage. She saw the apprehension upon his face. Apprehension for what? That she would say no? She raised her hand to his mouth, felt the whisper of his words against her spread fingers until they stopped.

"I love you. I wish to be your wife."

Very few words, but their future lay in them. Claire looped her hand through Aimery's strong arm. As they walked from the forest edge into the sunshine, she heard the happy shouts and laughter of Minerve's pride of children echoing towards them—children that both told the Montfort family history and shaped its future. It would take years and many events before she and Aimery might find the thread of their own story, might piece it together. But they had made a start.

# Embrace the Romance of
# **Shannon Drake**

# Discover the Magic of
# Romance With
# Jo Goodman

# Discover the Romances of
# **Hannah Howell**